To Jess.

Wells

#keepreading!

TAYLOR-MADE *for* ME

K.C. WELLS

This is a work of fiction. Names, characters, places, and incidents either are the product of the author's imagination or are used fictitiously, and any resemblance to actual persons, living or dead, business establishments, events, or locales is entirely coincidental.

Taylor-Made for Me

Cover Art by Lauren Dombrowski
Edited by Sue Laybourn
ISBN: 978-1-916853-68-3

Warning

This book contains material that is intended for a mature, adult audience. It contains graphic language, explicit sexual content, and adult situations.

ACKNOWLEDGMENTS

To Jason Mitchell for always being there

But especially to Parker Williams.
A girl couldn't have a better brother.
I love your humour, your patience.
This book is all the better because I followed your advice.

Prologue

Will Bryant looked around at the elegance of the Pfister Hotel. Okay, so he hadn't expected anything like this, but the lobby's opulence didn't change a thing.

Why did I ever agree to this harebrained scheme?

Except he knew why. Becca had pouted, and he couldn't say no.

What am I saying? She did more than pout—she lost her mind, and I did what every best friend would do in the circumstances—I caved.

He wasn't proud of that, not now he was standing in the lobby, holding Becca's hand as though he couldn't bear to be separated from her for even a second, while she chatted amiably with—Michael? Mikey?—some childhood friend or other.

Then someone shouted "Watch out!"

Oof. Something slammed into his back, propelling him through the lobby of the four-star, four-diamond hotel.

His only thought as he sailed through the air was that he must appear pretty stupid, his limbs in a tangle, and—*hey, I wonder if anyone has noticed that stain in the carpet before or did they have to be flying ass over teakettle to see it?*—and even though his inaugural flight hadn't been graceful, his first landing was worse.

Thud.

Expletive.

Expletive.

Expletive.

Thump.

Finally, he came to rest at the base of a statue of a cute young guy holding a spear. Or a halberd. He'd never paid much attention to weapon types when they'd played D & D. The next thing he knew, he was surrounded by people who—

Wait.

No.

If he was going to tell this story, it was probably better to start at the beginning.

Damn it, Becca.

Chapter One

Will Bryant Gets A Shock

November 4, 2022

Becca Taylor sounded like a lovesick puppy, and if she didn't stop sighing every time she read one of her girlfriend's messages, Will Bryant was going to beat her over the head with her phone. That, or smash it into a zillion pieces.

Okay, so he probably wouldn't do either of those.

Maybe. It all hung on the next thing to fall from her lips.

Becca sighed. "I hope she calls soon." She stroked the screen with a single finger.

That was it, he was done. That phone was going to Samsung Heaven.

Will held out his hand. "Give me the phone, Becca."

Her eyes narrowed. "Sure. You can have it—when you pry it from my cold, dead hands."

"Fine. Then either quit drooling over Kristen's picture, messages, whatever, or go do it someplace else. You're putting me off my lunch."

She glared. "I miss her, all right?"

Will rolled his eyes. "For God's sake, she only left an hour ago."

"But she'll be gone all weekend. And *I* can't help it if I feel things deeply. I'm in love." She pasted on a sweet smile. "You should try it sometime."

He snorted. "Not if it makes me act anything like you. How about a little perspective here? She's gone home for the weekend. She'll be back Sunday night. Surely you can survive *that* long without her?"

Becca gave her phone another wistful glance.

Apparently not.

Will peered at the clock on the cafeteria wall. His next class started in twenty minutes. No way was he putting up with Becca until then.

I'm being mean, aren't I?

For reasons Becca hadn't gone into, no one at home knew she was into girls. Will had thought her parents sounded cool, but if she wasn't willing to come out to them, then there had to be stuff going on that he knew nothing about.

"I think you need cheering up. They're showing *Glass Onion* at the Main this weekend. You liked *Knives Out*, didn't you? Or there's *Enola Holmes 2*. We could go for a pizza first." Anything to stop her moping.

Becca smiled. "And *this* is why you're my bestie. Yeah, that sounds cool." She turned her head to gaze through the windows at the snow-covered ground. "And *that* looks freezing."

"We've got coats, boots, scarves, gloves… I think we'll survive."

Her phone rang, and she pounced on it. "See? She loves me too." Then her face fell. "Aw crap, it's my mom."

"Want me to go?"

Becca shook her head. She held the phone horizontally, one end to her lips. "Hey, Mom."

"I wanted to catch you before you had a class or something." Her mom's voice was audible.

Will hoped the call didn't get too personal, not that Becca would be fazed by such a thing. She hadn't even blushed when her boob had popped out during a dance rehearsal last semester.

"Just finishing lunch."

"Then I suppose you'll have to change into… well, whatever it is you wear when you dance. Except… should you be dancing on a full stomach?"

Becca rolled her eyes heavenward. "Okay, I hardly think a salad and an apple are gonna make me bust at the seams. And who says I'm dancing? We do have real classes too, y'know, Mom. In a classroom? You can't get a degree in Dance with just performances. We study technique, choreography, dance theory, kinesiology…"

"Is that a real word, or did you just make it up?"

Will stuffed his hand into his mouth to stifle his laughter.

Becca gave him another glare. "Of course it's a real word. It means the study of movement."

Mom huffed. "Why couldn't you study a proper subject, like Aiden did?"

"Dance *is* a proper subject." She mouthed a yell.

"That's not what your father says. You know what he calls it?"

"Yes, I do, and please don't say it again."

She took a deep breath. "Was there a reason for you calling me?"

"You haven't forgotten about the party next weekend, have you?"

Becca rolled her eyes. "No, Mom. How could I forget your silver wedding anniversary? But I won't be coming home Friday. I've got a performance that night. I'll go straight to the hotel Saturday."

"Are you bringing a date? That would be okay."

Will gave her a sympathetic glance.

"No, Mom, it'll just be me."

"You know, I was talking about you just the other day to Josh. He's the new management trainee. Such a sweet boy. He's a little older than you, but such lovely manners."

"Mom…"

"And Richard works in the kitchens. He's a pastry chef, and oh my *lord*, the things that boy can make." There was a pause. "I could ask if either of them would like to take you to the party."

"Mom, we talked about this. You have to stop trying to fix me up with guys, okay?"

"But you're twenty-one and still single."

"So? What's wrong with that?"

"By the time I was twenty-one, I was—"

"Married, and you'd had Aiden. Yes, Mom, I know. But times change. Let's face it. You got married in the last century."

"It was only 1997."

"And now it's 2022. Are you trying to fix Aiden up with a date too, or is it just me?"

"I've invited a lot of the girls from the hotel.

I'm sure he'll like one of them."

My mom, Becca mouthed, with another eye roll.

Will kept his mouth shut. Matchmaking seemed to be her mom's favorite occupation.

Then Becca stilled, her eyes widening. Will noted the gleam in them and straightened. He knew that look.

She's up to something.

That was never a good thing.

"Actually, Mom, I was gonna call you. I have some news for you. Really exciting news, actually."

"Oh?"

"Yeah. You need to stop setting me up with dates because I…" She swallowed. "I just got engaged."

Will's jaw dropped.

"Oh my God. When were you going to tell me?" Her mom's voice went ultrasonic.

"It only happened last night."

Will gaped. "You and Kristen got *engaged*?" he whispered.

Becca fired him another glare. "Ssshhhhh!"

"What was that?"

"Nothing, Mom. Just someone on the next table talking way too loudly."

It seemed to be Will's day to be on the receiving end of a whole lot of glares.

"So tell me. What's his name?"

Becca stared at Will, her hand shaking. "Will. Will Bryant."

Will's jaw was scraping on the cafeteria floor.

What the fuck?

"Your best friend? *That* Will?"

"Yes, Mom, that Will."

"But we've never met him."

"What can I say? It was all kinda sudden."

So sudden, Will appeared to have missed it entirely.

"What does he study again?"

"Astrophysics." Becca averted her gaze. "He's really smart, Mom. You'll like him."

Yeah, you look away all you want, girl. Because when this call is over…

"Well, I hope we do more than like him, if he's going to be our son-in-law. You know your father will want to vet him, don't you?"

Will was going to kill her. Slowly.

"You know what, Mom? I gotta go. I'll call you on Sunday, all right? We can talk about it then."

"Okay. Wait till I tell your father. He'll be so happy—once he's picked himself up from the floor. You *will* be bringing Will to the party, won't you?"

"Yes, Mom, I'll bring him."

Will's jaw dropped for the second time in less than a minute.

"Then I'll book him a room. We'll have a houseful here."

"That's great. Thanks. Bye, Mom." She disconnected.

Will pounced. "Why the hell did you tell her we're engaged?" God, he was having heart palpitations. That sharpness in his chest worried the fuck out of him, and his heartbeat thudded in his ears.

"It was all I could think of to get her off my back, all right?"

"And you don't see any issues with this? Like… oh, I don't know… the fact that I'm gay?"

"Calm down, Will."

"Calm down? I'm so stressed, I can hardly breathe. You just told your mom we're engaged, and *then* you told her you're bringing me to their anniversary party next weekend."

"I know, it's sudden, but—"

"*Sudden*? Seriously?"

"It'll just be for one weekend, okay? Then we'll break it off."

"Oh really? And then what? You find yourself *another* fake fiancé for the next family occasion?"

Becca sucked in a long breath. "Please, Will. Do it for me? If I could take Kristen, I would, but you don't know my mom."

"Are you so sure she'd react that badly to discovering you're a lesbian?"

Another eye-roll. "Will, when anything remotely connected to LGBTQ+ comes on TV, you know what my mom does? She changes the channel. She doesn't say a word. Neither does my dad. And you want me to walk in there and announce I've got a *girlfriend*? Not gonna happen." She grabbed his hand. "Look, it's one lousy weekend, all right? You get to stay in a *beautiful* hotel—it's the Pfister, where Mom works, and it's real fancy—there'll be food, music, dancing…And all you have to do is shake hands with people, smile on cue, and act as if you're totally in love with me."

"That's all, huh?"

"You can totally do this. I've seen you act, remember? That amateur drama group you used to belong to, two years ago? You can do this standing on your head."

"Oh God, you want me to do tricks as well?" His heartbeat was returning to normal, however.

She chuckled. Then she grabbed his hand. "Please, Will. Do this for me?"

"You said that already."

"I swear, I wouldn't drop you into shit like this if it wasn't positively, absolutely, *extremely* necessary." Her face tightened., and she gasped as though breathing has become a chore.

Looks as if she's having a panic attack too. That cooled his jets a little.

"If I could take Kristen with me, I would, but—"

"You said *that* already too."

She swallowed. "I'll never ask you another thing, so long as I live."

He snorted. "Don't make promises you can't keep." She let go of his hand, and he glanced at it. "We need to talk props."

Becca frowned, and then she nodded. "We'd better find a ring before Saturday." At least she'd calmed down.

Will gaped again. "I am *not* buying you an engagement ring."

"I'll do that. It doesn't have to be much. We'll tell them you're an impoverished student. You can't afford anything fancy or expensive."

"And you promise, the engagement's off as soon as this party is over?"

Becca placed her hand over her heart and opened her mouth to say something, but Will held up a hand. "Please don't try to convince anyone you have a heart. If you did, you wouldn't be putting me in this awkward situation."

"How rude." Yeah, that was the Becca he knew. She pouted for a moment. "I have a heart." She glanced at her phone with a sappy smile. "It belongs to Kristen."

He couldn't argue with that.

She bit her lip. "Sometimes I forget how well you know me. Anyway, as soon as the weekend is over, I'll tell my parents the engagement's off. I'll be all broken up." She grinned. "In fact, your rudeness just gave me an idea. *That's* why I'm breaking up with you. I'll be so devastated, they might never want to see you again."

He managed a half-smile. "At least there's a bright side." He had no wish to spend time with haters. Thank God Becca was nothing like her parents.

She sagged into her chair. "Then you'll do it?"

He heaved a dramatic sigh. "What are friends for?" Then he gave her a hard stare. "But you *will* owe me, big time. Especially if you're dragging me to Milwaukee."

Ugh, even the name gave him the heebie-jeebies. All he'd ever heard about Milwaukee was the number of bars the place had. Not that he'd ever been there, but he didn't think anyplace that declared itself to be the beer capital of the world would hold any interest for him. Then again, at least he'd have no problem finding a place to get drunk if he needed to get away from Becca and her family.

And there was always the possibility

Milwaukee was inhabited by some of the world's sexiest men.

Maybe even the world's sexiest gingers.

Yeah, right.

CHAPTER TWO

Aiden Taylor Is On A Mission

Aiden Taylor forked Midnight's food into his bowl while the cat stood on its hind legs, front paws on the cabinet, yowling.

"Anyone would think I never feed you," Aiden grumbled. "I mean, look at you. You're obviously wasting away."

Sarcasm was wasted on Midnight because all that remark got him was another long meow. For all Aiden knew, that translated as *hurry up and gimme the damn kitty chow, slave.* And that right there was the main difference between dogs and cats, at least to his way of thinking. Dogs were grateful, whereas cats didn't give a fuck as long as there was food in the bowl, water in the dish, and rubbies on demand.

And what does that say about me?

Aiden was most definitely a cat person.

He set the bowl down on the tiled floor, and Midnight's head was in it in a heartbeat. Aiden grabbed the cup of tea he'd made before Mom had called, but one sip had him pouring the now cool liquid down the drain. He made himself another, then walked out of his small kitchen and into the living room.

That was Midnight taken care of—now to talk to Becca.

Except she'd be doing most of the talking.

He put his cup on the coffee table, flopped onto the couch, and fished his phone from his jeans pocket. He scrolled to her number.

"Hey. You just caught me." He heard voices in the background.

"Going anywhere interesting?"

"To a movie. What about you? What do you find to do in Milwaukee on a Friday night?"

Going to a gay bar. Not that he was about to share that information with Becca. Walls did indeed have ears, and Becca couldn't keep a secret to save her life. "I'm going to veg out in front of the TV, I think." He waited for her to explode with her news.

"You didn't need to call, y'know. You'll see me next weekend."

"I know. Maybe I just needed to hear your voice."

She snorted. "Are you sick or something? Last time we were in the same room, you called me an irritating brat, as I recall."

"Yeah, but that was September. And if *I* recall, the word wasn't brat, but it did start with a B. Besides, maybe I've missed you."

Becca chuckled. "Now I *definitely* know you're sick."

He waited, but she'd gone quiet on him.

Midnight let out another yowl as he strolled over to the couch.

"You haven't killed the cat yet, huh?"

"What does that mean?"

"Aide, you kill everything you touch."

"Since when?"

"That fish Dad bought you? You fed it too

much food."

"I was nine years old, for God's sake."

"And the cactus? I mean, how does anyone kill a *cactus*? And what about Snuffles?"

"That gerbil died of natural causes," he protested.

"Sure it did—only after you played dress-up with him. You wanted to make him all pretty, remember? That *was* you who put Mom's make-up on his little cute face, who sprayed him with Mom's Chanel No. 5? You wanna know what killed Snuffles? It was the shame of being turned into a crossdressing rodent."

"You weren't old enough at the time to know all this. You were still in diapers. The only reason you know about Snuffles is 'cause Mom told you." Aiden had heard enough. "And I didn't call you up to talk about my track record with pets and plants." He glanced at Midnight, who was sitting on the rug in front of him, staring at him.

Aiden could almost hear the words.

'Should I be worried here? Do I need pet insurance? If I'd known any of this shit, I would never have let you move in with me.'

"Then why did you call? And be quick about it. I need to be out of here in the next five minutes."

"That's long enough to share your news, don't you think?"

"What news?"

"Oh, I don't know… Maybe the fact that you got engaged?"

Crickets.

"Becca?"

"Oh. That."

Aiden blinked. "'Oh that'? You just agreed to marry some guy, and *that's* how you describe the proposal? And how come I had to hear about this from Mom and not you?"

"I was gonna call you."

He laughed. "No you weren't. You already said as much. So… tell me about this guy. Will, isn't it?"

"Yeah."

"How long have you known him?" *And why don't I know about him?*

"Three years."

"Wait—is this the same Will who's into sci-fi? The one you called a geek?"

"I don't remember saying that."

"Then there was the time you called him a nerd."

She snorted. "Well, the two terms *are* interchangeable, wouldn't you say?"

"Geek, nerd… *neither* of them explains why you're going to marry him."

"He's sweet." She sounded indignant.

"Okay, but how sweet? Are we talking thaumatin sweet or monellin?"

Crickets.

Aiden snorted. "Sorry, I forgot who I was talking to. So, like Reese's Pieces or more like Pixie Sticks? And how did he propose?"

"How does anyone propose? He asked, I said yes."

"But *how* did he ask?" Aiden's head was spinning. "Unless you get marriage proposals every day of the week, this has to be up there with your first kiss, right? You know, the kinda thing a girl remembers for the rest of her life? So did he get down on one knee? Where did he propose? Was it at least romantic?"

There was silence for a moment. Then he caught the sound of a door closing. "Okay, fine. We were in the university library," she said a moment later.

Aiden huffed. "I guess we can forget about romance then." Strike one for Becca's fiancé. *Who the hell proposes in a library?*

"It was sweet!"

"Again with the sweet. You really have to work on extending your vocabulary."

"But it *was*, really."

"Mm-hmm. Did he have a speech all worked out, or was it more of a spur-of-the-moment event? Did he have a ring?"

Another pause. "No. We're… we're going shopping for that tomorrow."

"He proposed and he didn't even have a ring ready? You *sure* you want to marry this guy?" And that right there was strike two.

Then it hit him. "Oh my God."

"What?"

"I know why you're doing this."

"I don't know what you mean."

Was he imagining the tremor in her voice?

"It's obvious. You're pregnant, aren't you?"

Her gasp was so loud, it hurt. "I am *not*."

"Aw, c'mon, sis. You can tell me. How far along are you? Did you tell Mom? Is she properly scandalized that her baby girl got knocked up?" He grinned. "Hey, I'm going to be an uncle."

"What? Of course you're not because I'm

not pregnant, okay? So there's nothing to tell. And… well… if you must know… we… we haven't even… done it yet."

Midnight puked up the food he'd scoffed in such a damn hurry, and Aiden snorted. "Yeah, I had the same reaction," he muttered. The mess would have to wait until he'd finished his call. He returned his attention to Becca. "You're telling me, you've known this guy for three years, you're going to marry him, and you have no clue what he's like in the sack? Because I don't buy it." And the fact that this Will character hadn't even *tried* to get into Becca's underwear?

Strike three.

So what if he was Becca's brother, which kinda made him biased as hell. She was beautiful. He could *almost* go as far as sexy, except that was way too weird to be thinking about his sis.

And he doesn't want that? What is he, blind?

"No one's asking you to. Look, you'd better not give him a hard time next weekend, you hear me?"

Aiden ignored the threat. He was used to them. "Mom says he's studying Astrophysics."

"That's right."

That brought on another grin. "He spends a *lot* of time in the library, doesn't he? I'm betting it's his second home." Yeah, Aiden could picture him: skinny, glasses, puny chest, a permanent dent in his shoulders from carrying his backpack full of books…

Not that there was anything wrong there. Aiden had wide and varied tastes when it came to men, and he'd had a few nerds after his own late-night D & D sessions. Nice thing about most guys like that, they were very enthusiastic when it came to sex, because they didn't often get it. Not that *all* nerds were lacking in the sexual activity department. After all, they came in all shapes and sizes.

I mean, Henry Cavil, for God's sake.

But Becca… and a nerd?

Why the hell is she marrying him?

He tried a different tack. "Is there anything you want to tell me? And I do mean anything. Because I'm trying to get my head around this, and I'll be honest, it doesn't compute."

"Can't you just be happy for me? Will is a sweet guy."

"You said that already. Doesn't he have any other outstanding characteristics?"

"He's smart."

"He studies Astrophysics. Duh."

"He plays Dungeons & Dragons."

She'd finally said something interesting. "Really? How many characters does he have? What level are they at?"

"Huh? Are you even talking in English?"

Aiden guessed it wasn't a shared interest. "Does he read?"

"He's always got his nose in a book."

Well, that at least told Aiden why he'd proposed in the library. It was probably the only place Becca got to see him, if they weren't sleeping together. Then he reasoned that would be difficult, seeing as she was in a dorm.

I'm damn sure I'd have found a way if it had been me. He grinned. *What am I saying?* He'd found a way, all right—he'd played hide the salami with one of his roommates.

"What about movies? He *does* go to the movies, right?"

She laughed. "Who do you think is taking me there tonight?"

"Great. So he gets out occasionally." Yeah, Aiden was going to add pale skin to his mental picture of Will. Dark hair framing his white face.

Oh my God. He's a vampire.

"Can't wait to meet him. Especially as he's going to be one of the family. Have you set a date yet?"

"Sorry, gotta go. I'll see you Saturday. Love ya." And she was gone.

Aiden placed his phone on the coffee table, then got up in search of paper towels to clean up Midnight's mess. He glared at the cat as he got down on his hands and knees. "Isn't it about time you learned to clean up after yourself?"

Midnight stared back at him. *'Sure, wiseass—the day I grow opposable thumbs.'*

Once cleanliness had been restored, Aiden flopped back onto the couch. Midnight was on his lap in a heartbeat, kneading Aiden's chest with his paws. "I don't recall ordering a massage," Aiden said softly, rubbing under Midnight's chin. He was rewarded with a loud purr. "This still makes no sense, kitty."

Becca was flighty, incapable of being serious, loud, funny at times, brash… And her fiancé sounded as if he were the complete opposite.

Maybe he needs that.

Maybe Becca provides him with some kind of balance.

Well, he'd know more on Saturday.

Aiden couldn't wait to meet his prospective brother-in-law. This guy already had three strikes against him, and if he wanted to marry Becca, he was going to have to do a *lot* better.

Chapter Three

The Road Trip To Milwaukee

November 12, 2022

Will could listen to Rihanna all day, especially if it meant he didn't have to talk to Becca who he *still* hadn't forgiven for getting him into this mess. Which was probably why he hadn't engaged in conversation for the first five hours of their drive to Milwaukee. The views didn't interest him—not that he could see much, thanks to the snow—and he was trying not to think about what awaited him when they arrived at the hotel.

I should have said no to this whole scheme.

I should have told her to call her mom and say we've broken up.

There were a lot of things Will should have done, but in the end, he'd kept his mouth shut.

Like she said, it's one weekend. I can be the perfect fiancé for one weekend. Well, not too *perfect. There's gotta be a reason for our eventual break-up, right?* Knowing Becca, she'd spin it so it was his fault. *What do I care? After this fiasco is over, I'll never have to see any of her family ever again.*

And speaking of family…

He stopped Rihanna mid-flow and removed his earbuds. "Want to tell me who's going to be at this shindig?"

Becca snorted. "Oh, so *now* we're talking?"

Will grinned. "I figure I'm gonna be having a lot of conversations when we get there, so I'm conserving my words. It's a well-known fact that males use fewer of them per day than females."

Becca indicated and pulled off the I-94, where a sign indicated the Lake Mills rest area. "We'll talk after I pee."

He chuckled. "TMI, but hey, I could go too." His stomach grumbled, and he decided to see what vending machines were available. A snack couldn't hurt. It would be hours before the party.

They got out of the car and headed toward the sand-colored building. Will was on autopilot, his mind churning now he had no music to lose himself in. He washed his hands in cold water, trying to remember how much Becca had told him about her family during the three years since they'd become friends. It came as a bit of a shock to realize how little he knew. Sure, he'd been told about her parents not being LGBTQ+-friendly, and he knew there was an older brother, but that was it.

She probably knows more about my *family than I do about hers.*

Will had really lucked out when it came to family.

He found the vending machines and grabbed two bags of chips, then walked with great care across the icy parking lot to the car, thankful he'd worn his thick coat and woolen hat. He smiled to himself as he gazed at his rainbow-colored gloves, his sister Emma's first attempt at knitting. They wouldn't win prizes, but they'd been made with love.

If I had hands shaped like these, I'd be worried.

Becca was already back behind the wheel. "We're almost there," she told him. "It's a straight run to East Wisconsin Avenue now." He fastened his seatbelt and she started the engine.

"What does your mom do at the hotel?"

"She works on the front desk. She's been there for years. She says the hotel has had its share of celebrities over the years: Mick Jagger, Robin Williams, Neil Diamond…"

Will ate a handful of chips to assuage his growling stomach. He pointed to the second bag on the central console. "Got those for you."

"Aw, thanks." Becca pulled back onto the I-94. "So you wanna know who's coming?" She huffed. "About every relative I possess, Mom and Dad's friends from college where they met, people they work with…"

"There's just you and Aiden, right?"

She nodded, her gaze locked on the road ahead. "But there are a *ton* of cousins. Mom is one of five kids, and Dad is one of four. Grandma Devlin will be there too—that's my mom's mom—and Granddad Taylor." She laughed.

"What's so funny?"

"You're going to get a lot of hugs tonight."

He smiled. "I can deal with that. I come from a family of huggers too."

"Mom says she's expecting about eighty people." Another grin. "And they will *all* want to meet you." Her phone buzzed and she glanced at it. Becca's face fell. "It's Kristen."

The fact she wasn't answering had alarm bells ringing.

"You *did* tell her, didn't you? About this whole plan?"

Becca jerked her head in his direction. "Are you crazy? If I did that, she'd cut off my… privileges. Besides, there's nothing to tell—or at least there *won't* be, once the weekend is over." She sighed. "She's pissed I haven't told my parents about us. I mean, we've been together a while now. And she asked if she could come home with me for Thanksgiving."

"I take it you said no." Will felt for Becca, he truly did. He couldn't conceive of not being out to his family. They were his biggest cheerleaders, and being the rainbow sheep of the family seemed like a blessed position.

Another sigh escaped her lips. "Yeah."

Will seized his courage. "Becca… you have to decide where you're going to go on this. What is more important to you—your future happiness with the girl you love, or keeping your folks happy and being miserable in the process?"

That earned him a glare. "Easy for you to say. You've never been in my situation. Hell, you've never been in love. Well, just you wait till someone walks into *your* life and turns it upside down."

Will snickered. "For that to happen, I'd need to actually go on a date. You know, *meet* people?"

She glanced at him. "What about the guys you play D & D with? Any likely candidates there?"

He guffawed. "God, no. You know my standards are flexible, but—"

That got him a derisive snort. "They're not flexible, you ass. You're a gay geek. That's why I was wondering about your D & D friends."

"Nope. Too nerdy, too…." He twirled his hand.

"Too what?" she demanded.

He sighed, as though it was painful for him to admit.

"They're too married."

Becca blinked. "How can they be 'too married'? Is that even possible?"

"I've met each of the guys' husbands. They've sat in on games. Marco's likes to bake snickerdoodles for us, and Richie's has a seemingly endless supply of pizza snacks and root beer for when we're at their house. No dick is worth giving those things up. Besides, they love their husbands, and I love them."

"So what's your type?"

He thought about it for a moment. "I like gingers."

She smirked. "Like me?"

"Similar." He flashed her a hopefully evil grin. "But not quite as butch."

Becca gave him the finger, chuckling. "Oh really? So how come you've never mentioned that before?"

"Because you tell people you like gingers, and they look at you funny."

"Not me." Becca twisted a strand of hair around her fingers. "In fact, you're gonna be in a ballroom full of 'em tonight." She narrowed her gaze. "And if a guy catches your eye, just remember one thing—you're there as my fiancé, okay? If I see you asking some cute server for his number, I'll—"

"You'll what?" he retorted. "Break off our engagement? Sounds to *me* like the perfect scenario.

We wouldn't even have to wait until after the weekend."

Becca arched her eyebrows. "And if that happened, care to guess where you'd be sleeping tonight? Because remember, you're broke, and my mom won't spring for your room at the hotel if you crush her baby's heart. So don't go thinking with your dick, and remember—*I'm* the love of your life."

The thought of spending a whole evening acting like some lovesick puppy was starting to turn his stomach.

"Tell me about your parents. What should I expect?" Forewarned was forearmed, right?

"Watch out for my dad."

"Why? Does he maim your would-be boyfriends?"

"No, he's the joker of the family. He's forever pranking us, even when we were little."

"What kind of pranks?"

"Okay, I think you're gonna be safe from his main line in pranks, because we're in a hotel. Dad *loves* the old trick poop. When I was about five, I remember going into the bathroom and seeing this little brown log on the toilet seat."

"What did you do?" Will asked with a smile.

"I ran out of there screaming, of course. Only, I screamed louder when Dad came in, picked it up with his bare hand—and took a bite off of it." She rolled her eyes. "Chocolate poop. What kind of sick mind invents stuff like that?" Another chuckle. "Probably someone just like my dad. There was that one time he smeared Nutella on a pair of Aiden's briefs and confronted him about them at dinner.

That was a whole different type of shit show, lemme tell you. Aiden started having a meltdown at the table. We're talking huge tears with him gulping for air and swearing he didn't do it. Mom glared at Dad, and he relented." She shook her head. "Aiden is still a little hurt over it, even after all these years."

"Did the pranks stop?"

"Lord no. There was the time he told us he'd baked a cake. It had white frosting on it, with blue frosting piped around the edge."

"It wasn't cake, was it?" he guessed.

"No, it was meatloaf covered in potatoes!" She laughed. "You'd think after that episode we'd be wary of anything Dad claimed to have made, but *noooo*, we fell for it again. Next time he presented us with this round cake covered in cool whip. Except when Aide tried to cut it—at Dad's insistence—it exploded. It was a balloon. There was whip *everywhere*. Mom was *so* pissed."

"Has she ever tried to get her own back?"

"No, even though Dad told her it would be totally okay to prank him." She chuckled. "Don't get me started on the chocolate parfait gag."

"I dread to think."

Becca was grinning again. "Aiden caught the worst of it that time. It wasn't cream on the top—it was Crisco. And then one time Dad put food coloring in our cereal, and the milk turned green."

"Your dad sounds like a fun kinda guy."

Her smile grew fond. "Yeah, he is. Mom's more straitlaced. But you know what? I have a feeling that if she ever decided to cut loose, she'd surpass him."

"Did you say Aiden is a teacher?"

She nodded. "He always wanted to do that. He studied physics at college, then did his student teaching program. He teaches science to grades 9 to 12 at Veritas High School. I think he's finding it tough—he's in his first semester there—but he'll stick it out. That's the kind of guy he is."

"Is he dating?"

"I don't know, and I don't ask. We don't talk much about personal stuff. He bawled me out because he had to hear about you from Mom, not me."

"So does he know about Kristen?"

"*No one* knows about her, all right? And I want it to stay that way." She fell silent.

"Hey." Will touched her lightly on the arm. "You okay?"

She gave him a warm smile. "In case I forget… Thanks for doing this. I owe you, big time."

"Don't worry. *I'm* not going to forget this."

He was still ruminating on how he was going to get his revenge.

"Except maybe I also need to apologize now," she added.

"For what? Dragging my ass into this mess?"

"No, for pulling you into the craziness of my family. I love them, sure, but sometimes they're just so… random, in a weird kinda way."

Tall buildings of concrete and glass rose ahead of them as they drove toward the hotel, and Will's stomach clenched.

Too late to back out now.

CHAPTER FOUR

Aiden Gets Attacked By The Green-Eyed Monster

Aiden sat on his parents' bed, watching his mom applying the final touches to her make-up. "No way do you look old enough to have a twenty-four-year-old kid."

She narrowed her gaze. "Okay, what have you done?"

He blinked. "Excuse me?"

Mom chuckled. "When you were little, any time you resorted to flattery, we knew you'd been up to something. So what is it this time? You haven't upset one of your students, have you? I remember you said some of them belonged in a zoo, but—"

"Relax, Mom. I haven't killed any of them—yet." Teaching was turning out to be different from what he'd imagined. It seemed less about inspiring young minds and more about targets. He recalled his own high school days. None of the students in his class would have dared come out with *half* the crap Aiden confronted on a daily basis.

"So there's nothing you want—or need—to tell me?" She gazed at him, a hopeful light in her eyes. "*You* haven't met someone, have you?"

"No, Mom. And before you start, please don't give me the names of some cute girls who work in the hotel, all right?"

She straightened, but he didn't buy the affronted expression for a second. "I wasn't going to give you any names. I'm sure you're perfectly capable of finding dates on your own."

Aiden laughed his ass off. "Okay, who are you, and what have you done with my mom?" She waved her hand at him. "When does Becca get here?"

She gazed at his reflection. "About four-thirty. She messaged to say they've passed Madison. Which reminds me. I need to call Lou on the front desk and make sure he knows Will's room is another one on the friends and family rate."

"And what gift is the hotel gonna leave in his room? The coasters or the tea cups?"

Another chuckle. "Neither. I thought the thermos mug was a better choice." She put down her brush. "I have to admit, this really surprised me."

"Becca getting engaged? Why? She's gorgeous. Any guy would be lucky to get her."

Mom rolled her eyes. "I know that. But this Will…" She pursed her red lips. "I don't think he sounds like her type, that's all."

Aiden put the remark down to a mom not ready for her chick to leave the nest. Then he reconsidered. "What do you know about him?"

She huffed. "Only what I told you." She peered at Aiden. "Did Becca tell *you* anything else about him?"

"I don't think so, apart from the Astrophysics part, the fact he's into D & D, the—"

Her mouth fell open. "I missed that piece of information. Well, at least you two will have something to talk about."

"And I don't think she wants us to know he's really a vampire," he teased. "Just be thankful it'll be dark when they arrive at the hotel. You watch. We get a sunny day tomorrow, and *poof*, he'll be reduced to a pile of ash."

Mom shook her head, laughing. "You're incorrigible."

He leaned back on his hands. "Gotta say, I'm curious now. What kind of guy did you *think* she'd pick?"

She shrugged. "Oh, I don't know. Someone… different."

"You haven't even met him yet. Wait and see. After five minutes, you'll probably love him." He glanced at the clock on the nightstand. "I guess I'd better get ready. What time do the guests arrive at the hotel?"

"A lot already have. Lou messaged me. They're serving drinks at six, and the buffet starts at seven. After that there's dancing, and—"

Aiden stared at her in mock horror. "Oh my God. Is there gonna be music from when you and Dad got married? What was trending in 1997? I'm afraid to Google it."

That earned him a glare. "No one said you have to dance to it."

"When do they close down the party?"

"Midnight. Will you take a taxi home? You can come back here with us in our taxi, if you want. Becca too."

Aiden grinned. "And what if she wants to spend the night at the hotel with her fiancé?"

They have to have sex sometime, *right?* And a

swanky hotel room seemed as good a location as any.

And speaking of sex, his chances of finding a guy to share his bed for the night would increase dramatically if that bed was *not* under his parent's roof.

"I think I'll go home. Don't wanna leave Midnight too long with Carol next door. He might decide he prefers her company to mine." He chuckled. "He's already got the hots for her Maine Coon, Candy."

Mom snickered. "Candy. Stupid name for a cat."

"It's better than calling a gerbil Snuffles." Another glance at the clock. "I'm gonna go get ready." He stood. "Gotta look my best to meet my prospective brother-in-law, right?" Aiden flashed his mom another grin. "You got any garlic in the house? I thought I'd better take some protection. Hey, maybe Dad can rustle up a wooden stake before we leave."

If looks could kill.

Mom rose and turned to stare at him. "I don't care if Will has fangs, hair down to his waist, claws… You *will* be nice to him, do you hear me? Because this is your sister's choice, and I don't want her upset."

"I'll play nice," Aiden assured her. "I'll make him welcome, I promise." He paused. "But I *will* take your make-up mirror with me, just to check if he has a reflection."

He scooted out of the bedroom before she could throw a hairbrush at him.

Aiden stood in the hotel lobby, gazing at his surroundings. He'd lost count of how many times he'd visited the Pfister, but it never ceased to impress him. From its rich carpet to its curved painted ceiling, it always had an air of opulence about it. Somewhere, someone played a piano, low, tasteful, unobtrusive music that seemed to blend in with the chatter of guests sitting on the couches and chairs. The front desk faced the revolving main door, and bellhops went to and fro, pushing luggage carts, carrying suitcases and bags, most of them with a smile.

He'd already recognized a few faces among the guests, exchanging nods with relatives and friends of his parents, some more familiar than others. Mom and Dad were up on the seventh floor in the ballroom, checking on the arrangements, and Mom had asked him to be in the lobby when Becca and Will arrived. Aiden had tried not to laugh—and failed miserably—when his mom asked him not to make any vampire cracks to Will.

"Hey, Aiden!"

He turned and grinned when he saw Mikey Pointer. "Looking good there, Mikey. Haven't seen you since your folks moved to Maine." They hugged, and when Aiden stepped back, he gave

Mikey the once-over. "God, you got *tall*." The Pointers had lived next door to the Taylors until Mr. Pointer's company transferred him when Mikey was fifteen. Aiden had fond memories of both he and Becca messing around in the pool with Mikey. "Where are your mom and dad?"

"They've gone to find your parents." Mikey scanned the lobby. "Where's Becca? I'm dying to see her." He grinned. "How did she turn out?"

Aiden chuckled. "I thought you'd have grown out of that crush by now. You always did follow her around like a lovesick puppy."

"Man, remember that time I was looking out my bedroom window and I saw her getting out of the pool after her midnight skinny dip? Her skin was so pale. Not that I could see her clearly—it was a dark night—but my mind sure filled in the details. I couldn't stop looking." He leaned in and whispered, "And as for what I did after that…."

It wasn't the first time Aiden had heard that story, but he'd never had the heart to break it to Mikey that the person he'd spied climbing out of the pool naked hadn't been Becca, but Aiden. Their hair had been a similar length back then, so he could understand the confusion. Lord, he'd *so* wanted to tell Mikey he'd been jacking off to Aiden's body, not his sister's.

"I hate to be the bearer of bad news, but… she's engaged."

Mikey seemed so disappointed Aiden wanted to give him another hug.

"Really? I suppose *someone* had to snatch her up sooner or later. What's he like?"

Aiden gave a wry smile. "No idea. We

haven't met him yet. Becca's bringing him to the party. The engagement only happened a week ago." He pulled his phone from his pocket. "Stick around. They should be here any minute."

Right on cue, the main door revolved, and Becca walked into the lobby, accompanied by—

You have got *to be kidding me.*

Will Bryant was freaking *gorgeous*.

He was tall, but not intimidatingly so. He wore a dark suit and his white shirt was open at the collar, a bag slung over his shoulder. Black hair, short at the sides and longer on top, and dark brown eyes. No pale skin, though—Will had the remains of a decent tan, and it looked perfect against the white of his shirt.

Aiden loved his sister, but right then he wanted to scratch her eyes out.

Then he realized Mikey was no longer at his side—he was striding toward Becca, who let out a whoop when she spied him, dropping her luggage to the floor. She and Will stood with their backs to Aiden, and fuck, that was even worse. The lower hem of Will's jacket rested against what appeared to be a gloriously firm ass.

Is there no *part of him that doesn't make my mouth water?*

Aiden stood rooted to the spot, watching as Will nodded while Becca performed introductions, talking animatedly.

This is so *unfair.*

It wasn't just the fact he was a beautiful man. *Noooo.* Because why would that be it? As Aiden watched, Will laced their fingers together, pulling her close. Aiden had dated a few guys in the last six years, once he'd gotten out of sight of his parents, but not *one* of them had done that for him. They were more the split-the-check types who were uncomfortable—at best—with displays of affection.

Will leaned in and spoke into Becca's ear, and her unmistakable laughter drifted over to where Aiden stood.

Why couldn't *he* find someone who whispered things in his ear that made him chuckle? Someone who'd brush a stray hair out of *his* face?

Why do I get frogs while she *gets the prince?*

Because his sister's fiancé was looking every inch a Prince Charming.

His sister who still stood with her back to him, a perfect target.

Where's a handy spear or rifle when you need one? He knew such feelings of jealousy were petty and out of place, but he couldn't help himself.

Then he saw it. An empty bell cart.

It would have to do. Not that he intended inflicting bodily harm—he wasn't *that* much of a bastard—but he could send it flying into her luggage, and probably scare the crap out of her the way he used to when they were kids.

Before he had time to change his mind, Aiden grabbed the cart, aimed for Becca's luggage, and gave it a shove, sending it rolling across the lobby.

Then Will moved and stepped into the path of the oncoming weaponized cart.

Oh shit.

CHAPTER FIVE

Will Gets A Grilling

Okay, that hurts.

Except Will wasn't sure which was more wounded—his body or his pride. Because finding himself flying through the air with curses exploding from his mouth wasn't his idea of making a good impression.

"Oh my God, Will, are you okay?"

The genuine concern in Becca's voice went a little way to healing his bruised ego. Before he could respond, however, two hands came into view, and someone helped him to his feet. Will got his first glimpse of the Good Samaritan—

And froze.

God had obviously been listening when Will had expressed a silent wish that Milwaukee would be inhabited by the world's sexiest gingers, because *would you look at him*. The guy was sex on legs. His longish, wavy red hair fell unfettered, framing cream-colored skin, blue eyes, and a smooth, square jaw Will yearned to kiss and stroke.

"I am *so* sorry."

Shit, his voice was as sexy as his appearance. Deep, resonant, the kind of voice Will could listen to all day long.

Especially in bed. Hell, yeah.

"How's your back?" his savior asked.

"My back?" Oh. Yeah. His back. Where something had plowed into him. "What hit me?"

"That would be a bell cart." Earnest eyes gazed into his. "I can't apologize enough."

His words registered. "Why are *you* apologizing?"

"Because he's a klutz, that's why." Becca glared at the object of Will's lust.

"You know this guy?" Will's brain decided to reboot at that moment, and he looked from Becca to the guy, and back to Becca. "Is he related to you?" The hair was a bit of a giveaway. And now that he took a third glance, there was a definite resemblance.

Becca bit her lip. "If I say no, would you believe me?" Will frowned, perplexed, and she sighed. "Unfortunately, yes. This is my brother, Aiden."

Wow. Talk about good genes.

Aiden regarded him with such an expression of abject horror and remorse that Will felt sorry for him.

"Hey, I'm okay." Will rubbed his back. "It only just caught me. I just won't be doing any dancing tonight, that's all." Aiden appeared stricken, and Will regretted his attempt at humor. "It's fine. I didn't intend going anywhere near the dance floor anyway. My two left feet cause misery and mayhem, usually for those around me, and *especially* for my dance partners. We're talking crutches afterward."

"I'm sure that's an exaggeration."

Fuck, that voice…

"If Aiden hasn't maimed you *too* badly,

would you like to go meet my parents?" Becca raised her eyes toward the ceiling. "They're probably on the seventh floor in the ballroom."

Will grimaced. "We've been driving for over six hours. I really could use a shower before I meet them. I don't want them taking one sniff of me and avoiding me for the rest of the night." He gestured to his suit. "This wasn't such a good idea. I should've worn my jeans and a sweater for the trip."

Becca widened her eyes. "It was *my* idea, if you recall."

"Yeah, that sounds like something *you'd* come up with," Aiden murmured.

"Exactly. That's why it wasn't a good idea." Will flashed Aiden a grin, and when it was returned, his world got a little brighter.

Damn it. Why does Becca's brother have to be so goddamn perfect*? Cute as hell, a wicked sense of humor, a voice made for sin, and smart too.* He had to be, if he was a teacher. And dummies didn't study physics.

Will wasn't sure if the thought of never seeing Aiden again—once Becca "*broke up*" with him and Will ended up on the family's death list—consoled or distressed him.

"Then get your key card and then you can go on up to your room."

Will headed for the front desk, doing his best not to turn to see what Becca's delectable brother was doing.

What did she say about not thinking with my dick?

Yeah, that ship had sailed.

When he'd checked in, he went over to where Becca, Aiden and Mikey stood.

"Where did they put you?" Becca asked.

He glanced at the card wallet. "804."

She grinned. "You're gonna like this. Mom got upgrades for all the family guests. Room 804's got a Jacuzzi."

"That'll help your back," Aiden added. "You've got time to have a soak in the hot tub before this evening."

Will wondered if Aiden's solicitous behavior would last the entire weekend, and for one brief moment he thought about milking the incident for all the attention he could wring out of the remorseful guy.

That's just mean.

Besides, what if he did get to meet the Taylor clan again sometime in the future? He wanted Aiden to remember him fondly, not as Becca's dick of an ex-fiancé.

"Let me carry your bag," Aiden said in a decisive tone.

Will bit back a smile. "Wow. You really *are* feeling guilty about trying to kill me with a bell cart, aren't you?"

"Yes, so it's useless to argue."

Will recognized the set of that gorgeous jaw. It was a Becca trait too. She could compete at Olympic level when it came to stubbornness.

You're not seeing the plus side to this, are you? He goes with you to your room, you get to spend more time with him—with no Becca around, if you're really lucky…

Yeah, that collision had definitely slowed his thought processes.

He gave as casual a shrug as he could manage. "Fine."

"I need to go find Mom and Dad." Becca

leaned in and kissed his cheek. "When you're ready, the ballroom is on the seventh floor."

"I'll make sure he gets there," Aiden assured her. He smiled. "I'll take good care of him."

Becca rolled her eyes. "Yeah, I've seen your brand of 'taking care'. Just get him to me in one piece, okay?" She flashed Will a smile. "Enjoy the Jacuzzi." And then she grabbed her bag and dashed through the lobby toward the elevator at the other end.

Aiden picked up Will's bag. "There's no rush."

Will performed a quick assessment. His back did ache a little, but it was nothing a hot tub couldn't alleviate. "I'm okay, honest." He glanced up at the ceiling. "This is really impressive." A chandelier hung from the middle, illuminating the painted curved panel of sky, clouds, and floating cherubs. Everywhere there was the glint of gold. He shook his head. "I guess they don't build hotels like this anymore." Not that he could make any comparisons with his limited experience.

Aiden led him toward the elevator. "There's a gift store down here that has just about anything you could need or want, and there's a coffee shop too." He leaned in conspiratorially. "And according to what Mom says, if you like your coffee, don't drink the stuff in your room."

Will grinned. "Now that's what I call useful info." He pressed the call button for the elevator, then took a step back, trying not to make it too obvious he was drinking in the sight of Aiden in black pants and an emerald-green shirt, open at the neck. "Becca looks good in green too." It was only as the words left his mouth that he realized the implication.

Aiden's eyebrows went skyward, and his lips twitched. "So I look good, huh?"

Thankfully, the doors slid open and Will darted into the small elevator. He stabbed at the seventh-floor button, and Aiden chuckled.

"It won't work without your keycard. Put it in the slot."

Which went to show how often Will stayed in hotels.

The doors closed, and Aiden leaned against the wall. "Something I have to ask. What does Becca think of you playing D & D?"

"She told you that?"

Aiden's eyes twinkled. "Why? Is it a secret?"

"Just surprised, that's all. She doesn't say much about it. Why do you ask?"

And what else has she told you?

Aiden's scowl caught him off guard. "She used to mock me for being a nerd or geek, depending on how bitchy she was feeling that day. I wasn't allowed to be around when her friends came over, because she didn't want them to know we were related." Then the scowl dissolved into his previous smile. "I can't believe she's mellowed out enough to have her fiancé meet her friends."

They arrived at the eighth floor, and Aiden led the way once more. Will used the card to open the door to his room—

And stopped dead. He hadn't been sure what to expect, but it certainly wasn't this. They were standing in a living room, complete with desk, fridge, a couch that appeared comfortable, an armchair that seemed to be its equal, and a glass-topped coffee table. On the table sat a thermal mug and a delicate pair of teacups and saucers, white china painted with deep purple flowers.

"Those are a gift from the hotel," Aiden told him. He gestured to the fridge. "There'll be goodies in there for you too."

Will went over and opened it. Sure enough, there was a tray laden with fresh fruit—apples, strawberries, melon, you name it—another plate with slices of different cheeses, and yet another with the most delicious-looking pastries Will had ever seen.

"I feel like royalty," he quipped. "Do they do this for every guest?" He closed the fridge.

Aiden smiled. "Only the special ones." He coughed and went through the door to the left, Will following. The bed was wide and high, and he guessed the door off that led to the bathroom. Will peered around the corner.

"They like their marble, huh?" The bathroom was as opulent as the rest of the hotel—well, what he'd seen of it so far. That Jacuzzi was *so* tempting, but it would have to wait.

He had parents to meet.

A role to play.

When Will thought about it, he realized he *deserved* that room for putting up with Becca's shenanigans.

"This is awesome," he said with a smile.

"Nothing but the best for Becca's fiancé." Aiden leaned against the bed. "So, how long have you two been dating?"

Okay, he'd expected to be grilled, but not

that soon.

"Oh, about nine days," he muttered, casting longing glances at the shower.

"What?"

Will jerked his head in Aiden's direction. "Maybe a year now?" He hated lying, but there was little he could do about it.

"You're studying Astrophysics, is that right?"

Will had no clue how many questions Aiden was going to put to him, but he was sure it would be better to answer them through the bathroom door.

"I really need a shower."

Aiden smiled. "Hey, I'm not stopping you. I only thought we could get to know each other, seeing as we're going to be related." He cocked his head to one side. "Can I stay while you take a shower?"

And what am I supposed to say to that? No? And look like an asshole after his mom has gone to the trouble of getting me this amazing room?

What made the situation worse was that Will couldn't make his mind up whether he felt awkward at having Aiden there—or grateful that he was staying.

"Sure."

Except there was the part where he had to take his clothes off.

Do I undress in the bathroom, or do I not give a shit and strip off right here?

Right then, Will was all for not giving a shit.

He removed his jacket and shirt, followed by his pants, underwear and socks. Naked, he ambled into the bathroom with a coolness he did *not* feel, left the door ajar, and turned on the jets.

"What are you going to do when you graduate?" Aiden called out.

"Aerospace Engineer. There seem to be plenty of positions about." Except that was a lie. There was only one place Will wanted to work, and it was going to take years to get him there. He paused. "Becca says you're a teacher." Aiden wasn't how he pictured a teacher to be. Hell, he didn't look much older than his grade twelve students.

"Uh-uh. I want to hear about *you*."

"You checking if my prospects are good? That I can take care of Becca?" he teased before turning his face toward the stream of hot water that felt glorious after six hours in a car.

"She'll need taking care of. A *dancer*, for God's sake. You watch and see. She'll be waiting tables or stuck in some depressing dead-end job, instead of starring in some hot show on Broadway." There was another pause. "You a player or a dungeon master?" Aiden called out.

Will laughed out loud.

"What's so funny about that?"

"It made me think of a joke someone once told me. 'How can you tell the difference between a nerd and someone into BDSM? Ask them what a dungeon master is.' He chuckled. He'd rather talk about D & D any day than be grilled about his future.

"So what are you?"

"Player. You?"

"Dungeon Master. In the non-BDSM sense."

Will let out another chuckle. "Good to

know." He flipped the shower off and grabbed a towel from the rail. "Wow. These towels are fantastic. I have no idea how I'm gonna be able to fit them all into my bag." When there was no response, he stuck his head around the bathroom door and grinned. "Just kidding." He retreated into the steamy space and toweled off. He wrapped the thick towel around his waist, secured it, then realized a part of his anatomy was *definitely* interested in the guy sitting on his bed.

Will gave his half-hard dick a stern glance. "Sorry, but you can't have him," he whispered. "Becca would kill me if I made a move on her straight brother." At least Will assumed Aiden was straight. Becca hadn't said anything to the contrary. And Becca *not* sharing stuff like that?

Yeah right.

He strolled into the bedroom as nonchalantly as he could, opened his bag, and removed a shirt, briefs, and socks. "Okay, back to D & D." That felt like safe common ground. "I know we've all done insanely amazing things, but what I want to know is, what's the *stupidest* thing you've ever done in a campaign?"

Aiden stared at him. "Uh, no," he said with a shake of his head.

Will laughed. "Aw, come on. Why not?" He gave Aiden an innocent glance. "You embarrassed?"

Aiden snorted. "You got that right. I was new, and the DM was a jokester."

"Tell you what," Will said as he turned his back to Aiden and dropped the towel. "You let me know what yours was, and I'll tell you mine."

The slight catch in Aiden's breathing had to

be Will's imagination—or wishful thinking.

Aiden sighed. "Fine. I hadn't been playing all that long. In fact, it *might* have been my first game, but I'm not really sure."

Will was ready to call bullshit on that, because who could forget their first game? But he bit his tongue and let Aiden continue.

"Anyway, the DM told us there were footprints all around. I wanted to see if I could discern any patterns, and he said to roll a perception check. *Then* he told me there were footprints from several races, including a set of human ones that were following behind me."

Will grinned as he stepped into his pants and zipped them up. "Oh, tell me you didn't."

"Well, I *could* lie, but I won't." Another sigh. "I spent thirty minutes trying to figure it out, and that asshole—and everyone else in the party—was laughing at me the whole time."

Will turned to face him and slipped his arms into his shirt. "How could you not realize they were *your* footprints?"

Aiden gave him a mock glare. "First game, remember?" He leaned back, his weight on his hands. "Turnabout is fair play. Now it's your turn."

"Okay, but this goes no further. And by that, I mean you don't tell your sister, all right?"

Aiden blinked. "*Now* you've got my attention."

"I was playing a satyr at the time. I had a personal quest to lay every race at least once."

"I think we've all been down *that* particular road," Aiden muttered.

"Yeah, well… During one, uhm, *encounter*,

he had me roll a disease check. I rolled a one."

Aiden winced. "Ouch. Critical failure."

"Yeah. It was so bad, my dick fell off. He thought that would be the end of it, but I reminded him I still had a tongue."

Aiden snorted. "A bisexual bard. Gee, what a surprise. They're notorious for trying to get laid. A hole is a hole, right?"

Will wasn't about to comment on *that.*

He gazed at his reflection. "Will I do?"

In the mirror, Aiden blinked. "Um, what are we talking about here? Are you asking if my bard would have bedded you or…? I need some context before I can answer that question."

Oh dear Lord.

He waved a hand at himself. "My clothes. Will they be okay?"

"Maybe, if you put on some socks. Bare feet freak Mom out." Aiden chuckled. "You look fine. You might wanna dry your hair, though."

He laughed. "No need. By the time we get to the ballroom, it'll be dry."

Aiden gave him a look that was unadulterated envy. "Wish I could say that. Mine takes forever if I don't attack it with a hairdryer. Not that I'm gonna cut it."

Will opened his mouth. "No, don't do that," he said quickly. Aiden's eyebrows shot up again, and he backpedaled. "I mean, you might look weird with short hair."

And you look awful fine just the way you are.

This weekend was going to put a real strain on Will. The chances of him letting something slip before he and Becca left on Sunday afternoon were increasing by the second, and it was Aiden's fault.

Why does he have to be so…

Perfect. He was goddamn *perfect.*

CHAPTER SIX

Will Has A Heart Attack. Well—Almost.

Will paused at the door to the ballroom. Music came from inside, and the murmur of voices.

"They won't eat you, y'know," Aiden assured him. Then he grinned. "Okay, they might nibble you a little, but only where the teeth marks won't be visible."

Will glanced at him. "You're not helping." It felt as though every single muscle in his body was twitching, and it was touch and go whether he'd throw up or not. He wiped his hands on his pants.

"What's to be nervous about? You're only marrying their only daughter, you're the first boyfriend she's ever brought to meet them… They've been waiting *years* for this."

He glared at Aiden. "I bet your students really hate you, don't they? They hang photos of you on the wall and throw darts at it. I'm right, aren't I?"

You've seen me naked. Not many guys had gotten to do that, and certainly none who ticked all Will's boxes.

To his surprise, Aiden placed his hand on Will's shoulder and gave it a gentle squeeze. "It'll be fine, I promise. They can't wait to meet you. How could they not like you? You're in love with their baby girl."

Yeah, that *really* set his stomach clenching.

This needs to be the performance of a lifetime.

Will squared his shoulders, and Aiden removed his hand. Will took a deep breath.

"Okay, let's do this."

He pushed the door open and walked into the ballroom.

Oh wow.

The square room was done in white and gold, with a blue carpet decorated with an elaborate paler blue pattern. Sepia prints beneath wall lights provided accents for the white walls and pilasters. Chandeliers sparkled, and recessed lights added to the effect, so that every corner of the room was illuminated. Round tables draped in white cloths, surrounded by brown chairs took up most of the floor space, with one end of the room obviously for dancing. There were already guests seated at the tables and standing around, chatting, and a table decorated with a huge floral display dominated the center of the room.

Becca stood there, talking with an older couple who had to be her parents. When she saw Will, she let out a squeal and hurtled across the room toward him. She planted an exuberant kiss on his cheek, then leaned in close.

"Where have you been?" she whispered.

"You wanted me to make a good impression, didn't you?" Will said while smiling and nodding at all the guests who'd turned to look.

Becca glared at Aiden. "You took your time. What did you do, walk up the stairs?"

Aiden held up his hands. "Hey, I got him here in one piece, didn't I?" He rolled his eyes. "I believe the next words from your mouth are 'Thank you, Aide'?"

That earned him another glare. "After that stunt you pulled in the lobby? You have got some *serious* ass-kissing to do before I utter *those* words."

Will cleared his throat.

The parents were advancing on them.

Becca turned and beamed at them. "Mom, Dad, this is Will."

Her dad shook his hand. "Good to meet you, Will."

It was easy to see Aiden took after his dad. They both had the same jawline, their eyes were the same shade of blue… Only difference was his dad's lack of hair.

Her mom gave him a polite smile. "Hello, Will. I'd *like* to say I've heard so much about you." She flashed Becca a glance. "Except that would be a lie. We're both really happy you could make it to the party." She gave him a brief hug. "So, have you two talked about a date yet?"

"Mom!" Becca gaped at her. "You've literally just met him, and already you're planning? And the answer is no, we haven't. We only got engaged a week ago."

"Nine days to be exact, but who's counting?" Her mom gestured to the center table. "Come and sit down, and we can talk."

Will felt like the proverbial rabbit caught in a car's headlights.

"Mom, you can interrogate—I mean, *talk* to him later," Aiden interjected. "Right now you're the hostess. So go mingle. We've got all night, remember?"

Will aimed a grateful glance in Aiden's direction.

"I guess." She grabbed her husband's arm. "Oh look, Carl, Harriet and Walt are here." She tugged him toward the door.

Becca stared at them. "Sometimes I have to wonder if we're really related."

Aiden snorted. "I hate to burst your bubble, kid, but you are gonna be *exactly* like Mom when you get older. The signs are already there."

The look of pure horror Becca gave him was almost comical. "Don't even *think* stuff like that."

"I need a drink." Will hadn't meant for the words to come out so bluntly, but it had been a long day, and the evening promised to be even longer.

"How about a glass of champagne?" Aiden suggested. "I saw someone walking around with a tray. I'll go grab us a couple." And with that he hurried off.

"Yeah, I'd love some too," Becca hollered after him. She shook her head. "Jerk."

"I don't think he's that bad," Will murmured.

Becca narrowed her gaze. "He's a jerk, because I say he is, okay? It's all right for you—*you* don't have to share living space with him. Why do you think I don't come home all that often?"

Will coughed. "Because you're too busy in bed with Kristen?"

Her eyes blazed. "Okay, that's the last time you get to mention her all night." She pasted on a bright smile. "Aunt Deborah. I haven't seen you since last Christmas. How's Kelly doing? Mom said she's going to be a chef."

Aunt Deborah turned out to be another redhead, not that there was any shortage of them in the ballroom. She beamed. “Yes, she’s in her first year of culinary arts. So far, she’s loving it.” Deborah glanced at Will. “And you must be the fiancé.” Another smile. “Welcome to the family.”

“He isn’t part of it yet,” Becca said quickly.

“But look at the two of you. I was watching from across the room. I don’t think I’ve ever seen a couple who were so smitten with each other.” She walked away, and Will chuckled.

“Wow, my acting must be better than I thought.” He buffed his nails on his jacket.

“And you’ve only got another….” Becca glanced at her watch. “Five hours to go.”

That was a dose of reality Will didn’t need right then.

Aiden was a man on a mission.

After almost disabling Will, he was going to make sure the rest of the evening went as smoothly as possible, and with Aiden’s family, that meant only one thing—rescuing Will when he was floundering. Aiden recognized his glassy-eyed stare at once. It was the same one Becca sported when she was trapped in a room full of relatives every holiday. The least Aiden could do would be to dive in and drag Will away from whoever was grilling him.

Of course, saving Will from the Taylor clan was just an excuse. Aiden wanted to stick close to him because… because….

Yeah, he didn't need an excuse. Will drew him like a moth to a flame.

He's marrying Becca. Don't forget that part.

As if he could.

And right then, Will was drowning.

Aiden walked over to the table where Will gave perfunctory nods as Grandma Devlin rattled on at him in what was probably a torrent of questions. It was a torture Aiden had endured on many occasions, and Will didn't deserve such a grisly assault.

"Your champagne." Aiden handed Will a glass, trying not to smirk when Will gulped it down and promptly erupted into a coughing fit. "Yeah, you might wanna take it a bit slower than that."

Will wiped his lips, and Aiden did his best not to stare.

Aiden pointed to the far end of the room. "Hey, Grandma, isn't that Uncle Tim and his new girlfriend?" Not that he had a clue as to the identity of the woman clinging to his uncle's arm, but it was just the distraction he needed.

Grandma widened her eyes. "Who *is* that?" And before Aiden could get another word out, she was off.

"You keep that up, and I might have to pay you to be my bodyguard all night," Will muttered.

"Deal."

Will peered into his empty glass. "Oh, that

is *not* good."

"It's fine. I'll just get you another one."

He jerked his head in Aiden's direction. "That isn't what I meant. I'm not a big drinker, and that went down *way* too fast. I'm going to have to watch myself tonight."

"What kind of drunk are you?" Aiden couldn't help asking. "Do you get the giggles? Do you dance on tabletops? Strip?"

Will let out a wry chuckle. "Nothing that interesting. I talk really fast, and then I pass out, usually in a quiet corner someplace."

"We could always find that quiet corner right now and talk D & D," Aiden suggested, knowing full well it wasn't going to happen.

Becca would see to that.

For a second, Will's face brightened, then fell just as fast. "I can't. Not that it doesn't sound like a really good idea, but…." He gazed at his surroundings.

Aiden got it. Will was a good guy.

"Let me find you another glass, and that'll be it for tonight. But I *will* stick close by, and if you need rescuing, you just give me a nod and I'll dive in and pull you out."

Will's dark brown eyes were warm. "Thank you."

A voice came from the middle of the room. "Ladies and gentlemen, the buffet is open, so please, help yourselves."

Aiden grinned. "Finger food. The perfect base for alcohol."

Will's eyes sparkled. "Now *there's* an idea."

As they headed for the long table groaning

beneath the weight of a mountain of nibbles, salads, bread rolls, and hot dishes, Aiden scanned the room. Becca was with three of their numerous cousins, laughing and chatting.

Some fiancée. She's deserted him.

Well, Aiden wasn't about to leave Will to the mercy of the wolves.

You know this is so *wrong, don't you?*

He ignored the voice in his head.

You were flirting with him just now.

Aiden told himself it wasn't flirting, it was merely being friendly.

Oh yeah? So you want to be friends *with Will? As in* really *close friends?* How *close, exactly?*

Maybe more alcohol would silence Aiden's fucking *annoying* conscience.

Will should have known the reprieve wouldn't last long. No sooner had he piled his plate with a heap of deliciousness, than Becca appeared to tug him toward her parents' table. Will peered over his shoulder at Aiden, giving him a beseeching help-me glance.

His single nod gave Will a sliver of hope.

It was difficult trying to eat and drink while under a constant barrage of questions, but he did his best. Now and then Aiden diverted their parents' attention, and Will took the opportunity to cram a little more food into him. Then it was back to the interrogation.

I'm not surprised Becca has never brought anyone home to meet them.

He'd totally forgiven Aiden for almost cutting him in half with a luggage cart: since then, Aiden had been a godsend, nothing like the aggravating brother Becca had made him out to be.

And once this weekend was over, the possibility of seeing him again was remote, but nowhere near as remote as the possibility of confessing to Aiden that one, Will was gay, two, he was attracted to Aiden, and three, even if Aiden wasn't into guys, Will would still like them to be friends.

Yeah. Snow in hell was a more likely prospect.

"So what about the wedding?"

Becca's mom was like a dog with a bone.

"Mom, give it a break? We're still in school, remember? Then we'll have to find jobs. It could be years before we ever get around to a wedding."

And a matter of days before Becca and I go through an irrevocable break-up that will probably put me on her dad's shit list for the rest of my life.

Will could deal with that. After all, he was never going to see any of the Taylors ever again, with the exception of Becca, and he had to be honest, he'd seen less of her this past year. He'd been replaced by Kristen, not that he minded all that much. That left more time for other pursuits.

Such as finding someone to burn up the

sheets with.

What followed that thought was an image of Aiden under him, that red hair spread out over Will's pillow, those long legs wrapped around him…

You don't want to see the back of all *the Taylors, do you?*

Oh God. Now *there* was an image. Aiden's back, an expanse of creamy skin, narrowed at the waist, Will's fingers gripping his shoulders as he—

Yeah, it had been far too long since he'd gotten laid.

Then he realized eyes were boring into him.

Becca gave him a hard stare that plainly said *Say something, you doof.*

Her mom blinked. "What's wrong with being married students? Your dad and I married before we finished our studies." She gave Becca a pointed glance. "*Remember?*"

"But I'm not you, Mom."

Will didn't miss the desperation and frustration creeping into Becca's voice.

"Besides, Mrs. Taylor, we—"

"Louise. Call me Louise. And this is Carl."

"Okay—Louise. We'll need a couple of years to plan for a wedding. When my sister got married, it took them ages to find a venue, and then there was a waiting list…"

"See, Mom? These things take time." Becca flashed him a smile that told him he was back in her good graces once more.

With everything he was doing for her, Will deserved a lifetime membership for Becca's good graces.

"Louise? You're pushing," Carl said in a low

voice.

Louise stood. "Would you all excuse me?" She walked away from the table.

Aiden stared after her in obvious surprise. "What was that all about?"

Carl chuckled. "You're asking *me*? I've only been married to her for twenty-five years. I don't have all the answers yet." His eyes twinkled. "And it might take me another twenty-five to find them."

Will liked that. He was used to being around his parents whose constant displays of affection had been part of Will's childhood and teenage years, to the point that he believed all parents were that loving. Listening to some of his friends had been an eyeopener. And here was another loved-up couple, still going strong.

I want to be as happy as they are when I reach their age.

"Quick, she's gone. Eat something," Aiden muttered. "We don't know how long it'll be until she comes back."

Will laughed and ate some of his pasta salad.

Becca leaned in. "You took your time," she said from the corner of her mouth. "I thought for a minute there that you were gonna leave me to deal with my mom on my own."

"You were doing fine," he assured her.

Becca snorted. "You don't know my mom. She isn't done yet. I know the signs."

"Do you come from a big family, Will?" Carl asked.

"I have a brother and two sisters, sir. I'm kind of in the middle."

Carl gave an approving nod. "Can't tell you

the last time someone your age called me sir. Not that I don't like it, but lord, it makes me feel old. Please, call me Carl. And what do your parents do?"

"Mom is a teacher and Dad is a professor of mathematics."

Aiden smiled. "That explains why you're studying astrophysics. It's in the genes, obviously."

"I hear *you're* no slouch in the brains department," he remarked.

Brains, good looks, and a Dungeon Master to boot. Plus, he was a nice guy.

Aiden had everything Will could ever want, except for one tiny but significant detail.

He's Becca's brother. And after this, my name will be poison around here.

Carl raised his head. "Will, I hope you've gotten enough food into you. My wife is heading this way." The twitch of his lips told Will what else was in the Taylor family genes—a sense of humor.

Louise came to a halt behind her chair. "I have some really exciting news." Her eyes sparkled, and her face was flushed.

"Who for?" Aiden asked.

"Becca and Will." She beamed. "You are going to be *so* happy."

The roiling in the pit of Will's belly was the exact sensation he'd encountered the night Becca had announced their *engagement.*

"Mom?" The tinge of alarm in Becca's voice told him he wasn't the only one who was getting a very bad feeling about this.

She saw this coming, remember?

How could Becca have ever thought such a hare-brained scheme would work?

"I popped down to the front desk to check on something." Louise pulled out her chair and sat. "And wouldn't you know it? There was a call from the catering manager. The hotel has *just* had a cancellation." She gave a triumphant smile. "Literally two minutes after I walked through the door. It's like an answer to a prayer."

Oh God. Will was praying too. *Don't let her say what I think she's about to say.*

"Mom, what are you talking about?" Becca's eyes were huge.

"I've penciled you in already. I wasn't going to pass up such a wonderful opportunity."

"*What* 'wonderful opportunity'?" Carl demanded. "Louise, will you just spit it out, please?"

Louise smiled. "Becca and Will can have their wedding here. In this room, actually. And who would pass up the chance to have their wedding in the Imperial Ballroom?"

I would. In a heartbeat. Will wasn't sure whether he wanted to run out or throw up.

Throwing up was more likely.

"When, Mom? When *exactly* did you pencil in this wedding?" Becca's face was white.

"December twenty-second."

"You managed to get them the hotel for next year? That's awesome," Carl declared.

Louise chuckled. "Not next year, silly—*this* year. They can have their wedding in just under six weeks' time. A Christmas wedding. Isn't that fantastic?"

Holy fuck.

Will was going to kill Becca. Slowly.

CHAPTER SEVEN

Will Prays For An Alien Invasion To Get Him Out Of This Nightmare.

Will cast an agonized glance in Becca's direction.

You got us into this mess. Now get us out of it.

All she had to do was tell them the truth, right?

"Mom, we can't get married in December."

He held his breath, waiting for the outbursts from her family when they realized they'd been lied to.

"Why not?"

"Because… because…"

Tell them! For God's sake.

Becca's breathing hitched. "We won't have finished for the holidays by then. We'll still be at school."

Will gaped at her. *What the fuck?*

"You won't. I checked. The fall semester finishes December twenty-first." Louise gave her a satisfied smile.

"But we have exams! They don't finish until the twenty-first."

She isn't going to tell them, is she?

The hole Becca had dug was getting deeper

by the second.

I *could tell them.*

Except he knew he wouldn't.

The only person who could stop this merry-go-round was Becca, and for some reason he couldn't fathom, she wasn't ready to do that.

"I know—I went online and checked that too—but that's fine. Just get here as soon as you can."

"Mom? Are you not listening? Neither of us have time to spare, and wedding preparations eat up a *lot* of time."

It was Becca's turn to send an agonized look in his direction.

Welcome to my *world, Becca. It's called Hell—and* you *created it.*

"I know. There's so much to do, isn't there? There's the cake to order, the flowers, the catering…" Louise's eyes widened. "And let's not forget the most important part—the dress."

"Exactly. So you do see why we couldn't possibly—"

Louise beamed. "It's not as if you need do anything. Just leave everything to us."

"Us?" Carl chuckled. "Oh, so now *I'm* riding this steamroller too?" He gestured to Will and Becca. "Don't they get a say? After all, this is *their* wedding, right?"

Louise rolled her eyes. "Will you just *look* at them? Have you ever *seen* two people more in love? I only want my baby to be happy." She glanced at Becca. "You *do* want to be happy, don't you?"

"Yes, of course I do, but—"

"And it's not as if either of you has to

contribute a cent. We'll pay for everything."

"And there you go with that *we* business again," Carl murmured. "Is that like the royal *we*? Or will I be taking out my wallet too?"

Louise glared at him. "We've only got one daughter, and she's getting married. Are you telling me you're not going to make it the most memorable day of her life? We're already making it the easiest wedding ever. All they have to do is show up."

"There's going to be a wedding?" Aunt Deborah's face lit up.

Louise nodded. "Next month. Becca's getting married, and the whole family will be invited."

That did it. Will was in deep shit up to his eyeballs, stuck in a nightmare where he couldn't see a way out, short of aliens invading the planet and abducting him.

Hell, even an alien probe up his ass was a better prospect than marrying Becca.

"There's gonna be a wedding!" Deborah hollered, and Will was engulfed in a sea of bodies as the guests surged forward, whooping, cheering, shouting out their congratulations, shaking his hand, hugging him, planting loud, smacking kisses on his cheeks…

I didn't know it was possible to drown in a ballroom.

Will was sinking like a Mafia dude wearing concrete boots.

"Well, it looks like you'll be my brother-in-law sooner than I thought."

Will gazed at the second glass of champagne that Aiden held out to him.

Fuck it.

He took it, tipped the glass, and drank it in several gulps, the bubbles finding their way into his nose, champagne going down the wrong way, making him cough until he was certain his face was crimson.

"Hey, take it easy." Aiden patted him on the back.

Will held out the empty glass. "Another."

"I don't think that's such a good idea. We'll have to carry you to your room at this rate."

Will couldn't help it. "As long as you're the one who carries me." He grinned. "I've always wanted to be slung over a hunky firefighter's shoulder. Not that *you're* a firefighter, but you'll do."

"What?" Aiden blinked.

Shit.

Becca would kill him if he let *that* cat out of the bag.

'Hey, Mom? Why does Becca's fiancé want to be manhandled by a firefighter?'

The solution was obvious—drink himself unconscious. At least that way he couldn't open his mouth and put his foot in it.

Then he realized Louise was talking to him.

"Sorry. I must've zoned out for a moment there. What did you say?"

"I asked who your best man would be. You'd better pick someone because they'll need to organize your bachelor party."

Bachelor party? *Oh dear Lord.*

"Aiden can make himself useful and organize that," Becca interjected, an evil glint in her eyes.

"Excuse me?" Aiden's mouth fell open.

Carl burst out laughing. "Well, if *I'm* getting roped into this wedding, you might as well join me."

"Oh, can I join in too?" Deborah said with a grin.

Sure, why not? The more the merrier.

Will scanned the room in desperation for a passing server with a tray of drinks, but it seemed Aiden had the same idea. He grabbed two glasses and handed one to Will, who downed it.

"What have you got in mind?" Louise asked.

Ooh, let me guess. Your poodle will be the ring-bearer. You want to make me a groom's cake in the shape of the door from Dante's Inferno, with "Abandon all hope ye who enter here" *written above it in red frosting. Hey, do I get a sexy guy jumping out of the cake too?*

Yeah, Will was as drunk as a skunk.

"I'll throw a cocktail party for the happy couple," Deborah announced, her phone in her hand. "In fact, I'll add it to my calendar right now. Hey everyone! December third, my place, for a party."

More whoops and cheers broke out, but by now Will's head was starting to spin—or was that the room?

He couldn't tell anymore.

"Where's my phone?" Becca's voice rose above those of her relatives. "Will, have you seen my phone?"

He blinked. "What would I be doin' with your phone? Besides, isn't it surgically attached to you, or something?"

She gave him an icy glare. "I'll take that as a no, then, shall I?" Becca peered at the table. "It isn't there."

"It'll turn up." He grinned. "What's wrong? How long has it been since you spoke to…." He winked. "*You* know. Well? How long? Five minutes? Ten? Or has been as long as…" Will gave a dramatic gasp. "Half an hour? OMG."

That earned him another glare. "You're drunk."

He flashed her another grin. "Hey, you're good. Fancy workin' that out all by yourself."

Louise joined them. "Here. I found this on your chair. I was afraid someone would sit on it." She held out Becca's phone.

Becca grabbed it. "Oh, thank you." She pocketed it.

"So, Will, have you thought about whether you'd like a Christmas-themed wedding?"

Will squinted at his watch.

He wasn't going to make it to midnight.

Aiden scanned the ballroom, searching for Becca. Music blared from the speakers, and at least half of the guests were gyrating on the dance floor, moves he vaguely remembered seeing his parents trying to perform at Christmas, when Mom did her usual trick of drinking way too much eggnog, and

Dad put on one of his ancient vinyl LPs.

Watching your parents grooving to the Spice Girls who were asking what you really really want had to be up there as one of the most cringe-inducing, embarrassing moments of all time.

Then he spied Becca, sitting alone in the corner, her phone in her hand, held flat as she spoke into it. What struck him most was her forlorn expression.

What's eating her? She should be out there with her fiancé, having a good time.

Come to think of it, he hadn't seen Will for a while now. The temptation to go find him was huge, but then he got a twinge of guilt.

His sister came first.

Aiden walked over to her, and as he drew closer, he caught the last four words of her conversation.

"I love you too." She finished the call and slipped her phone into her pocket.

He had to smile. That dopey smitten look spoke volumes.

Aiden sat on the blue carpet beside her, leaning against the wall. "That is so cute."

"What is?"

"You can't bear to be apart from him for five minutes while he goes to the restroom?" He leaned in. "Word of advice, though. Guys don't like to talk while they're taking a leak—or God forbid, doing anything else that requires concentration."

He did his best not to think about the two or three occasions when he'd taken a guy's ass while he stood with one leg bent, his foot on the toilet. He'd even ridden a guy once in a toilet stall. And if *his* phone had burst into life while he was… busy, he'd have dropped it into the toilet bowl.

Then he reasoned that in Will's present state, he could be doing something equally demanding.

He could be throwing up.

Becca regarded him with a puzzled expression for a moment, then widened her eyes. "Oh. Right. Sure. I'll try to remember that."

Aiden stared out at the dance floor, noting that not one of his cousins under the age of thirty was anywhere to be seen on it. "So… great party."

Becca snorted.

"Classic dance tracks."

Snort.

"Wanna tell me what you're doing over here when you should be out there?"

She stared at him. "You *were* there, right? When Mom decided to ruin my life?"

"All she did was find you a beautiful wedding venue, offer to pay for everything, organize everything… Yeah, I can see why that would totally ruin anyone's life."

"You're telling me I should be *grateful*?"

"I'm telling you that it's still your wedding. If she's going to do something you don't like, tell her. Like she said, she only wants you to be happy." He leaned in, their heads meeting. "Besides, this is what she does, right? We should be used to it by now."

"Yeah, sure, tell her. As if it would be *that* easy."

Aiden turned to face her. "You do *want* to marry Will, don't you?" He took her left hand in his, gazing at the plain gold band adorning her ring finger. Nothing fancy, but hey, they were students. "I mean, you said yes, after all."

Becca pulled her hand free of his. "Of course I want to get married. It's just…"

"Just Mom doing her thing. I know." He smiled. "You know what? I'm gonna go find your fiancé, send him your way, and the two of you should wait for a slow number and get out there and do something really romantic." He inclined his head toward the dancers. "You know, like our parents are doing right this second."

Becca gazed at them as they circled the floor slowly, Mom's head resting against Dad's shoulder, her hand on his neck, his hand on her waist.

"They *are* amazing, aren't they?" Her lips twitched. "And totally aggravating." She sighed. "Go find Will."

He stood and held out a hand to her, hauling her to her feet. To his surprise, Becca hugged him.

"What was that for?" he asked when she released him.

"I just felt like it, that's all. No other reason." She pointed toward the door. "Now, go do your impression of a Saint Bernard puppy dog—just without the brandy barrel. I think Will's had enough for one night."

Aiden had the same idea.

He wove his way through the partygoers until he reached the door. Outside, the hallway was quieter, and he breathed a little easier.

Where are you, future brother-in-law?

Aiden went to the nearest restroom, but Will was nowhere in sight. He rode the elevator downstairs, searching for any sign of him.

Then he saw him, standing in the middle of the lobby, gazing up at the painted ceiling, weaving a little.

Aiden walked up to him. "It's beautiful, isn't it?"

Will jerked his head toward him. "Hey. Yeah, it is." He gestured to their surroundings. "When was this place built?"

"1893." Aiden pulled on his arm. "Come with me, and I'll show you photos of the hotel that go back years."

"I'd like that."

They walked across the thickly carpeted floor to the far end of the lobby.

"The hotel usually has an artist-in-residence," Aiden told him. He glanced at Will. "You okay? You look a little green."

"I just drank too much, that's all. But I could sure use some water."

Aiden had a change of plan.

"Then let me take you up to your room. You can drink water, lie down, go to sleep, whatever you want."

"But what about the party?"

He smiled. "Don't you worry about that. They're going to have a good time whether you're there or not. Think about it. Which is better—to go be quiet in your own room, or go back to the party and throw up over your future mother-in-law's best shoes?"

Will frowned. "Wait. I didn't know that was an option." He sighed. "Yeah, when you put it like that, maybe getting some rest would be the best thing for everyone right now."

Sure, that wasn't at *all* weird. Aiden guided him back to the elevator.

It wasn't until they reached the eighth floor that he realized something had been niggling him ever since he'd left the ballroom. He'd asked Becca if she wanted to marry Will. How had she answered, exactly?

'Of course I want to get married."

But that doesn't answer the question.

Chapter Eight

Will Has A Hangover

Sunday, November 13, 2022

The first thing Will did once he'd opened his eyes was check everywhere on his body to make sure he hadn't gotten himself a tattoo. One of his classmates had done that their first year, and on his belly there was the goofiest looking dinosaur *ever.*

He heaved a sigh of relief to find unmarked skin. It appeared all the tattoo shops had been closed. Thank God.

He hauled himself into the shower and let the hot water work its magic. That got him about halfway to feeling human again. Breakfast would accomplish the rest, but no way was he going downstairs to eat in a restaurant filled with the people he'd gotten drunk in front of the night before.

His room was a much safer option.

He called down and ordered eggs, sausage, bacon, an English muffin, and coffee.

The latter would probably need to be refilled.

His phone buzzed while he was waiting, and he glanced at the screen.

Becca.

Oh yeah. He had a bone to pick with her. Several bones, in fact.

You awake?

He snorted and typed. *It's seven-thirty. Of course I'm awake.*

Mom was worried when you didn't come back to the party.

He frowned. *I didn't? Oh. Right.* He recalled Aiden helping him to his room. He also recalled telling Aiden he needed help getting undressed.

Oh God.

He couldn't think about that right then. His head was already complaining.

He typed. *Sorry to disappear on you like that, but I wasn't at my best.*

An eye-roll emoji. *You didn't miss much. Only my Uncle Tim doing a* Dirty Dancing *number with his girlfriend. Then Aunt Deborah climbed onto a table and stripped to a Rihanna song.*

OMFG. Seriously?

Several laughing emojis. *You are so gullible, Bryant. I get you every time.*

Then he remembered what had really happened.

So what do we do now?

Nothing came through for a moment. *About…?*

She had to be kidding. *Oh, I don't know. How about the fact that you're marrying me next month?*

Oh. That.

Will looked around for one of the hotel notepads so he could start writing down all the imaginative ways in which he was going to kill her. *Yes, that.*

So you do remember that much?

He laughed out loud. *Pretty hard to forget the reason I got drunk in the first place.*

She was typing. *Right now I have no idea what we're gonna do.*

He blinked, his fingers stumbling on the screen. *Really? Because I can see one obvious solution. Tell. Your. Mom.*

I can't. Not yet.

Then when, Becca? When she asks if we've got the marriage license sorted? When you go for the final fitting of your wedding dress? Just before your dad walks you down the aisle?

There is no aisle. It's a ballroom.

You're gonna nitpick details like that at a time like this?

There was a knock at the door, and Will groaned.

Coffee. Food.

Once the server had gone, a five-dollar tip safely stowed in his pocket, Will poured himself a steaming cup of coffee, ate a strip of bacon, and checked to see how Becca was planning to extricate them from the pile of shit she'd dropped them in.

I'll tell her, okay? Just… when the time is right. What are your plans for this morning?

Will knew avoidance when he saw it, but he was too hungover to continue with this dance.

Right now, to stop my head from banging. Maybe I'll go for a walk. He glanced at the window where an inch of snow covered the sill. *Or maybe not. What time are we out of here? Check out is 11.*

The front desk will stow your bag until you're ready to leave. I'll pick you up outside the hotel at 2. Don't wanna get back too late tonight. Oh. And you're invited home for Thanksgiving.

Will forked eggs into his mouth and typed at the same time. *When did this happen?* Great. Another chance to look like an idiot in front of Becca's family.

In front of Aiden.

Last night. Sometime before everyone stopped dancing. You know what? A walk is a good idea. Fresh air to clear your head. I'll call Aiden for some suggestions. He's the hiker of the family.

Yet another thing to like about Aiden. Except Will wasn't sure he wanted to be around him after the previous night.

Don't… don't ask him, okay? I don't want to put him out.

No response.

Becca?

You didn't tell him, did you?

What? No. At least, he hoped he hadn't. That part was a little… hazy.

Not even a hint?

*Well… there *was* one tiny slip up.* Okay, two. Possibly. *But I'm sure he'll put that down to me being drunk off my ass.*

He'd better. Oops. Mom is calling. Breakfast. See you at 2.

Will finished his breakfast and poured himself another cup.

Never mind a walk. A couple more hours sleep would do him a world of good.

Except he knew what would be waiting for him behind his eyelids.

A certain ginger, with the most beautiful

blue eyes Will had ever seen, and a smile that both warmed and thrilled him.

A certain ginger to whom Will might have given away way too much.

Aiden had just finished his breakfast when the doorbell rang. He smiled as he went to open it. Carol stood there, holding a pet carrier.

"One feline, reporting for kitty duty."

From behind the wire panel, Midnight glanced at him then turned away.

Great. I'm in the dog house with my cat.

He took the carrier. "Was he okay?"

Carol smirked. "If you call catching him in the closet, humping Candy, then sure, we'll go with that. I keep meaning to get her fixed. Maybe now is a good time. You know, before there's the pitter patter of tiny claws around my place."

Aiden chuckled. "Do they fix horny boy kitties too? Maybe I should look into that—unless they're human, in which case send them here."

Aiden put Midnight's carrier on the kitchen floor and opened the door. The cat was out of it in a heartbeat. Aiden grabbed the bottle of wine he'd stood on the countertop and held it out to Carol. "Thanks."

She grinned. "Any time."

Aiden closed the door and turned to find Midnight sitting in the middle of the floor, tail curled around him, covering his front paws.

"Hey, kitty. Miss me?"

Midnight yawned.

"Don't be like that. You had a great night by all accounts so don't you go giving me the cold shoulder. Because we both know that the minute my back is turned, you'll be doing a little furry paw pump, and scratching another notch on your cat tree."

Midnight yawned again.

Aiden grinned. "Maybe I should go with Carol. Think we can get a discount on having you *and* Candy fixed?"

He'd never seen a look of horror on a cat's face before.

Aiden's phone buzzed, and he grabbed it to peer at the screen.

Aha. The bride-to-be.

He clicked answer. "Good morning. How's your head this morning? Better than your fiancé's, I suspect."

"He needs some air. Any ideas where I should send him?"

Here. Send him here, so we can become better acquainted.

Aiden's version of getting acquainted required a bed and no clothing.

Except you'd be just as happy to talk D & D with him, wouldn't you?

Yeah, that was sad.

"Aide? You still there?"

"Still here. I could always drive him to the lake. It's pretty to look at."

"That's your idea of a good time, is it? Now I know why you don't have a girlfriend."

No, you don't. You really don't. And it's going to stay that way.

"Leave it with me. Send me his number. How long do you have left in Milwaukee?"

"We're leaving at two."

That gave him a few hours to play with.

And remember that. Play with the hours, *not Will.*

"Have a great morning with Mom and Dad." Aiden grinned. He wouldn't swap places with Becca right then, not for all the gold in a dragon's hoard.

His phone buzzed again, and he chuckled. *Now what?*

It was Mom's number.

He answered the call, and the first sound that reached him was a familiar bird song.

"Mom? Is that a chickadee?" The song always made him smile, ever since his dad had said it sounded as if the bird was singing cheese burger. And now he could never un-hear it. "Where are you?" It was way too loud to be inside the house.

"I'm in the backyard," she said in a low voice. "And I'm freezing, so this is going to be a quick call."

"But *why* are you out in the yard?"

"Because I don't want Becca to hear me, all right?"

Okay, something was up. "Talk fast, Mom, before something freezes and falls off."

"Last night, your sister left her phone on her

chair, and—"

"I know, I was there, remember?"

"Fine. But I… I didn't give it back to her right away."

He managed a mock gasp of horror. "Mom, tell me you didn't snoop."

Her snort filled his ears. "I'm a mother. Of course I did."

He knew he was going to hate himself for asking, but… "And? What did you find?"

"What did you think of Will?"

The randomness of the question threw him for a second.

"I like him. Why?"

"Oh, I'm sure he's a lovely person, but is he really the kind of boy you imagined Becca marrying?"

"Oh my God. What did you find on her phone?"

"It's what I *didn't* find that concerns me."

What? "Mom, you're not making any sense."

"I only looked because I was certain he wasn't the man for her, okay? And after going through her photos, I—"

"You did what? Mom, that's awful."

"But there were no pictures of them together or anything."

"So? You still shouldn't have done it." When she didn't reply, the hairs on Aiden's arms stood to attention. "Mom? What else did you find?"

"Nothing that need concern you."

"You know what? It doesn't concern *either* of us, because it's Becca's business, you got that?"

"Your father's calling. I have to go inside."

"Mom, don't you hang—"

Up on me.

Aiden stared at his phone, his mind racing.

This is weird.

A soft *whump* frightened the life out of him when Midnight jumped into his lap.

"Oh, so *now* you're talking to me? Does this mean I'm forgiven for allowing you the opportunity to get laid?"

Midnight bumped Aiden's chin with his head, and Aiden absently stroked the silky fur. He couldn't explain the lack of photos, not when Becca had known Will for three years and they'd been dating for at least one.

There was only one course of action.

Aiden reached for his phone and dialed the number Becca had sent him. It rang about three times before Will answered.

"Hello?"

"Will, it's Aiden. Becca gave me your number. Listen, you wanna go down to the lake with me? We can take hot drinks and snacks from the coffee shop, and sit and look at the water."

And talk. We're definitely *going to talk.*

There was a pause. "Sure. But as for snacks, I could just bring what's in this fridge. Otherwise, it isn't going to be eaten, and that would be a crime."

He chuckled. "Bag 'em, and I'll meet you in the lobby in about thirty minutes."

"Great. See you there."

Aiden disconnected the call, and scritched behind Midnight's ears. "Sorry, but I'm gonna leave you alone for a while."

The purr made Midnight sound like the

epitome of the perfect cat, but Aiden knew better. He knew Midnight.

'Fine. Leave me again. And I'll leave you lots of little gifts all over the place. Where you least expect them.'

Aiden took a sip from his cup. "So you and Becca have been friends for what, three years?" Beyond the windshield lay Lake Michigan. Even though the day was overcast and the sun wasn't causing the water to sparkle like normal, the lake had a certain majesty of its own. How often had he come down here and whispered his problems to the lake, just knowing the lake would carry them away on the tide?

Will nodded. "Though there are times when it feels longer."

He laughed. "I know where you're coming from."

Will smiled. "She can be utterly adorable, though. Like when she's listening to music, and she dances in front of the mirror."

Aiden cackled. "She still does that? What about when she thinks no one's looking, and she blows her—"

"Cheeks up! Oh my God, how long has she been doing that?"

"Since she was about six."

"Did she used to eat her dessert before the main course back then too?"

Aiden laughed. "God yeah."

"Did she freak out back then when other people tried to eat stuff from off her plate?"

He pointed to his right hand, to a tiny scar on his pinky. "Yup. I got that when I tried to sneak a fry off her plate. She stabbed me with her fork."

Will gasped. "Seriously?" Aiden started laughing again, and Will smiled. "You've got a great laugh." Then he cleared his throat. "What's so funny?"

"When she was little, she had this weird idea that if she used shampoo all over her body, not just on her head, that she'd grow hair everywhere and turn into a monkey."

"That is so cute." Will chuckled. "You know what's *really* cute? When we're in town, shopping, and we go to cross the street. She waves her hand at the lights and—"

"And they change! She still does that? She used to say it was her secret power." He took another long drink from his cup. "It's good to know some things *don't* change."

His mom might not think Will was right for Becca, but the affection in Will's voice when he talked about her eased Aiden's mind.

He really does care for her.

Mom was worrying about nothing, he was sure of it.

"I guess I'll be seeing you for Thanksgiving," Will said in a low voice, staring out at the choppy waves that lapped the lake shore.

"I guess so."

Only eleven days to go.

"About my bachelor party… You don't have to organize it, you know." Will bit his lip. "Becca doesn't have to get her own way in *everything*."

"No, it's fine. I don't mind, really."

"And who knows? I might not even *want* a bachelor party. A lot can happen before then."

Such as what?

"Something you want to tell me?"

Maybe Mom's thinking wasn't that far out after all.

Will blinked. "No, of course not."

Aiden wasn't convinced.

"I think we should be getting back to the hotel. Becca will be there soon."

Aiden gave a huge sigh. "All the way back to Minneapolis—with my sister. I feel for ya."

And you want to change the subject, don't you?

What bothered Aiden was *why*.

"About last night… I didn't do anything… foolish, did I? Or say anything stupid?"

Aiden arched his eyebrows. "No more than any of us do when we're drunk." He tilted his head to one side. "You don't remember?"

"Yes… well, no… it's a bit… blurry."

Aiden couldn't resist. "So you don't recall asking me to take your clothes off and put you into bed?"

The horror on Will's face was everything he'd expect from a straight guy.

"Oh God. It's all coming back to me now. Do me a favor? Don't tell Becca about that, please?"

Aiden snickered. "Your secret is safe."

"I didn't ask you to get into bed with me, did I?"

No such luck.

Aiden gave him a kind smile. "You weren't *that* drunk."

Great. I can see my future now. Years and years of Christmas Days, Thanksgiving, birthdays, family get-togethers… and there I'll be, lusting after my extremely straight brother-in-law.

God hated him, that was it.

CHAPTER NINE

Will's Life Is Suddenly Not His Own

Tuesday, November 15

"You're *what*?" Kristen's shriek could probably be heard from space, let alone the small kitchen area where Will was standing. "How the *fuck* are you engaged to Will? Are you for real?"

He'd been asking the same question ever since the party.

A second later, the door to Becca's room was flung open, and Kristen strode out, eyes blazing and jaw set as she grabbed her coat from the chair where she'd dumped it.

The front door closed with a *bang*.

Will winced. *That went well.*

Becca appeared in the doorway, eyes red, face blotchy. "You heard?"

He snorted. "I think all of Minnesota heard. And maybe even parts of Iowa, Wisconsin, and South Dakota." He gaped at her. "How did you think she was gonna take it? *'Oh, Becca, that's wonderful. I'm so happy for you'*?" Will narrowed his gaze. "You *did* tell her we're not *really* getting married, didn't you? That this was all your idea of surviving your parents' party without your mom setting you up with every hotel employee who was eligible—you know, so long as they had a pulse, they were in?"

"She isn't *that* bad," Becca retorted. Will simply stared at her, and she crumpled. "Okay, yeah, she is. Who am I kidding? She's gotten worse this year. It's as if she's on a mission from God to get me married off." She gazed at the front door. "I think Kristen was more upset that I hadn't just come clean—come out—and told Mom and Dad about her."

Will had heard enough. "You know what? I can't deal with this. I've got exams to prep for, and so do you." He didn't need this crap messing with his head.

Becca put her hands on her hips. "Well, here's something you *have* to deal with. Mom is busy filling my—*and* your—weekends for the next five weeks."

He froze. "What the fuck?"

She nodded. "Aunt Deborah's party you already know about. Now Mom has booked me an appointment on Saturday morning at the Strike Bridal Bar." Will smirked, and she glared at him. "You think that's funny?"

"Sure. *I* won't be the one being pinned into something that resembles a meringue."

Her eyes gleamed. "I hate to spoil your enjoyment of the situation, but I wouldn't laugh if I were you. Not when you're coming along to decide on the flowers—*and* the cake. Mom also says she wants us to okay the menu. And the following weekend is Thanksgiving, where you get to meet all my relatives again."

Will threw his hands up in the air. "For a

wedding that isn't even going to happen, it's sure taking over my life." And Becca didn't seem to give a shit. If anything, she was enjoying it.

He froze when a sob burst from her. "I'm sorry, okay? I had no idea Mom would go this far. I know I promised it'd all be over by now, but this has really railroaded me." Becca wiped her eyes. "Just don't fall out with me over this, okay, Will? I couldn't bear it if I lost you for a friend. We've been through too much for that to happen."

He gave her a hug. "Hey. It'll be okay."

"Ya think?" Whatever Becca was about to say was lost when the door opened, and Kristen walked in, wiping her eyes. She came to a halt in front of Becca.

"Babe, you *have* to do something."

Will huffed. "I've been saying that since Saturday. See if you have more luck than I did." And with that, he walked out of the three-bedroomed university apartment, heading for his own that he got to share with no one.

As he walked across campus, Will's mind was busy exploring all the options, but so far he'd only come up with one.

Kill Becca.

A bit harsh, maybe? That was no act just now. She was really upset.

Okay, maybe he wouldn't kill her. Just… torture her a little.

His phone vibrated, and Will knew it would be a message from Becca, asking him to return.

Fat chance of that. She'd already ruined his afternoon—he wasn't letting her anywhere near his evening.

Then it buzzed again, and Will groaned. *Leave me alone, why don't you?* He removed it from his jeans pocket, ready to tell Becca where to get off, and came to a dead stop in the middle of the cleared path when he saw Aiden's name—right before someone bumped into him from behind.

"You need brake lights, dude," a voice hollered.

"Sorry!" he yelled as they passed him. He made sure he wasn't going to be someone else's obstacle before reading the message.

Mom says you'll be here this weekend. Wanna talk about the bachelor party? I was thinking December 10.

Great. First Becca, now her brother.

Her hot-as-fuck, straight brother, who was going to make every family get-together awkward as hell once he and Becca were mar—

Okay, that did it. He was starting to sound as crazy as Becca.

We are not *getting married, remember?*

Will hit speed dial, and when Becca answered within two rings, he let rip.

"I'm not playing anymore. You got that?"

"Oh sure. Like it's *that* easy."

"I'm gonna tell Aiden the truth." It was easier than telling her parents, and besides, once Aiden knew, they'd get to hear about it pretty swiftly after that.

"You can't!" Becca blurted.

"Ya think? Watch me."

"But Will, I—"

"'But Will' nothing. What's the alternative? Play along until you're suddenly standing in front of a room full of guests, with me in a suit, looking like the Penguin from those old *Batman* shows my dad used to watch, and then you say 'Oh, sorry, hundreds of guests, this wedding isn't happening. It was a joke, all right? You know, ha ha ha'?" He took a breath. "There's still time. We can break up. Tell your parents I took one look at your family and changed my mind."

"What? What's wrong with my family?" Becca's voice was laced with righteous indignation.

Will rolled his eyes. "To quote your girlfriend—you know, the one you *do* want to marry—'are you for real?'"

"Who says I want to marry Kristen?"

"Wait—you *don't* wanna marry me?" Kristen shrieked in the background.

"Oh fuck." He listened as Becca pleaded with Kristen not to walk out again, whined that of *course* Becca wanted to marry her—she'd do it in a heartbeat—and then went so far as to tell her she'd even picked out a dress for the occasion.

When he heard Becca's labored breathing at the other end, he snickered. "See? You *do* want to marry her. Tell her I think she'll make a beautiful bride."

"I heard that. Thanks, Will. It's good to know I've got *someone* on my side," Kristen called out.

"Babe, I'm on your side, honest." Then Becca snarled down the phone. "*Now* see what you've gone and done?"

"What *I've* done? Girl, you are delusional. So here's the deal. I'll go with you to Milwaukee this weekend, but on one condition. Before your mom lays out any money for a dress, flowers, catering, whatever—you tell her it's off. *We're* off. You got that? One party, you said. We'll break up right after it, you said. Well, this has gone *way* beyond what we agreed, and if you think I'm gonna let you walk all over me, then think again."

"Will… I… I can't tell her, not yet." The catch in her voice was all too real, and it sobered him.

He took a deep breath. "Then give me one good reason why. Why are we still playing at this… farce, Becca?"

"Because…."

"Still here. I'm waiting."

Her sigh tugged at his heart. "I love my family, okay? I'm trying hard to figure out a way that I won't lose them, but no matter how I look at it, once the truth comes out, they're gone." She paused. "I know I'm asking a lot, but please, just give me a little longer. I *swear* I'll fix it. I just have to figure out how."

He sighed too. He could understand that desire to keep the family. He'd had friends who'd come out and it hadn't gone well.

"I… I guess I can understand. But so we're clear, I am *not* marrying you." He snorted. "And we are *not* having babies."

Becca choked. "Don't say things like that!"

Then he sighed once more. "And for the record, I really like your family, okay?"

"Yeah, it sounded like it."

"Not that it matters if I do or I don't because we're not really getting married, remember? But Aiden seems cool."

"Huh. He likes you too. I guess because

you're both nerds. It's a pity you won't be his brother-in-law. He'd have liked that." Another pause. "I gotta go. Got a girlfriend to spoil."

"You got that right." Will hung up.

By the time he reached his own apartment, he'd pushed aside his bad mood, all thoughts of weddings, bachelor parties, killing Becca…. He had a lot of work to do, and he needed a clear head. No sooner was he in his room than the phone rang again.

Great, now what?

It was his dad.

"Hey, how are the studies going?"

They'd be going better if everyone just left me alone to study. Except that wasn't fair. Dad only called once in a blue moon.

"Okay, I guess."

"You *guess*? That doesn't sound like you. Is everything okay?"

Fantastic. Now he'd gone and worried his dad.

"It's… complicated, all right? Nothing I can really talk about." *And definitely not to you.* His dad was an awesome father, but the present situation would be beyond his comprehension.

Who was he kidding? It was already beyond Will's.

"Boy trouble?"

Will laughed. "Oh Dad, that would be so easy compared to what I've gotten myself into." Well, what *Becca* had gotten him into, even if she *had* been motivated by her love for Kristen.

"You know, if you ever need to talk, we're right here."

"Thanks, Dad. Give my love to Mom."

"Will we see you for lunch on Sunday? We missed you last week."

His heart sank. "Yeah, sorry, but I can't make it."

"Okay, I'll let your mom know, but don't leave it too long, all right? I mean, we're not exactly a million miles away from the campus."

"I know. I'll come over soon." He hung up, grabbed a glass of milk from the fridge, a couple of cookies from his stash, and spread his textbooks out over his bed.

Finally.

Five minutes later, his phone buzzed, and Will raised his eyes to the ceiling.

You're just toying with me now, aren't you, God? You're doing this for shits and giggles.

He glanced at the screen. Ethan.

Will closed his book and stabbed at the phone.

"Hey. Your little brother is just fine, okay? Never mind whatever Dad has told you. And don't tell me he hasn't called you, because we both know that's a lie. He's been doing this since I was old enough to have a phone."

Ethan chuckled. "Okay, you got me. He said you sounded—and I quote—'a little weird'."

"He'd be weird too if he was in my shoes," Will muttered.

There was a pause, and Will wondered if he'd said too much.

"Sally's Saloon, ten minutes. Be there, or the next thing you'll hear will be me hammering on your door at University Commons."

"Don't you have better things to do than annoy me?"

"Sure I do. I could be helping Dad tidy the garage."

Now Will got it.

"You just wanted a get out of jail free card, didn't you? And I'm it." He knew when he was beaten. "Fine. See you at Sally's in ten." He hung up.

Is this my lot in life, to be used by everyone?

Will gazed at his books. "Just one beer, all right? Then I'll be back."

He chuckled. *Now who's delusional?*

Ethan was already sitting at the white marble-top bar when Will walked in, his gaze focused on the TV screen at the end of it. A re-run of a football game was playing, and Ethan was yelling at the players.

Will laughed as he slid onto the stool next to Ethan. "You already know how it ends, dumbass." He picked up the tall, frosted glass and clinked it with Ethan's. "Here's to the Dwarfs for their great brews, and may we all live longer than our foes."

Ethan arched his eyebrows. "Whatever."

The beer was crisp and refreshing, and exactly what Will needed.

"So…. What's going on that you couldn't tell Dad?"

Will chuckled. "Finish your beer first."

"Why?"

"Because you'll only spit it out when you hear what I have to tell you."

Ethan blinked, then downed his beer. "Okay, what's bad enough to get you to a bar on a school night?"

Will finished his own beer, set the glass down, and started at the beginning. Ethan listened, peppering Will's account with the occasional 'What the fuck?' and 'OMG'. When Will got to the end, Ethan shook his head.

"I was going to ask how you got yourself into this mess but I think you just answered that question."

"I keep asking myself the same thing."

Ethan laced his fingers on the bar. "Okay, let's look at the positives. You're *not* marrying Becca. Sure, you're going to upset a ton of people when they learn the truth, but if you don't let it get too far, you might avoid that. I'll be honest, you've stuck it out far longer than I think *I'd* have done."

Will gestured to the bartender. "Same again, please." Then he realized Ethan had gone quiet. He shot him a darting glance. "What?"

Ethan smirked. "All right…. What is it you haven't told me?"

He feigned innocence. "I don't know what you mean."

"You're not still playing along because Becca wants to keep her family sweet. And sure, she's your bestie, but there has to be more to it than that."

"I don't want to sour relations with Becca's family," Will protested.

Ethan's gaze bored into him. "And the rest."

He sighed. "Okay…I don't want to sour relations with her brother, all right?"

That got him a grin. "Aha. *Now* we're getting someplace. I knew there had to be a guy in the equation somewhere. What's his name?"

"Aiden."

"Right age?"

"Perfect."

"Is he hot?"

"God, yes."

"Is he into guys?"

Will groaned. "I don't know! All I *do* know is he's a D & D Dungeon Master, he's cool, smart, and even if he *isn't* gay or bi, he'd be a great friend. And I don't know why I'm in such a mess over him because I only met him on Saturday."

Ethan chuckled. "In which case, I have the perfect toast, one I even researched and saved for just such an occasion. Well, almost perfect."

"I dread to ask, but what is it?"

Ethan grinned. "Bottoms up and tops down."

Will was glad he'd chosen to wait before taking a drink.

"So what does Aiden look like?"

It was Will's turn to smile. "He's a ginger."

Ethan laughed. "Oh yeah. Perfect for you."

"And what does that mean?"

"Little brother, who was on your bedroom

walls when you were sixteen, seventeen, eighteen…? Prince Harry. And remember when Mom found your *Red Hot Exposed* calendar under your mattress when you were sixteen?" He grinned. "I think your cheeks were the same color."

"Can you blame me? She stood there, leafing through it, saying things like, '*he's* got a nice bottom' and 'ooh, look at those muscles.' And *then* she wanted to know where I got it, because she was thinking of getting a copy for herself. Not that I ever told her."

Ethan coughed. "Thanks for that, by the way." He studied Will. "You really have no idea if Aiden is into guys or not?"

"No."

"But you want to know, don't you?"

Oh yes, he wanted to know, all right.

"We're meeting this weekend, to talk about the bachelor party."

Ethan's hand froze, his glass stopped on its journey to his lips. "Say what?"

He huffed. "It was Becca's mom's idea. She asked Aiden to put it together."

Ethan put his glass down, his gaze narrowed. "Now wait just one minute. The bachelor party? That's the remit of the best man, right? So does that mean *Aiden* is gonna be your best man? Because I can think of someone else who should be at your side, and it isn't him."

Will gaped at him. "At my side when? On the day I *don't* get married? Or did you forget that part? I don't *need* a best man. I don't *need* a bachelor party. Because I am *not* getting married, do you hear me?"

The bartender snickered. "Preach. You're better off single." When Will and Ethan turned their heads to stare at him, he flushed. "Just sayin'. Marriage is for morons. Who needs a stupid piece of paper? Play the field, man. Sow your oats. Love 'em and leave 'em, that's what I say."

Will bit his lip. "You don't date much, do you?"

The bartender blinked. "How d'you know that?"

With a sigh, Will returned his attention to Ethan. "Thanks for that. You've given me a reason to go to Milwaukee." He took a mouthful of beer. "I'm going to tell Aiden he is *not* organizing any party for me."

"Thank God for that," Ethan muttered. "Besides, putting together a bachelor party for you would be a freakin' nightmare."

"Why?" Will glared at him. "What do you mean?"

Ethan chuckled. "You don't have three friends to rub together. I can see it now. Sitting around a table playing your games till the wee small hours, eating chips and drinking beer."

Will was about to retort that he *had* friends, thank you very much—until he realized Ethan was correct.

He didn't have many.

That's why I don't want to piss Aiden off.

Aiden was the kind of friend Will would love to have. So whatever he was going to say when they came face-to-face, it had better be diplomatic.

I'll let him down gently. He'll understand.

Gods, Will hoped so.

CHAPTER TEN

Will Puts His Foot Down

Saturday, November 19

Will sighed. "I wish Becca had told me where she was dropping me off before we got here. I'd have said anywhere but here." Not that the Pfister wasn't a beautiful hotel, but now it stirred memories of things he'd rather forget.

Like, did anyone who works here see me that night when I was stumbling through the lobby, staring drunkenly at the ceiling?

From the armchair facing him, Aiden chuckled. "That doesn't sound good, considering you're getting married in here." He sounded as chilled as he looked. His faded jeans, folded up at the bottom, clung to long, lean legs, and whoever had said redheads shouldn't wear red was full of shit in Will's opinion. The thick red sweater also made Aiden appear eminently huggable.

"You know what? Forget what I just said. I'm an *adult*, for God's sake. I should have asked Becca where we were going."

What's the number one rule? Never trust Becca. Ever.

Especially after this mess.

Then Aiden laughed, a bright, delightful

sound that rose above the tinkling of the piano.

"What's tickled you?" Will drank a little of his soda.

Aiden grinned. "Oh, I was just thinking of Becca and Mom, looking at wedding dresses—and how glad I am not to be with them."

Will had made it clear to Becca before he'd gotten out of the car that in no way was she allowed to let her mom fork out any money, unless it was a returnable deposit.

He had to do *something* to limit the fallout from this fiasco.

Aiden removed his phone from the front pocket of his jeans. "Okay, I've been thinking about where to hold the bachelor party, and I've come up with a few options. There's Cathedral Square, the South Shore Terrace beer garden, Burnhearts…. If you want to do something completely different, there's the Paddle Tavern—"

Will had to work really hard not to shower Aiden with soda.

"Please, tell me that has nothing to do with the kind of paddles you use to smack someone's ass."

Aiden's laughter caused heads to turn in their direction. "No, it doesn't, but at least I know that sort of party is *not* what you have in mind. No, in this instance, you get to spend a couple of hours cruising down the river, alcohol included."

Will was all for cruising, but on dry land.

"Unless you have ideas of your own?"

And there it was, the opening Will needed.

"Yeah, we need to talk about this."

Aiden stilled. "That sounds serious."

"That's because it is." Will wanted to be gentle, but maybe ripping off the Band-aid was the way to go. "Look, it was sweet of Becca to suggest that you could organize this, but to be honest…" Except sweetness didn't enter into it.

It was Becca's evil nature. Okay, maybe not *totally* evil, but definitely mischievous.

"You don't want me involved." Aiden delivered the statement in a flat, neutral tone that gave nothing away, but it had to be a fair assumption that Will had just hurt his feelings.

"Look, when I get married, my best man will be my brother, Ethan. I've only got one brother, after all. Besides, how could you organize it? You don't know my friends—"

He could hear Ethan's snort all the way from Minnesota. *What friends?*

Will wasn't finished. "So what would you do—go to Rent-A-Crowd? Have a room full of strangers there to watch me get drunk—again? Unless you intended turning it into a massive game night, and—"

Aiden held up his hand. "Whoa there."

He took a breath, his heart pounding. The words had poured out of him, and while everything he'd said was true, what lay at its root was the deep desire not to have Aiden put himself out in any way whatsoever.

He's going to be pissed when Becca announces the engagement—and the wedding—is off. Will didn't want Aiden bearing him a grudge.

Why not? Do you really think that once Becca calls a halt to this business, you can come out and say, 'actually, I'm gay, and I was wondering if you'd ever contemplated going on a date with a guy'? Do you seriously *think that's gonna happen?*

Not a fucking chance.

Then Aiden smiled, and that light in his eyes was a joy to see, rekindling expectations Will knew were groundless, but he couldn't help himself.

"Thank God. You're a logical man. I was hoping you'd say something like that. Not that I don't want to organize the party—I can be a party animal when the occasion calls for it—but you're right. Of *course* it should be your brother. And it should be in Minnesota or wherever you damn well please. It's *your* party, *your* wedding, right?"

Yeah, Will wanted to keep Aiden in his life.

Oh, come on. If you had to choose between staying friends with Becca or with Aiden, it'd be a no-brainer.

Maybe.

"But since you brought it up… a game bachelor party? I like that idea."

Will liked it too, but that would take some organizing, and—

There I go again. There isn't going to be *a bachelor party, remember?*

What was it about Becca's family that lowered his IQ and made him forget his good intentions?

"And now we've got *that* out of the way…" Aiden smiled. "What else is happening this weekend?"

"Once Becca gets back here, I think your mom said something about flowers." Not that he had a clue what they expected *him* to do.

What do I know about flowers?

"Want me to tag along?"

Stupid question.

"Don't you have stuff to do? Classes to prepare for?" Will didn't want to appear *too* eager.

Aiden's lazy grin was like sunshine on Will's skin.

"That's why I was up until very late last night and way too early this morning, making sure I got everything done. So now, I'm all yours."

Will wished.

"Sure, you can come along. But right now… can we go down to the lake again, until Becca calls? Unless you think we should stay here."

Aiden snorted. "They've only been gone half an hour. I think we're safe for at least another two." Will gaped, and he chuckled. "Okay, maybe that's an exaggeration. An hour and a half?"

Aiden had to admit, he enjoyed Will's company. Many of the guys he went with were all too keen to fill silence with conversation, whereas Aiden preferred the comfortable quiet that happened way too infrequently.

Will seemed to be of the same mindset. He stared out at the lake, smiling as he watched a puppy, all legs and tail, tugging its bundled-up mom along.

"Do you like dogs?"

Will turned his head, his smile still in evidence. "I like all animals."

"Cat or dog person?" It was an important fact to know.

He stroked his chin. "I think cats have the edge. I want at least one of each once I've got a place of my own."

Aiden cocked his head. "Don't you mean when you *and Becca* have a place of your own?"

Will blinked. "Yeah, of course." He went back to staring through the windshield again.

There was one thing about Will and Becca's relationship Aiden still didn't get.

No time like the present. And no mom around either.

He cleared his throat.

"So what's wrong with Becca?"

Will frowned. "What?"

"She's beautiful, isn't she? I mean, let's be honest here. She's nowhere near as good-looking as *me*, but she's not exactly chopped liver."

Will snickered. "Are you always this modest? And as for her being beautiful…" He gave the tiniest shrug. "I guess." Then he stilled, his eyes widening as though he'd just realized what he'd said.

Too late.

Aiden folded his arms. "You *guess*?"

Will coughed. "Okay, sure, she's beautiful."

"Then why haven't you and she… *you* know…?"

"Excuse me?" Will looked as if he wanted to throw up. Again. "I don't think that's any business of yours."

He had a point, but Aiden had gotten this

far.

"Is it God?"

Will gaped. "What?"

"Because I'm pretty sure God would be happy if you two played hide the Polish sausage. He *invented* sex, right?" He widened his eyes. "Oh, wait. Maybe it *isn't* a Polish sausage. Is it more like a bratwurst? Or a hot dog? Oh, *please* tell me it's not a hot dog. I'm not sure I could look you in the eye ever again."

Will arched his eyebrows, his lips twitching. "Right now I'm seeing why Becca doesn't go home all that often. And can I remind you that you know *exactly* what I'm packing because you saw every naked inch of me in the hotel room. When I took a shower, remember?"

Aiden grinned. "*And* when I put you into bed."

Will blinked. "So I didn't dream that part?"

He managed a nonchalant shrug. "Hey, you asked for my help, so I helped."

"I was drunk."

"Yeah, but you're a cute drunk."

"And you took advantage of my inebriated state, so no *way* am I telling you anything about me and Becca."

Yeah, he wasn't going to answer the question, not that Aiden was all that surprised.

Then Will leaned back in his seat. "So, do I get to ask you some equally embarrassing questions now?"

I deserve that.

Aiden shrugged. "Sure." He flashed Will another grin. "I might even answer some of them."

That earned him a rough chuckle Aiden would have loved to feel reverberate through him, preferably when Will buried his face in Aiden's neck while he slowly filled him…

Fuck. He needed camouflage, and there wasn't a cushion in sight.

"Are you dating anyone?"

Of all the questions Aiden had anticipated, that was pretty tame.

"Not at the moment." He snorted. "Mom would like to fix that, however."

Will's smile was a welcome sight, even if it didn't help Aiden's boner to subside.

"Yeah, I figured. Has she ever set you up with someone from the hotel? From what Becca says, it seems to be the pool she dips into the most."

"So far, I've managed to escape. I think she's given up on me."

Will fell silent, and Aiden considered himself lucky that his future brother-in-law seemed to be a nice guy. Then Will turned his head.

"So what's your type?"

It was on the tip of Aiden's tongue. *I'm looking at him.*

"They've gotta have a brain," he said at last.

Will chuckled once more. "I think we've all got one of those."

"Yeah, but some people are really good at not using it much—or bypassing it altogether."

"What else?" Will asked. "Do they have to be a 'looker'?" he air-quoted.

What was it about Will that made Aiden want to tell the truth? He didn't want to feed him a line, to say stuff that would make him sound intelligent, sexy, whatever…

"I'm not gonna lie. The way someone looks is the first thing I notice, but…" He deliberately avoided female pronouns, the same way he did when Mom grilled him about his love life, because that would also have been a lie, and Mom's Shit-O-Meter was hyper-sensitive. "There has to be something more."

Will was so still, almost as though he was hanging on Aiden's every word, and *damn*, it felt good. "Such as?"

"I want someone who's caring, tender, affectionate…. Selfless. Someone I could spend the rest of my life just making them smile."

The same kind of smile you gave me a moment ago.

Will's breathing caught, but then he relaxed into his seat once more. "I'm sure there's someone out there who is perfect for you."

Yeah, and he's sitting next to me.

Okay, so maybe Aiden had known Will for about five minutes, but it was enough to realize there was more to him than a pretty face.

Aiden finished his bottle of water. "Tell me about you."

"What do you want to know?"

What he *really* wanted to know, he couldn't ask because he had to remind himself that the gorgeous guy next to him was marrying his sister.

"Family first."

Will grinned. "First? You have a list or something?"

"It's a good place to start."

"I guess. Okay, I'm one of four kids—" He tilted his head. "Weren't you there when I told your dad all this?"

"Maybe? And if you did, I forgot. I had a lot on my mind that night."

"Like what?"

He gave Will a smile. "I was trying to make up for almost cutting my future brother-in-law in half with a bell cart."

Will laughed. "Forgiven and forgotten. So yeah, Ethan is the oldest, by three years, then it's me, then Dee—she's twenty—and finally there's Emma. She's the baby of the family, at seventeen." He smiled. "She's just taken up knitting as a hobby. At least, I hope it stays a hobby and she doesn't decide to make a career out of it."

"That bad?"

He smirked. "Let's just say she's untroubled by such constraints as shape or size."

Aiden snorted once more. "Oh, now I *have* to see some of her handiwork." Then he realized he had a more burning question. "Can I ask—why astrophysics?"

Will's face lit up. "Why not astrophysics? Who *wouldn't* want to delve into the fundamental nature of the universe?" Then he chuckled. "Actually, I already know the answer to that—your sister."

Aiden sighed. "She asked me once if I could make a recording on her phone, talking about physics." He paused. "She says it's the best way to cure insomnia."

"Ouch. Okay, where was I?"

Aiden grinned. "Delving into the nature of the universe."

"Oh. Right. There are so many mysteries out

there—the origin of the universe, how time works—"

"I can tell you about that last one. It flies, especially when you're having fun, apparently."

It was Will's turn to laugh. "I see what you did there. I can go one better. Time flies like an arrow. Fruit flies like a banana."

Yeah, Aiden could listen to Will Bryant talk all day.

"But there are also black holes, dark matter, dark energy—other intelligent life. So much to explore… the birth, life, and death of stars, planets, galaxies, nebulae…" He sighed. "NASA's goal summed up for me why I wanted to study astrophysics: 'Discover how the universe works, explore how it began and evolved, and search for life on planets around other stars.'" Will flung out his arm. "How *does* the universe work? How did we get here? Are we alone?"

Aiden smiled. "Those are pretty big questions. Would you like to work for NASA one day?"

Will's eyes sparkled. "Yes! That's my dream. I'd love to work on dark energy, dark matter… Do you know, seventy percent of the universe is dark energy? And that dark matter accounts for twenty-five percent?"

Aiden did know, but he wasn't about to stop Will when he was in full flow, excitement in his voice, unable to sit still.

"Dark energy… I like to think of it as gravity's evil twin. An 'anti-gravity' force providing a negative pressure that fills the universe and stretches the very fabric of space-time. And if I couldn't get a job with NASA, then I'd try CERN." He paused, his gaze meeting Aiden's. "But… you know all this. You studied physics."

"Which is why it's refreshing to find someone else who digs it too."

Both their phones buzzed at exactly the same moment. Will glanced at his. "Becca. She says they're done."

Aiden peered at his own phone and laughed. "That's more polite than what Mom has said." He turned it around to show Will, who burst out laughing.

"Oh, I know that reaction all too well."

You just came *this close* to becoming an only child.

Aiden pocketed his phone and turned the key in the ignition.

"It's good to know I'm not the only one Becca bugs the hell out of."

Will had a feeling Becca wouldn't win any contests for the florist's favorite customer. So far, he'd muttered disparaging remarks whenever he was out of earshot, wincing when she chose colors that clashed.

Okay, Will had felt bad about coughing up a lung when Louise introduced the florist as Mr. Pink, but one glance at Becca told him he hadn't been the only one.

"What color will your bridesmaids be wearing?" Mr. Pink inquired. "Because whichever color you choose for their dresses? Don't have that color in your arrangements."

Louise gave Becca an inquiring glance. "How many bridesmaids were you thinking of having?"

Becca bit her lip. "I haven't given it much thought."

Give Becca her due, at least that's the truth.

Mr. Pink took the folder containing examples of the floral arrangements from Becca's hands. "Much as I love putting butterflies, feathers, even birds in the displays, I really don't advise you to have *all* of them. It will just look too…"

"Busy?" Louise suggested.

"I was aiming more for hideous," Aiden said under his breath.

Becca glared at him. "You didn't like the tulips either."

"But Sir is correct," the florist piped up. "Tulips wilt."

"And wilting is bad," Aiden remarked sagely.

"You got that right," Will muttered.

Aiden jerked his head in Will's direction, his mouth open, eyes wide.

"No one wants a sagging mess in the middle of the table," the florist continued.

"No one wants a sagging *anything*," Will muttered again.

The strangled noise coming from Aiden was

definitely stifled laughter.

"What about chrysanthemums?" Louise said in a bright tone.

Mr. Pink gazed at her in obvious horror. "No, madam. They're just pollen parties waiting to explode."

"Lilies?" It was clear Becca was trying to be helpful.

"Yes, they're lovely," the florist agreed, and Will saw Louise's shoulders sag with relief. "However…"

He rolled his eyes. "I knew something was going to spoil it."

Mr. Pink gave him the side-eye. "I was *going* to say, lilies can be hazardous around children and pets."

"I think I'll leave Midnight at home," Aiden commented.

Will frowned. "Midnight?"

"His cat," Becca told him. "That damn cat is the only one who'll put up with him." She gave Mr. Pink a hopeful smile. "Maybe we should go with fake flowers?"

His look of abject horror said it all.

"Sure—if you want your wedding to look cheap," Louise said dryly. She smiled politely at Mr. Pink. "Send me the details. I'll make a decision."

"I don't get to choose my own flowers?" Becca remonstrated.

"Based on what I've just heard?" Louise grimaced. "No. And if you weren't already engaged, I'd have said you shouldn't even be allowed to choose the groom." She walked with the florist to his office at the rear of the shop. Aiden went to sniff the lilies.

Becca stared after her. "I'd hate to have her nerve in a tooth." Will gave Becca's arm a strong pinch above the elbow, and she glared at him. "Ow!"

He leaned in and whispered, "Can I remind you that you don't *need* flowers?"

Becca's eyes glinted. "And can I remind *you* that I'm playing a *role* here? You know, keeping up appearances? If I just rolled over and said 'Sure, Mom, pick whatever you like', she'd smell a rat."

"I don't want your mom paying out her money for things we don't need."

Becca made a low growling noise at the back of her throat, then raised her voice. "Excuse me? Mr. Pink?"

He poked his head around the door. "Yes?"

"Once we've made a decision, if we change our minds, would you be able to cancel this order and come up with another?"

"Well, yes, but—"

"And what would be the deadline for any changes?"

"A week before the wedding."

Becca smiled at Will. "Just checking. Thank you."

Louise shook her head. "And now we've got that settled… Will, do you have any plans for this evening? Are you and Becca going out? It *is* Saturday night after all."

Will hesitated for a moment. "Actually? I wanted to see Aiden's cat." Becca blinked, and he shrugged. "What? I like cats."

Louise chuckled. "He *is* allowed to have an

evening away from you, Becca. I expect you see a lot of each other when you're in school. And after all, you're going to spend the rest of your lives together. Right?"

Becca didn't break eye contact with Will. "Right, Mom."

Will had a feeling the temperature inside Becca's car on the trip back to Minnesota was going to be even frostier than outside. He reckoned it would warm up a little when Will reminded her of the really huge favor he was doing her.

Then he remembered his manners.

"If that's okay with you, Aiden," he added quickly.

Aiden nodded. "Sure. I'll even throw in a pizza or two."

Will grinned. "You just said the magic word."

A few hours alone with Aiden sounded magical too—as long as they stayed away from the subject of weddings.

"Although I should warn you. Midnight isn't too keen on visitors, so keep your shins covered unless you want them punctured."

Will snickered. "If he's handy with his claws, that could prove useful. I've been meaning to get my ears pierced."

Aiden's eyes twinkled. "Nipples are more in his line."

He had to fight the urge to say, 'you could always kiss them better.'

Will's libido was going to be the death of him.

CHAPTER ELEVEN

Will Sees A Whole New Side To Aiden

"So which neighborhood are we in?" Will gazed at the neat front lawns, the single-story houses set back from the road.

"This is Wauwatosa," Aiden informed him. "My place is only twenty minutes' drive from my parents."

Will couldn't resist. "But those are awfully important minutes, aren't they?"

Aiden laughed. "Yup. Eleven precious miles separate me from Mom. Even *she* can't see me from Bay View, much as she would love to." He pulled up outside a two-story, red-bricked house, its wide front lawn bifurcated by a stone-slabbed path leading to the front door flanked in stone.

Aiden pointed to the second floor. "My apartment is on the right. On the left is my neighbor, Carol, AKA Midnight's sitter." He switched off the engine.

"Is the pizza place near here?"

Aiden nodded. "Down Wauwatosa Avenue about five blocks, then onto West North Avenue. Maggio's. Best damn pizza *you'll* ever taste."

"Any recommendations?"

Aiden's eyes lit up. "Garlic bread bites for

an appetizer, then I usually go for one of three fave pizzas. Fig and prosciutto—"

Will grimaced. "Figs? On a *pizza*?"

Aiden arched his eyebrows. "Do you eat Hawaiian?" Will nodded. "And do you like it?"

"Yeah."

He gave Will a mock glare. "Then you've got nothing to say on the subject. Because pineapple… on a pizza?"

Will had been known to start a flame war on that subject at D & D nights, and he definitely didn't want to head down *that* route. "What are the other choices?"

"Raclette—that's made with raclette—"

"I know what raclette cheese is," Will interjected with a chuckle.

Aiden snickered. "Then maybe you can educate Becca. She didn't have a clue. So… raclette cheese, purple potato, roasted garlic creme fraiche and green onions. I usually add sausage."

"Who doesn't like sausage?" Will murmured.

Aiden coughed. When he stopped, he said, "And finally there's the SS Garlic. A garlic cream base, sausage, spinach, and mozzarella. You can add mushrooms, pepperoni, sausage…" Aiden's eyes twinkled. "You can even add pineapple—if you absolutely have to."

Will bit back a smile. "I'm seeing a theme here. Got a thing for garlic? Or are you trying to keep the vampires away?"

Aiden laughed out loud.

"It wasn't that funny," Will observed.

"Oh, it really was, but I'll tell you why after

we've eaten. So… have you got a thing about garlic too, or should I just hit reorder?"

"Garlic works for me." It wasn't as if he was going to be kissing anyone, right?

More's the pity.

"Which one would you like?"

Will grinned. "Both of them."

Aiden chuckled. "A man after my own heart." He scrolled.

"*Now* can we get out of the car? Because it *has* to be warmer inside."

"You're right. Pizza will be here probably just before we start looking at Midnight and thinking he'd make a tasty snack." They got out of the car and Aiden led the way up the path. Inside, they climbed the wooden staircase.

Aiden paused at the front door. "This is where I warn you. Midnight's claws can penetrate denim as easily as a knife through butter." He opened the door.

There was no sudden flash of fur, teeth and claws, but a cat sitting on the rug a few feet away from them, tail curled over its front paws.

A cat with the darkest, glossiest coat Will had ever seen.

"Whoa, you certainly live up to your name, don't you, kitty?" He crouched in front of Midnight, hand extended, and to his surprise the cat bumped his face-down palm with its head, nudging it. Will smiled. "Well, hello there." Midnight rubbed against his knee, his motor running, and Will stroked along the sleek back, making sure to scritch the base of the tail.

Midnight's engine shifted into high gear.

Aiden snorted. "Oh, I get it. You heard every word I said out in the hallway, didn't you, you little bastard? You just wanna make me look stupid."

Midnight yawned, and Will laughed. "Is he saying he doesn't have to work too hard at it?"

Aiden snorted. "Knowing him? Probably." He held his hand out. "Give me your coat. Then I'll show you around. It'll take all of ten seconds."

Will chuckled. "My mom showed me photos of the place they had when she first started teaching. She said no one becomes a teacher to get rich and have a swanky place to live. They do it because something in their soul tells them to." He removed his coat and handed it over.

"I like the sound of your mom."

Aiden hadn't lied about the size of the place—it was tiny—but it had a warmth Will appreciated. The living room was cozy, with windows on two sides, and the setting sun fell on the brown leather couch beneath one of them.

"How many bedrooms?"

"Two, but I use the guest room as an office." Aiden pointed to the fireplace. "The reason I picked this place. Wisconsin can be cold as a witch's tit most of the year."

Will beamed. "Can we light a fire?"

Aiden laughed. "Exactly what I was about to do." He knelt on the rug in front of the hearth and began putting twists of newspaper behind the grate.

Will took the opportunity to sit on the couch where Midnight joined him, climbing him like a tree to bump his head under Will's chin.

"Yeah, he likes doing that." Aiden grabbed a couple of logs and placed them in the fireplace. He aimed a gas lighter at the paper and it caught fire.

Midnight was off Will's lap in a heartbeat, heading for the rug.

Aiden chuckled. "Sorry, but he's a cat. A fire beats rubbies every time."

Will surveyed the room, taking in the hardwood floor's varnished glow, the warm tones of the cabinets in the kitchen, seen through the open door, the thick red throws over the couch and the armchair…

"You have a nice place."

Aiden shrugged. "Not bad for a rental. One day I'd like a place that belongs to me—well, me and the bank." He sighed. "With a backyard like my mom's. Somewhere to sit out in summer and catch some rays."

"I'm always happy to get through another winter," Will admitted. "It's great right now on days when the sun shines, but it's too damn cold to be outside." Aiden laughed again, and Will's curiosity was piqued. "Okay, just what is so funny?"

Aiden cleared his throat. "You weren't exactly what I expected."

Will blinked. "Elaborate, please?"

"It was just an assumption, based on a couple of things Becca said."

"Such as?"

"Oh, you know, the bit about you proposing in the university library, the fact you were always reading, the—"

"You got something against reading?" Will gestured to the bookcase with its overburdened shelves. "Because… hello?"

"Not a thing. Some of my best friends are

books. But it kinda built up a picture in my mind: dark hair, pale skin from the lack of sunlight… *you* know…" He cleared his throat again. "Just your common, everyday vampire."

Will stared at him for a moment. Then he smiled. "If I were a vampire? Trust me, there would be *nothing* common about *me*."

Aiden met his gaze. "I can believe that."

Something about the husky quality of Aiden's voice and the way he didn't break eye contact sent a shiver through Will. Then Aiden's phone buzzed, and the moment shattered.

"Pizza's here. I'll go down and get it." Aiden lurched to his feet and left the room.

Will glanced at the cat stretched out on the rug, as though he was trying to get every inch of him warm.

"Hey, Midnight. Your daddy is gorgeous, you know that?"

And funny. And smart. And sexy as fuck. And—

And straight, remember?

Midnight licked his paw clean, avoiding Will's gaze.

Will let out a sigh. "Yeah, you know."

Oh, Aiden. If only I'd met you instead of Becca.

If only Becca hadn't come up with this stupid scheme of hers.

If only I had the nerve to tell you the truth.

Except he wouldn't do that.

It wasn't only his truth to tell.

Aiden pointed to the box containing what remained of the SS Garlic. "You want the last piece? Please don't feel you have to say yes, by the way. This is equally yummy for breakfast, so it won't go to waste."

Will smiled and patted his belly. "I'm stuffed. And there's a slice of the raclette left too."

"Great." Aiden placed the slices of both pizzas in one box. "I'll just put this in the fridge. You want something to drink? There's hot chocolate, beer, coffee, juice—"

"You had me at hot chocolate."

Aiden grinned and headed into the kitchen. He glanced at the wall clock. Seven o'clock already.

Time really does fly when you're having fun, doesn't it?

Except it wasn't flying—it was zooming—and the last hour hadn't been anything so mundane as fun. They'd talked D & D, and Aiden realized his idea of a game bachelor party was something he needed to make happen, because damn it, he wanted to play with Will, in many, many different ways.

Some of them didn't involve clothing.

"Just how did you and Becca meet?" Aiden called out as he squeezed the pizza box into the fridge. He wouldn't have matched them. The more he saw of them together, the clearer it became that their personalities were diametrically opposed.

"I was in the audience at one of her first ever performances back in our first year in college. She was dancing with this ribbon on the end of a wand… you know, twirling it, using it as a prop…"

"Was she any good?"

"Yes—until she let go of the wand, it sailed through the air, and hit me smack in the forehead." Will chuckled. "She spent weeks trying to make up for that." He gasped. "Oh my God. I never realized it until just now."

"Realized what."

"That clumsiness is a gene, an inherited trait."

Aiden laughed. "You know what? Neither did I?" A rush of heat surged through him.

Except you weren't being clumsy, were you?

You were being evil. Jealous. And Will paid the price.

He wasn't going to think about that. Forgiven and forgotten, Will had said.

"Does Becca ever visit you when she's home?"

Aiden snorted. "Yeah right. As if I'd invite her here. Too much stuff I don't want her to see."

And why did I say that?

"Now I'm intrigued."

There was *one* thing he could share, and now that he thought about it, he knew Will would probably love it.

More importantly, it was something Aiden *wanted* to share with him.

He crooked his finger. "Come with me."

Will chuckled. "Now I'm *definitely* intrigued."

Aiden took him to the guest room and opened the door. Will went inside.

"Ah, this is where you do all your—oh my God!" He swung around to face Aiden, open-mouthed.

Aiden smiled. "My secret hobby."

The walls were lined with framed photos he'd taken during the last three months, but he knew they weren't what had provoked Will's reaction.

The cause of his outburst sat in front of the window.

Will gave him a huge smile. "You have a telescope."

"You noticed that, huh?"

He laughed. "Becca never told me about this."

"That's because she doesn't know. She already thinks I'm a nerd because of D & D."

Will walked over to it and stroked a finger along its length. "It's a beauty. What's the aperture?"

"Sixteen inches."

"And it's what, about forty inches focal length?"

Yeah, this had been a good idea.

Will was still smiling. "Is it portable?"

"Yeah, it can easily be dismantled and put in the back of my truck for when I go stargazing."

"However did you afford it?"

Aiden gave a shrug. "Actually… I built it."

Will's jaw dropped for the second time in less than a minute. "Holy shit. It's awesome."

"'Holy shit'?"

Will flushed. "What—am I not allowed to swear?"

"Of course you can swear if you want to. It's just…"

Will tilted his head. "Just what?"

"Well… when you talk…. You're usually so… precise. You sound so… intelligent. And definitely not your age. I play D & D with guys your age and trust me, you don't sound like you're twenty-two."

"More like forty-two, huh?" Will gave a half smile. "Blame that on my parents. From the moment I started talking, they wouldn't let me be a kid. I had to speak properly. And *you* try growing up with a teacher and a professor for parents. When I was little, the other children used to tease me about the way I spoke."

"I like the way you speak," Aiden confessed. "It suits you."

"Thank you." Will's flush deepened. "I don't resent what my parents did, by the way." His eyes sparkled. "And if I'm honest? I liked being different. My brother Ethan, however? He hated it. When he isn't around them, he sounds so… relaxed, so chilled. It's as if he's adopted a cooler vocabulary. I'm trying." He chuckled again. "Becca encourages me to swear more." He shook his head. "The first time I said *gonna* instead of *going to*, I think she was going to burst with pride, as though I'd done something amazing." Will gazed at the walls, and his breathing hitched. "Did you do these?" He pointed to the photos.

"Yes. Once a month I go to Harrington Beach State Park. There's an observatory, and the

Northern Cross Science Foundation meets there regularly. There's a twenty-inch Panarusky telescope, and the roof rolls right off, so the views are fantastic. The only thing is, there are only about sixteen nights a month when there's enough darkness to use it." Aiden went to his laptop and opened it. "This is the Harrington Beach Clear Sky Chart. It shows what's going on every night—cloud cover, transparency, how many hours of darkness…"

Will walked over to the photo of Jupiter. "This is awesome." The note of longing in his voice unfurled something deep in Aiden's belly.

He glanced at the screen, and grinned.

"How would you like to go look at Mars and Jupiter? And maybe Saturn, except it's only average visibility tonight."

Will spun around, eyes shining. "Could we?"

"Harrington Beach is only thirty-five miles north of Milwaukee." Another glance at the screen. "If we leave now, we should have a great view of Jupiter by the time we get there. Mars won't be at its most visible until around one this morning."

"I'd love that."

Right then, Aiden loved the joy in Will's voice—and the fact that he'd put it there.

Will had to admit he liked that they were the only ones at the observatory. It was also pretty neat the Foundation trained its members how to operate the telescope and deal with the roll-off roof. He was glad of his thick coat, and Aiden had loaned him a beanie. The night air was cold enough for him to be able to see his breath, but he didn't care about that.

This had been a wonderful night.

Will peered into the eyepiece. "Look at that," he said softly. "Every time I look at Jupiter through a telescope, I have to remind myself that what I'm seeing is mostly ice-crystal clouds made of ammonia and ammonium hydrosulfide."

Then he became aware of Aiden moving closer, until they were almost touching. "Let me see."

Will pulled back a little to give Aiden a turn—and caught a whiff of Aiden's hair.

Gods, that smells good.

Will wanted to bury his face in Aiden's long hair, to breathe him in, to wrap himself up in that scent. The smell of warm, clean cotton mingled with the scent of shampoo and soap, an overpowering fragrance that *spoke* to Will, conjuring images of naked flesh, mouths, and fingers, of intimate embraces and sensual abandonment.

Then Aiden turned his head without warning, and their noses met in the darkness.

Actually, their noses *smashed.*

"Ow."

Aiden straightened immediately. "I am *so* sorry."

Will clutched his nose. "Is everyone in your

family this lethal to be around?"

"Want me to kiss it better?"

Oh dear God, the temptation to say yes…

"It'll be fine," he said quickly.

"As much as I hate to say it, maybe we should go."

"Why?"

Aiden grinned. "Remember how you *ooh*'d and *aah*'d over Mars? Remember me telling you it wouldn't be visible until one in the morning?"

Oh crap. "Yeah?"

"It's almost one-thirty," he said brightly.

Will blinked. *Where did the last five hours go?*

That was easy. They'd been swallowed up in stargazing, good conversation, and even better company. He'd been amazed to find out how knowledgeable Aiden was when it came to astronomy.

I don't want this night to end.

The next day would bring the trip back to Minnesota, another five hours in the car with Becca…

Will already knew conversation with her would be a chore. He didn't want to chat—he wanted to close his eyes and remember his magical evening.

"Will?" Aiden turned on the flashlight on his phone, and the bright light gave his face a ghostly appearance.

Will's mind had gone off on a tangent again.

"I lost all track of time," he said as he helped put the telescope to bed and the roof back on.

"I can't take you to my parents' house," Aiden said decisively as they walked toward Aiden's truck.

"Why not?"

"Because you'll wake everyone up." He paused. "But there *is* an alternative."

"Which is?"

"Spend the night at my place. There's a sofa bed in the guest room."

Will swallowed. "I… I can't put you out like that."

Aiden chuckled. "You wouldn't be. Just be prepared to share your bed."

For one heart stopping moment, Will thought he was suggesting…

Then sanity returned.

"You're talking about Midnight."

"Of course. What else could I be talking about?"

What indeed?

Will's brain was trying to kill him. Well, either his brain or his libido.

Aiden was waiting for a response to his kind offer.

"Thank you," Will said earnestly. "It's a good idea. Only, I don't—"

"There's a new toothbrush in the bathroom cabinet," Aiden told him. "I've got plenty of sheets and pillows, there's a spare comforter… It's a quilt Mom made for me when I first left home to go to college." He grinned. "You'll love that, by the way. I was just discovering the awesomeness of space at the time, so she covered it with the planets and stars. And in the morning, I'll take you for breakfast." Aiden smiled. "I promise to have you back with Becca in plenty of time."

There was no way Will could say no to that.

Even if what he *really* wanted was to spend the night with Becca's brother.

CHAPTER TWELVE

Will And Aiden Stay Up Late

Aiden should have been sleepy, given the hour—it was two a.m. for God's sake—but the prospect of talking some more with Will had him wide awake. He reasoned they could stay up a while longer. They didn't have to be up early, breakfast might as well become brunch… and Becca could deal with being alone with Mom and Dad for a few more hours before they had to head back.

That last thought made him smile.

The first thing he did when they got home was to relight the fire, and to his surprise, Will chose to sit on the rug in front of it. Of course, he had to share its warmth with Midnight, but the kitty didn't appear put out by this. He'd already crawled into Will's lap, his chin resting on Will's thigh, eyes tight shut.

"You're not ready for bed either, are you?"

Will chuckled. "I seem to have found my second wind." He glanced at Midnight. "Unlike your kitty."

"I once tried to log how many hours Midnight slept in a day."

"And? How many?"

Aiden snorted. "Well, as impossible as it

seems, in a twenty-four-hour period, he sleeps at least twenty-six. He's even sleeping when he eats. And in case you decide you need a little help in dropping off, I have a couple of remedies that'll do the trick." He eased a book from the shelf and held it out to him.

Will gave a mock gasp. "*Moby Dick*? It's a classic."

Aiden stared at him. "And have you ever *read* this 'classic'?"

"Well, no, but—"

"But nothing. This is one of those books people say 'Oh, you *have* to read this.' So I did. I wanted to see what all the fuss was about. Then I reached page six and wondered what the hell I'd gotten myself into. Sure, if you *really* want to know everything about whaling in the nineteenth century, and what a shit job it was to be a sailor on a whaleboat, then fine, *this* is the book for you." He replaced it on the shelf. "Or there's *Anna Karenina*, which I have to admit that while being as boring as whale shit, it did teach me something."

"What was that? And by the way, I liked the link. 'Whale shit'?"

Aiden grinned. "I try. And I learned that in Russian high society—again in the nineteenth century—highborn ladies died from self-inflicted fevers brought on by shame or embarrassment. I'm not kidding. They literally fell down dead."

"I think I'll pass on the books. What's the other remedy?"

"Beer," Aiden replied promptly.

"I'm not a beer connoisseur," Will confessed. "I don't really see the attraction. They all taste the same to me." He coughed, then gave an apologetic glance. "Frog in my throat."

"Ah, but this isn't your ordinary, everyday, run-of-the-mill beer."

Will leaned back, his weight on his hands. "You keep coming out with stuff that makes me curious." He smiled. "I like that. So what is this beer you're dying to tell me about?"

Aiden perched on the arm of the couch. "One group I used to play with had a beer run every weekend. We'd take turns buying a couple cases of beer to last us the three days we got together to play." He peered at Will. "Your groups don't do that?"

Will snorted. "They're more the soda-snacks-and-chips kinda players. With the occasional root beer. I like the sound of yours better."

"Well, one of the guys, Jimmy, brought out this beer, and we all went nuts. And that was before we'd even tasted a drop." Aiden chuckled. "He told us about finding a list online that had the most outlandish beer names we'd ever seen. And of course we had to try them all."

"Well, of course," Will replied in a deadpan voice. "What kind of names?"

"There was one called Dark Helmet, with a sort of Darth Vader mask on the can. The Imperial Stout Trooper was a hit, a mix of coffee beans and fruit flavors. Another was Empire Brewing's Strikes Back."

Will laughed. "Okay, they sound awesome. What was your favorite—or did you like them all?"

Aiden went into the kitchen, and returned with two cans. "This one. It's an IPA and the best of the bunch. It's not easy to get, so I don't share it with most people, but you're an exception."

Will gazed at the can. "*Pan Galactic Gargle Blaster*? The 'Best Drink in Existence'? Whose effects are similar to—and I quote—'having your brains smashed out by a piece of lemon wrapped around a large gold brick'?"

Aiden beamed. "You're a *Hitchhiker's* fan."

Will put down his beer can, picked up Midnight, deposited him on the rug, lunged toward his messenger bag he'd left on the floor next to the couch, and reached into it. He handed Aiden what looked like a Kindle in its plain black cover.

Aiden frowned. "Am I missing something?"

"Turn it over."

He did as instructed, and found a rectangle in the center, on which was printed in large, friendly letters, *Don't Panic*.

"Oh, I fucking *love* that."

Will popped the can open and took a long drink.

"Well?"

He smiled. "I like this."

Aiden put the Kindle on the couch and joined Will on the rug. He opened his own can, and held it up to Will's. "A toast."

"To Douglas Adams?" Will suggested.

"I thought you'd want to drink to your upcoming wedding."

Will stilled. "Oh. Yes, of course. To the wedding." They clinked cans.

Aiden sat cross-legged, staring into the fire. "I think it's fantastic, you know. You and Becca getting married, I mean. At your age, too."

"What does my age have to do with it?"

"Well, you're only twenty-two. I guess most guys your age wouldn't feel ready for marriage."

Will gave a wry chuckle. "And there you go with the 'your age' line again. I suppose you can say stuff like that when you get to the age of *twenty-four*." He rolled his eyes.

Aiden sighed. "You're right. I've got no business coming out with shit like that."

Will gazed at him, his head tilted to one side, his eyes bright, his cheeks flushed. Then he cleared his throat. "To be honest, I hadn't given the whole marriage thing a lot of thought. I wasn't ready for it to be this December, I'll tell you *that* for nothing."

"Yeah, when Mom drops a bomb, it's a doozy." Aiden glanced at him. "But you're okay with it, right?" Then he waved a hand. "Forget I asked. You wouldn't be here if you weren't."

"What about you?"

"What about me?" Aiden repeated with a frown.

"You think *you'll* ever get hitched?"

Aiden took a drink from his can.

"Have I touched a nerve or something?"

He smiled. "I look at my parents. They met in college, and *bam*, they knew they were meant to be together. They were married before they'd graduated, and twenty-five years later, they still hold hands, go out on date nights, act like loved-up teenagers…. And yeah, I want to be like them." He sighed. "I always told myself I'd only marry when I met someone who…"

"Who what?" Will sat upright, his gaze focused on Aiden's face.

"Someone who took my breath away. Who, when I was with them, made me feel as though all the oxygen had been sucked out of the room. Someone who made me feel good about myself. Someone I wanted to be the very best version of me that I could be—for them."

Someone who's a whole lot like you.

And suddenly Aiden didn't want to talk any more. He'd steered way too close to a precipice, and if he kept on talking, he might say something that had no business being said.

"I've got a question for ya." He held up his can. "Is beer better from a bottle or a can?"

"Ooh, a philosophical debate." Will smiled. "I want to hear your opinion first."

Aiden shrugged. "Okay by me. I'm for cans."

"And your reasons for this stance are…?"

He counted off on his fingers. "Cans don't let light in. They're more durable. You can store them anywhere. And let's not forget the most important factor."

"What's that?"

He grinned. "They hold more beer."

"What about the complaint that they make the beer taste of metal?"

Aiden let out another snort. "Anyone who says that doesn't know how to drink from a can. Besides, kegs are metal, right? Most beer is served in kegs and *those* don't taste of metal because of it, now do they?"

"So bottles have *no* redeeming features?"

He stroked his jaw. "Okay, if you wanna age some beers, then bottles win. You know, leave them alone for three or more years, like wine." He cocked his head. "You can't argue against any of that logic, can you?"

He was starting to enjoy this conversation.

Will straightened, took a long drink, and then locked gazes with him. His eyes gleamed. "Right."

Aiden couldn't help feeling he'd just opened a can of worms.

Or should that be a bottle?

"To start with, you can't say that cans are better. It's a beer-by-beer thing. Secondly, there are too many variables to take into consideration."

"Such as?"

"I won't argue that canning technology and affordability have improved a helluva lot in recent years. But…" Will mimicked Aiden, counting on his fingers. "Cans are still a lot harder and more temperamental to use than a bottling line. And then you need to look at TPO."

Aiden blinked. "'TPO'?" Will was talking another language.

"Total Packaged Oxygen. Because what a canning line producer *says* their oxygen pickup is, versus what the *actual* operational TPO coming off the line? We can be talking about two very different things."

"We can?"

Will nodded. "Unless you're talking about packlines that the *big* boys have, but most craft breweries can't afford those type of packlines." He stroked Midnight, who started purring. "On any given day at the same craft brewery on the same canning line, the difference in TPO can be massive.

The amount of packaging required can influence the speed of the line. Then there's the staff's level of competency."

"Is that it?"

Will's eyes twinkled. "As Marisa Tomei said in *My Cousin Vinny*… 'No, there's more.'"

'Not a connoisseur of beer' my ass. Then his words registered. "Wait a sec. Hold up. *You* like *My Cousin Vinny*?"

Will gazed at him with obvious amusement. "For a smart man, you ask some dumb questions. Now, *beyond* the packline, there are issues with logistics of beer supply, followed by how it's handled by retail outlet and the customer. You know, things like… how long has the beer been stored for and how has it been stored? How and at what temperature has it been transported?" Will's smile was almost smug. "I'd take a one-month-old IPA in a brown bottle that was packed with low TPO, that was cold-stored, cold-transported, and sold cold, over a two-week-old can with much higher TPO that has been kept at ambient temperatures."

"*Now* you're done."

"Not quite. You also need to consider what *style* of beer. Some styles are more welcoming to the ingress of oxygen. Bottles can withstand more pressure than cans, therefore the liquid contained can hold more carbon dioxide. The resultant beer is fizzier, and packs a greater flavor hit. Not for things like bitters and stouts, but for lager, sure." Will gave him a satisfied smile. "So yes, while the *potential* is certainly there for cans to be better for beer than bottles, it's patently wrong to say that canned beer is better than bottled beer."

Aiden stared at him in silence for a moment, then burst out laughing. "Wow. I feel as if I just took a crash course in brewing beer." He drained his can. "Want another?"

"Sure. You got any bottles?"

He rolled his eyes. "Damn it, I ran out." They laughed.

Fuck, that was one sexy smile. *And how come I never spotted those cute dimples?*

Aiden schooled his features. "So, you don't see the attraction of beer? They all taste the same?"

Will had the good grace to flush. "Okay—I lied." Then he grinned. "But you believed me, didn't you?"

"Totally. Remind me never to play poker with you." He paused. "So, you want to sleep, or should I find us a movie on Netflix?"

"Movie."

They got up off the rug and sat on the couch. Aiden aimed the remote and scrolled. "Okay, what are you in the mood for?"

"Not a clue. What's new?"

Aiden peered at the screen. "*A linguistics professor and her family find their bonds tested when she is diagnosed with Alzheimer's Disease.*"

"Er, no. I'm sure it's a great movie, but not tonight." Will chuckled. "Or should I say this morning. Next."

"*A rookie cop spends his first day as a Los Angeles narcotics officer with a rogue detective who isn't what—*"

"And you can stop right there."

Aiden laughed. "Well then, how about a romance?"

"I could stomach a little of that," Will said grudgingly.

He snorted. "Is that Will-speak for Aiden, romance is my jam. Bring it on."

Will laughed. "Just don't tell Becca, all right? I'd never hear the last of it."

Aiden looked at the screen. "Oh, that's perfect. You've got a choice. *The Bodyguard* or *Notting Hill*."

"The latter," Will replied in a heartbeat.

Aiden waggled his eyebrows. "You've got a thing for Julia Roberts, huh?"

Personally, he thought Hugh Grant was gorgeous, and as for that accent…. Aiden believed he could come just from listening to Hugh read his grocery list.

"Bring us two more beers, and put the movie on."

Aiden shook his head. "You've got a bossy streak. Does my sister know about that?"

"What she doesn't know won't hurt her."

"Until after the wedding," Aiden added.

Except he didn't want to think about Will standing there in a suit, waiting for Becca to join him. Will smiling at her as she walked slowly toward him on Dad's arm, her wedding dress spread out behind her in a cascade of satin and lace.

Will kissing her as the celebrant announced they were Mr. and Mrs. Bryant.

And then the full force of Aiden's longing swamped him.

I'd be Mr. Bryant for you any day.

A thought he'd never had for *anyone* his entire life.

Dammit, we have so much in common. We're both into D & D, we like the same movies, we enjoy a cold beer—even if we do hold different views on which is the best container. Why the hell *did you have to be straight and fall for my sister?*

A miserable future loomed before him, filled with the family gatherings from hell. Because hell it *would* be, to see Will and Becca, all smiles and laughs. To watch as he kissed her, Aiden wishing fervently it was *him* on the receiving end of those kisses. To listen as he and Becca announced they were having a baby. To see their family grow.

All of this is gonna gut me. Every single time.

Maybe it would be better to skip those events. He needed to start weaning himself away from the family until either he got over his infatuation or....

Except he knew he wasn't likely to get over it.

Even now, he could picture Will aging, the hair growing darker, then start to lighten as the years progressed. The first gray hairs, sprinkled amidst the black. The fretting about getting old. Aiden telling him he'd never looked more amazing.

Damn you, Becca. You had to find the one perfect man, didn't you?

Will's eyes felt as if they were glued shut. He tried to raise a hand to rub them, until he realized it was trapped—behind Aiden.

What the…

Will blinked a couple of times, turning his head. Aiden leaned against him, his arm across Will's waist, his head resting on Will's shoulder, his breathing slow and even.

Oh wow.

He didn't want to move a muscle for fear of waking Aiden. He gazed at his face, which had taken on an expression of serenity in sleep. His long hair curled on his shoulders, shining in the lamplight.

He's even more beautiful than when he's awake.

Aiden opened his eyes and looked into Will's, then glanced down.

"Okay, this is embarrassing." He straightened, disengaging them. "I guess we fell asleep, huh? I don't recall seeing the end of the movie."

Neither did Will. He'd even missed his favorite part, when Julia Roberts did her famous line about being a girl, standing in front of a boy…

A line Will had wanted to use some day on his own boy.

He pulled his phone from his pocket and squinted at the screen. "It's nine-thirty."

Aiden grabbed his phone and groaned. "Oh shit. I have about a gazillion missed messages from Becca."

Will clicked on his messages. "I have just the one. *You *are* planning on coming here at some point, right? Unless you wanna make your own way back to*

Minnesota?"

"Oops. Well, that's better than what she sent me." Aiden read aloud.

Have you kidnapped Will?

You took him out on the town and got him drunk, didn't you?

Do you need bail money?

Then he flushed, his cheeks scarlet, and erupted into a coughing fit.

"I dread to ask what you just read," Will remarked.

"Brother-and-sister shit. Nothing to do with you." Aiden pocketed his phone. "I guess I'd better feed you and get you back to your fiancée." He stood. "I'm gonna grab a shower before we leave." And with that, he walked out of the room.

Will frowned.

What on earth did you say to him, Becca?

Aiden stopped his truck in front of his parents' house and switched off the engine. The curtains in the front window twitched violently, and he chuckled.

"Uh-oh. We've been seen."

And when he got Becca alone, he was going to kill her for almost choking him to death with that message.

Man, after this stunt I am so glad you're not my maid of honor. Even if you would totally rock it in a dress and heels.

Aiden prayed she'd never seen any of the photos from that drag party he'd gone to during Pridefest a couple of years ago.

The door opened, and Becca stood there, her hands on her hips.

"Get used to that look," Aiden muttered.

Will laughed. "I've seen it many times before." They got out of the truck and walked toward her. Mom and Dad appeared behind Becca, who gave Will a pointed stare.

Yeah, Aiden knew *that* look too. Will was in trouble.

Becca inclined her head toward the trunk. "Your stuff's already in the car. We need to get a move on if we're gonna miss the traffic."

"You can't stay for lunch?" Dad remonstrated.

"It's a great idea, but I hadn't counted on losing Will for most of the morning." Becca aimed another cool glance at Will, and Aiden winced.

Yeah, it was going to be a frosty trip back to Minnesota.

"We'll see you in a few days anyway," Mom said brightly. "If you don't want to drive again so soon, your dad'll send you the money for the train. You might have to miss some classes Wednesday afternoon but at least you wouldn't get here so late."

"Lots of students will be heading home, so that's not a problem," Becca told her.

"You *are* still coming, aren't you, Will?"

Mom asked.

There was a moment's hesitation before Will replied. "Yes, of course."

It wasn't as if Mom had given him much of a choice. An edict had been issued, right?

On impulse, Aiden grabbed Will in a tight hug. "Safe trip back. And thanks for last night." He released him and took a step back.

Will chuckled. "Thank you for a highly entertaining—and instructive—evening. I think we both learned a lot." His cheeks pinked.

"You can say that again," Aiden murmured.

A strident *beep* told him Becca was anxious to be on her way.

Aiden leaned in. "Want some advice? I think you need some sleep. In fact, if I were you, I'd sleep the whole way back to Minnesota."

Will laughed softly. "Now there's an idea." He went to say his goodbyes to Mom and Dad, and Aiden walked over to Becca's car.

She rolled the window down. "Did you have fun last night?"

He snorted. "Shit, Becca, whoever said you were good at sarcasm? They lied. And yeah, I had fun. I think Will is a pretty cool guy. And if you're gonna blame anyone for him staying over, blame me."

Her eyes flashed. "Oh, I do." She gave him a sweet smile. "Just wait until you bring a girlfriend home. I'm gonna monopolize her the way you did Will."

There was an undercurrent to her voice Aiden couldn't quite identify. "You okay?"

She gazed at him with wide eyes. "Why

would I not be okay?"

"Because you sound… I don't know… nervous. Is anything wrong?"

"No, nothing is wrong. Everything is absolutely fine. Dandy. Awesome. I'd even go so far as peachy."

"I'd believe you if it weren't for the fact that you said all that through gritted teeth."

Becca rolled her eyes heavenward. "I said I'm—"

He held his hands up. "Okay, okay, I get the picture." Will came around to the passenger side and climbed in. Aiden stepped back. "Drive safe. And message me when you get there."

That earned him another eyeroll. "Sure—*Dad*."

Will gave him a smile. "*I'll* message you, all right?"

"Thanks." He watched as Becca pulled away from the curb, and through the rear window, he saw Will raise his hand in a wave.

Then the car turned the corner, and they were gone.

"You coming in?" Mom rubbed her arms. "It's freezing out here."

"You know what? I'm gonna go home. I've got some stuff to get ready for tomorrow."

Dad nodded. "Good boy. We'll see you Thursday morning, bright and early, okay?" He grinned. "You know your mom likes to have all hands on deck for Thanksgiving."

He knew.

Aiden climbed behind the wheel of his truck and headed out, giving his folks a final wave. He hated lying to them—his work was all done—but he couldn't stand the thought of getting the third degree from Mom.

Besides, he wanted to cuddle Midnight and watch *Notting Hill* again.

And remember waking up to find himself in Will's arms.

CHAPTER THIRTEEN

Thanksgiving In Milwaukee

Wednesday November 23

"I saw Kristen leaving as I got to your apartment this afternoon." One look at her red-rimmed eyes and blotchy cheeks was all Will needed to know all was not well in Becca and Kristen's world. He hadn't asked questions, but instead gave her a hug.

"Good for you." Becca didn't glance in his direction but kept her attention on the road ahead.

"Becca… she was upset."

She set her jaw. "Change the subject," she said in a low, firm voice.

"Uh-uh. I like Kristen. She's funny, sweet, and she loves you beyond reason, which makes her both a saint and a masochist."

Becca jerked her head toward him and glared. "Hey!"

Will pointed to the windshield. "Eyes front, please."

Becca grumbled but did as instructed. "I don't know what you're talking about. I'm a nice person."

He chuckled. "Don't give me that butter wouldn't melt act." He twisted in the passenger seat to stare at her. "Deny you can be a total bi—"

"Don't say the B-word," she said with a growl. "And if you must pry, we… we had a talk last night. She told me to tell Mom and Dad the truth."

"It seems Kristen and I are in agreement, then."

Becca let out a noise of pure exasperation. "Great. Gang up on me, why don't you? Now all we need is for Aiden to find out and it'll be three for three." She darted a glance at him. "He still doesn't know, right?"

"No, he doesn't," Will confirmed. He'd hated lying to Aiden, and the longer this fiasco dragged on, the worse it was going to be when Aiden finally learned the truth.

Three days of thinking of ways to extricate himself from this mess.

Three days of coming up with no solutions but a whole lotta guilt.

"You've been avoiding me."

Will blinked. "I don't know what you mean."

Becca never was slow on the uptake.

"Bullshit. You slept the whole way home Sunday. I turned the music up loud and even *that* didn't wake you."

"You did what?" *Who does that?*

She ignored him. "And when we got back, you went straight to your apartment. That was the last I saw of you until two hours ago."

"I have exams coming up—in three weeks' time, to be exact—and so do you."

That observation sailed right over Becca's head too.

"But back to Aiden. What went on between you two?"

Nothing. Unfortunately. How could anything go on when he thinks I'm his sister's straight fiancé?

Will was struggling not to resent Becca landing him in this pile of crap, and fuck, it was hard work. Another reason why he'd avoided her all week.

"What *are* you talking about?"

Becca tightened her grip on the steering wheel. "He *hugged* you. Aiden isn't a hugger, but he hugged *you*. So yeah, I'm asking—what happened?"

"We talked. All night—literally. Which is why I was dead to the world, by the way. Oh, and we drank a couple of beers."

That earned him another head jerk. "*You* drink *beer*?"

He snorted. "And you call yourself my bestie? Yes, I drink beer."

Becca laughed. "Now, if you'd said you *talked* about beer, that I could believe."

Maybe Becca knew him better than Will had imagined.

"By the way, I didn't notice any scratches. I guess he kept Midnight locked up. Either that, or Midnight knew another nerd when he saw one, and you made a new friend."

"He's a nice kitty. Obviously a much maligned one. And with good taste in humans."

"Well, here's a word of advice. Don't get too friendly with Midnight's human. Because once we break up, your name is gonna be mud."

"*My* name? Don't you mean *our* names?"

"Not if we go with the original plan, and *you*

call off the wedding."

"Oh, so *I* get to be the bad guy? Gee, thanks, Becca."

Silence fell, and Will was in no mood to fill it with conversation.

Then Becca sighed. "I couldn't do that to you. The whole point about calling off the wedding is so that I can eventually tell them the truth—tell them about Kristen. So when it all goes tits up, I'll make sure they knew you were against this from the start."

He swallowed. "Now *there's* the Becca I know and love." Yes, she drove him to distraction sometimes, and he'd lost count of how many times in recent days he'd been tempted to tell her he'd had enough. But he couldn't imagine having someone in his life that he couldn't take home to meet his family.

It must really hurt her.

Still, the prospect of three days with Becca's family filled him with dread.

I'll have to be on my guard the whole time.

I'll have to remember I'm supposed to be in love with Becca.

Even if right then he could have throttled her.

Hey, don't give too *good a performance, not if you want to give credence to the whole 'calling off the wedding' scenario. Let them see a few cracks. Then the break-up will be less of a shock.*

Despite his sympathy for Becca's situation, Will couldn't wait to be out of this shitstorm.

"So will it be just your parents and Aiden?"

"Yup, and enough food to feed four."

"Four people?"

She chuckled. "Four families. But we'll have to work for our dinner. You and Aiden can prepare the veggies."

"What did we do to be so honored?"

Another chuckle. "I hate doing them, so you just drew the short straw." She paused. "Were your folks okay with you not being there today?"

Will smiled. "They've had me at the Thanksgiving table for twenty-one years—one year without me won't kill them. Besides, I'll be there next year. And there's always Christmas."

By then, he'd be a single man again.

You're single now, remember?

Will told himself he was just getting into the right mindset.

Less chance of getting caught out that way.

Thanksgiving was starting to look like the tranquil lake where his parents owned a cabin, its waters still and inviting.

And rocks hidden below the surface, waiting to hurt the unwary swimmer.

Something landed on Will's bed with a soft *whump*, and he opened his eyes to be confronted by a furry black face with long whiskers, bright eyes focused on him.

He smiled. "Midnight. Good morning." He stroked behind the kitty's ears, and Midnight got comfortable, snuggled up to Will's side, purring. "Do you get a special Thanksgiving Day meal too?"

The door to the guest room opened, and the wonderful aroma of freshly brewed coffee wafted in.

"Are you decent?" It was Aiden.

"Me? Sure. Midnight's naked, though."

"No surprise there. He's a brazen kitty cat." Aiden came into the room, carrying two mugs. "Good morning. Mom said you didn't get here until late last night."

"Mm." He sniffed. "That smells good." Will sat up, scraping his fingers through his hair and yawning. "What time is it?"

Aiden perched on the edge of the mattress. "Seven-thirty. Mom's already making a mess in the kitchen. To be honest, I was kinda surprised to find you here."

"But you knew I was com—"

"Oh, I don't mean *here*, I mean in this room."

"Where else would I be?" Will sipped the fragrant brew.

His eyes twinkled. "In Becca's room? Then again, she could have been in here."

Will arched his eyebrows. "And then again, maybe I like my balls where they are. Imagine if your dad walked in. This *is* the twenty-first century, but I don't think fathers' attitudes have changed all that much, not where their daughters are concerned." Not that it was a likely scenario, but Will had a role to play, and that meant saying the right things.

The *expected* things.

"Next you'll tell me you're saving yourself for marriage." Will choked on his coffee, spraying the comforter, and Aiden appeared stricken. "Oh dear Lord. You're not a…" He clammed up.

Will wiped his lips. "Were you about to ask if I'm a virgin?"

"No. Absolutely not." A pause. "Okay, yes." Before Will could respond, Aiden surged ahead. "Forget I asked. It's none of my business."

He laughed. "No, it isn't. And no, I'm not. Haven't been since I was sixteen. And a half." Will wasn't about to regale him with the story of Andy, the guy next door, who used to mow the lawn in nothing but shorts and sandals. Or how he'd asked Will to help him get the grass stains off his legs, which required him to get very, very close.

As close as he'd like to get to Aiden, given half a chance.

"So tell me—are you going to ask your sister the same question?"

Aiden gaped at him. "God no. I like my balls where they are too."

Midnight chose that moment to let out a loud meow, and Will chuckled. "I don't think he's happy with all this talk of genitals, but I don't see why. He *is* a cat, after all, and they do like to bat at dangly things."

"Oh, trust me, I'm very well aware. Those claws are lethal weapons." Aiden shuddered.

Will let out a mock gasp. "Midnight, did you hurt your daddy?"

Midnight blinked as if to say, *'Me? As if. I'm*

an angel.'

"*Hurt* me?" Aiden snorted. "The doctor couldn't stop laughing when he stitched me up. On the plus side, I get some strange looks when I tell people at the gym it's a circumcision scar." He chuckled. "It was my own fault, and it taught me a valuable lesson—never play with the kitty while naked."

Will stroked the warm, sleek cat. "How come you brought him with you?"

"I'm staying here tonight, and my neighbor has gone to see her parents, so that would mean leaving him alone."

"You live twenty minutes away, dude. You could always go home."

"True," Aiden admitted. "But since I moved out, Mom kinda put her foot down and said she expects both kids under her roof for Thanksgiving and Christmas. Besides, the day after Thanksgiving is usually a lot of fun around here." He grinned. "Dad raids the garage for all the Christmas decorations. By Sunday, you won't recognize this place."

"It takes that long?"

Aiden gave an evil chuckle. "You'll be able to see for yourself. Because *you're* gonna help."

"We're not just talking Christmas lights here, are we?"

"You're going to be part of this family, so you might as well learn now. In this street during the holidays, there's a kind of competition every year for who has the most decorated house."

"And how does the Taylor family usually fare?"

Aiden's eyes gleamed. "You're looking at the champions." He cocked his head. "What about *your* family? Are they Christmas nuts too?"

"I think we'd be in the minor leagues." Something Will had pushed to change every year, but his parents had always put up staunch resistance. The idea of being part of—

But you won't *be part of it. In fact, after this all blows up, you probably won't want to be anywhere near the Taylors again.*

There was something about this family that sucked Will right in, made him lose his reason, his perspective…

*Well, some*one *in this family.*

Aiden stood. "I'd better let you get dressed. Mom will be hollering for everyone to come down to breakfast any second now."

Will held up his mug. "Thanks for the coffee."

"You're welcome. I remembered how you like it."

"Aiden!" Louise called out. "You're doing toast duty this morning. Get your butt down here."

Aiden sighed. "No rest for the wicked." He left the room.

Midnight stayed put, and Will scritched his ears. "I'm going to have to disturb you now. I need to get out of this bed."

The cat rolled onto his back, his paws curled, exposing a fluffy white tummy that was impossible to ignore.

Will laughed. "You fight dirty."

He could almost hear Midnight's response.

'Duh. Of course. I'm a cat. Now rub me, slave.'

Will hoped Becca's prediction was correct. The thought of spending time in the kitchen with Aiden was a pleasant one.

He stroked Midnight's soft belly. "Can you keep a secret?" Midnight blinked twice, and he chuckled. "I hope that means yes." He leaned over and kissed Midnight's paw. "Your daddy is as adorable as you are."

And just as difficult to ignore.

Then he chuckled again. "And don't tell him, but I'd really like the chance to rub *his* tummy too."

Mom's To Do list made prepping the vegetables sound like a simple exercise.

It was anything but.

Aiden stood next to Will as they peeled and chopped carrots, ready for roasting with a coating of oil, garlic, and parmesan. The kitchen wasn't small, yet they managed to brush shoulders continually as they worked, and each light contact sent a shiver through Aiden. Now and then he stole a glance at Will, only to jerk his head back when he found Will doing the same thing.

Did Mom turn up the thermostat in here?

They worked at the kitchen island, and the

combination of Will's shampoo, soap, and warm, clean skin took Aiden's mind on a decidedly carnal tangent.

Stop this. Stop this right now.

He reached for the knife, and their hands touched. Aiden pulled his back as though stung, his skin tingling. Then Mom came back into the kitchen, and he shifted sideways, putting space between them.

What surprised him was that Will did the same thing, almost simultaneously.

Mom glanced at the countertop. "Aren't you finished yet?" She narrowed her gaze. "And no eating, Aiden James Taylor. I know your little ways." She went over to the oven to peer through the glass at the turkey. "That smells amazing." Then she left the room.

"It does, doesn't it?" Will said in a rough voice totally unlike his own.

It took Aiden a second or two to realize what he'd heard. He beamed.

"*Muppet Christmas Carol.* Miss Piggy as Mrs. Cratchit." Aiden laughed. "That was really good. It even sounded like her."

Will glanced toward the door and said, "Just tell your mom 'I was merely testing them. It's a chef thing.'" He was an excellent mimic.

Aiden had to know. "Can you do Becca?"

Will widened his eyes. "Are you kidding? She could walk in here any second."

He snorted. "Yeah right. She's not gonna be anywhere near here, in case Mom gives her something to do." He batted his lashes. "Please, Will? For me?"

Will stared at him for a moment then shook his head. "You fight as dirty as your cat. Hell, Midnight probably learned it from you." He cleared his throat, gave another furtive glance toward the door, and said, "Maybe we should go with *fake* flowers."

Aiden roared with laughter. "Oh my God, that *is* awesome. You totally nailed her."

Will picked up a carrot baton. "Quick, before your mom comes back."

Aiden's heart beat faster. Instead of taking it from Will's hand, he leaned in and took it in his mouth, his lips brushing Will's fingers. He bit off the end, then drew back slowly, his gaze locked on Will's parted lips.

Okay, that was so wrong.

Aiden grabbed a head of garlic and busied himself with it, removing the papery outer skin. "I'll get started on this."

Will coughed. "We have to keep the vampires at bay, right?" His voice was a little husky.

"Right."

Except I don't want to keep you *at bay.*

On the contrary, Aiden wanted Will as close as it was possible for two bodies to get.

How is it possible for a day to be both fun and *torture, all at the same time?*

The preparation had been an exercise in sensual torment, and Will had been relieved when Louise came in and told them to leave so she could work without them under her feet. He'd gone to his room, giving the excuse of calling his parents.

Okay, so he *had* called them, but that wasn't why he'd fled.

Avoiding Aiden was his prime motivation.

When it was time to gather for the meal, he'd chosen the chair next to Becca. Aiden sat facing him, and Louise and Carl at opposite ends of the dining table. The deep red tablecloth was covered with dishes that were empty but for the odd smear of food, and Will was about to cross the line between comfortably full and stuffed. The food had been delicious, and he'd tried to hold back, leaving a little room for dessert, but right then he wasn't sure he could manage it.

He'd enjoyed the banter, particularly as the topic of the wedding hadn't cropped up once, a welcome reprieve. And when one hour became almost two, he relaxed enough to join in the conversation. But throughout the meal, he was conscious of a weight across his shoulders, pressing down on him.

This feels so good. And Becca is going to wreck it.

Becca's phone buzzed, and she slipped it from her pocket to peer at the screen.

Louise made a noise of disapproval. "Not at the table."

Becca tapped the screen and replaced it in her pocket. Seconds later it buzzed again.

"Are you going to answer that?" Aiden asked.

Becca gave a tight smile. "No, it can wait." The phone vibrated for a third time.

"Well, obviously *someone* wants to talk to you," Louise observed.

Becca's eyes flashed. "I said it can wait."

Carl cleared his throat. "I think a toast is called for." He raised his glass. "To Will, whose sanity is in doubt because he wants to join this family." His eyes sparkled.

Everyone clinked glasses.

Will chuckled. "Any more compliments like that, and you'll lose a willing pair of hands tomorrow."

Carl's face lit up. "You're going to help with the decorations? Good man." He beamed at Becca. "I like him."

"I like him too," Louise added.

Aiden raised his glass. "Let's make it unanimous. We all like Will."

That last part set Will's stomach churning.

But I don't want you to like *me.*

He wanted so much more than that.

"And now all we need is for Aiden to find someone," Louise declared with a smile.

Will was a realist. He knew he was fixated on a man who didn't bat for Will's team, who probably couldn't be *tempted* to switch teams, and who wouldn't want anything to do with him once the dust of the breakup—and the cancellation of the wedding—settled.

That left only one option—enjoy it while it lasted.

CHAPTER FOURTEEN

Will Gets Entangled In More Ways Than One

After two hours with no sleep in sight, Aiden gave up the fight and headed to the kitchen in search of a cup of hot chocolate. The light showing under Will's door gave him another idea.

Better make that two cups.

He stood in the kitchen, waiting for the kettle to boil. The reason for his insomnia could have been the amount of food he'd eaten, but Aiden knew that wasn't the root cause.

His mind was full of Will.

Aiden couldn't put his finger on it, but something seemed… off during the meal. He recalled the way Will and Becca had been at the hotel, the night of the anniversary party. It had been as though they couldn't bear to be parted for more than a minute, always touching, always sneaking glances at each other. But since that night?

Something's changed.

It couldn't be anything huge—they were still engaged, for one thing—and whatever it was, Becca hadn't said a word. But her manner during the meal had been a little strained, especially noticeable with that business of her phone. And the rest of the evening she'd been quiet.

Becca? Quiet?

Aiden sensed a disturbance in the Force.

He poured hot water into the cups, stirred, and crept out of the kitchen, switching the light off with his nose. When he reached Will's door, he nudged it twice with his foot. He heard the wooden bed frame creak, and a moment later, Will stood there in his shorts, pulling a tee over his head.

Aiden held up the cups. "Thought this might help."

Will smiled. "Well, come on in, fellow insomniac." He closed the door behind Aiden, then climbed back into bed.

Aiden glanced at the book lying face down on the comforter, and chuckled. "*A Brief History of Time*? Not exactly a light read."

"And not a good choice for sending me off to sleep either. It's way too interesting." Will smiled. "Where's *Moby Dick* when you need it?"

Aiden sat on the bed, his back resting against the high footboard. "I deliberated bringing you a turkey sandwich," he teased.

Will gave a low groan. "Don't mention food. I haven't eaten that much since…"

"Last Christmas?" Aiden suggested.

"Yeah, possibly." He wrapped his hands around the mug, inhaling the aroma. "Your parents…"

"What about them?" Aiden smiled. "You're a hit, by the way."

"Good to now." Will took a sip before continuing. "It's just… well, they're not what I expected."

Aiden arched his eyebrows. "Now you've got me curious." Whatever expectations Will had harbored could only have been fueled by Becca.

Will stared into his hot chocolate. "Becca has talked a lot about her family."

"I dread to think how she painted me."

Will bit his lip. "I think 'nerd' pretty much nails it. But I had an idea of what your parents would be like."

"And is reality better or worse?"

Will smiled, and it reached his eyes. "Better." He took another sip.

Aiden got the sense Will didn't want to continue with the present topic. "So… where will you be spending Christmas?"

Will gazed into his cup again. "I don't know."

Aiden chuckled. "Well, surely it's one of two places, dude."

"I… I can't think that far ahead."

"I hate to break it to you, but Christmas is three days after your wedding—which is *exactly* four weeks from today."

"And right now I have other things to think about, okay?"

Aiden regarded him thoughtfully. "College stuff? I know you have exams coming up." But from what Becca had told him, Will would breeze through them.

Whatever was on Will's mind, it wasn't school.

Well, something *sure is. And it's keeping him awake nights.*

Aiden frowned. "You and Becca…

everything's okay, isn't it?"

"What? Oh, sure. Everything's fine."

Aiden studied him. "Let me guess. You'd go so far as to say it's dandy. Peachy, even."

Will reached back to touch the base of his neck. "What does that mean?"

"Nothing. Just something Becca said."

Okay, something didn't add up, but maybe Aiden's math was at fault.

Maybe I'm reading too much into this.

Yeah, and maybe it was time he went back to his own bed and stopped thinking about Will.

Aiden got off the bed. "If you like, you can borrow Midnight. His purrs will soon have you falling asleep."

"Thanks for the offer, but I think your need is as great as mine." Will smiled, only this time there was none of that captivating light in his eyes. "Sleep well."

Aiden went to the door. "You too." He left the room and crept along the hallway.

Near the footboard, Midnight didn't even stir as Aiden entered.

Oh, to sleep like a cat.

He climbed back into bed and sat, finishing his hot chocolate. Then he placed the cup on the nightstand, snuggled down the bed, and pulled the comforter up over his head, creating a warm cocoon. Midnight was a warm lump near his feet.

You mess with my head, Will Bryant.

Friday, November 25

Will gazed at the string of lights coiled on the living room floor. "How many lights are there?"

"No idea. Mom says there were a hundred originally, but they'd added to them since." Aiden laughed. "She claims they make baby lights during the time they're in the attic, when no one is watching."

He grinned. "Really? That is freaking adorbs."

Aiden nodded. "She's been saying that for years, and when I was little, I believed it. *Now,* of course, I know the truth—smart lights wear condoms."

The more time Will spent around the Taylors, the more they enchanted him.

"And every year it's my job to test them first, to check all the bulbs are working," Aiden continued. "Then I replace any dead ones."

Will coughed. "You know, most Christmas lights these days don't have bulbs. They're usually LED lights."

"Which tells you how old these are." Aiden plugged them in. He grinned when the room was filled with cool blue and warm white lights. "Hey, whaddaya know? They all work." He snorted. "That was the easy part."

"Where's your dad?"

"In the garage with the compressor, getting all the inflatables ready."

"How many is 'all'?" Will pictured the front of the house with its four raised flower beds retained behind low brick walls, and the expanse of lawn that reached the sidewalk. A lot of room for decorations.

He won't fill all *of it—will he?*

"Let me see." Aiden counted off. "There are three Santas, one Santa in his sleigh, eight reindeer, eight snowmen—"

"Eight?"

"Sure. They line the path to the front door, four on each side. Then Dad puts a wire arched tunnel over the path, and strings little white lights all over it."

It sounded magical.

At least I'll get to see it before Christmas.

Aiden picked up the end of one of the coiled cables. "Hold this, would you?"

Will grasped it. "What am I supposed to do with this?"

"Just stand still."

Before Will could ask what on earth Aiden was doing, Aiden began to wind the cable around his body, looping it under Will's arms.

"What—what are you doing?"

"Trust me. You'll look amazing." Aiden wound the cable around Will's neck, even going so far as to give him a coiled crown of lights.

"I am *not* a Christmas tree!" Will called out, doing his best not to laugh.

"Really? Are you sure?"

"Perfectly sure. And watch what you're doing with that," Will said as Aiden passed the cable between his legs, up his back, and over his shoulder. "There's a word for this, you know."

Aiden grinned. "Yes, there is—Shibari. Never seen it done with lights before. Maybe I'll start a new trend."

"And maybe you can unwrap me *right now*."

The door opened and Becca came into the room. She took one look at Will, burst out laughing, and a nanosecond later, her phone was out and she was taking a picture.

"Becca!" he remonstrated.

"What? You look so cool. I bet Dad would *love* to plop you out in the yard, next to the sleigh." She waggled her phone. "You know what? I'm gonna save this and print it. Then I'm gonna stick it on the noticeboard in the Astrophysics faculty."

"Do that and you're a dead woman," he growled.

Except it was hard to get the words out, he was laughing so much.

Becca held up her phone for him to see. "Aw, don't you look pretty?"

"You see those gold-painted pinecones in that bag by the fireplace? When I get out of this, I am going to shove them where the sun doesn't shine. And that goes for both of you."

Aiden bit his lip. "There's a word for that too." He started to untangle Will with obvious reluctance, winding the cable as he went.

At last Will was free. "Thank you." Then he darted across the room to grab the bag of pinecones, and Becca let out a shriek. She fled, leaving Aiden holding his hands up defensively.

"Now, Will… don't do anything you'll regret."

Will grinned. "I'll give you a ten second head-start. Two…four…six…eight…TEN!"

Dinner was predictably turkey-based, with nowhere near the quantity of the previous day, for which Will was grateful. It wasn't until the pumpkin pie made its appearance that the meal became a little awkward.

"You've organized your suit for the wedding, haven't you, Will?" Louise asked as she passed the plates around.

"My suit?" The words came out as a squeak, and Aiden chuckled.

Becca wasn't laughing, however. She gave Will an unwavering stare.

"Yes, your suit. And while I think on it, what do *you* plan on wearing, Aiden?"

Will took refuge in the momentary distraction to think fast.

I can't lie. I hate *lying.*

Aiden blinked, and a wave of sympathy washed over Will.

"To be totally honest, I haven't given it

much thought," Aiden replied.

"Then I suggest you remedy that situation—tomorrow. I'm taking Becca to try on her dress, so you might as well come along and find yourself a suit."

Judging by Aiden's look of misery, he couldn't think of anything worse.

Will to the rescue.

"I've got a confession."

Becca stilled, her face paling a little.

"I think I know what you're going to say." Louise cocked her head to one side, and for one scary moment, Will had the feeling she saw right through him.

Becca seemed to have stopped breathing.

"You haven't organized a suit yet, have you?" Louise gazed at him with warm eyes.

"How did you know?"

She huffed. "Because I know you've been working very hard at school." Louise smiled. "Don't worry—you can join Aiden tomorrow, and we'll kill two birds with one stone." She forked off a piece of pie, and Will took the opportunity to breathe.

Becca appeared to be doing the same.

"But you *have* made arrangements for Will's bachelor party, haven't you, Aiden?"

It was Aiden's turn to do the old rabbit-caught-in-the-headlights routine.

"It's all in hand," Will blurted out. "Just a bit of-fine tuning left to do." He met Aiden's gaze. "Isn't that right?"

Aiden swallowed. "Yeah, that's right. We can talk about this after dinner."

"Lou, give them a break." Carl smiled.

"They've worked so hard today, the last thing they need is to be grilled by you. Stop worrying. This wedding will go off without a hitch. You'll see." He resumed eating his pie.

Will could see one pretty humongous hitch heading straight for them. One thing was certain, however. He was *not* about to let Aiden organize a bachelor party.

As to how he was going to get around it—without letting the cat out of the bag—he had yet to work out.

Chapter Fifteen

Aiden And Will Hatch A Plan

Saturday, November 26

Aiden lay in bed, staring at the ceiling. As yet no sound penetrated from below: Mom wasn't up yet. Midnight was curled up on the pillow next to him, his little nose and paws twitching.

I wonder what cats dream about? Mice? Birds? He smiled. *Stupid question. World domination, of course.*

The prospect of shopping for a suit didn't thrill him. He had better things to do with his time. Then he reasoned it might not be as bad as he anticipated. There was a silver lining to the trip, after all.

Will would be there.

He'd had two days of Will's company, and it wasn't enough. If anything, it had given him only a taste and he wanted more.

Shit, I have it bad.

Except he'd passed bad twenty-four hours ago.

A soft knock at the door had Midnight opening his eyes, stretching his front legs out, and yawning. Aiden knew it wasn't Becca out in the hallway—she never knocked—so that left—

"Are you awake?" Will asked in a low voice.

Aiden sat up and straightened the comforter. "Yeah. Come in."

The door opened, and Will stuck his head around it. "Can we talk?"

With a rush of hot guilt, Aiden realized he'd reneged on the promise he'd made during dinner the previous night. "Sure." Before Will reached the bed, he blurted, "I'm sorry about last night. I did intend to talk about the bachelor party, but I had an email I had to answer." Work was yelling at him, but it would have to wait until Sunday.

"That's okay." Will sat on the edge of the bed, and Aiden did his best not to stare at his lean legs, his feet looking so cute in little white socks. The rest of Will's body was hidden beneath a pair of white shorts and a grey tee.

"I sort of got the impression last night that you were in a jam, which is why I said we'd discuss it." Aiden smiled. "Mom can't turn off her organizer button."

"Thanks for that, by the way. I know I said my brother would arrange the party, but I've been thinking…" Will squared his shoulders. "There won't be a party."

Aiden blinked. "At all?" Will shook his head. "But why not?"

"Because none of my friends can make it. They all said the same things: too close to the holidays, exams, commitments… And Ethan can't make it either." He flushed. "I don't mind, not really. Besides, a bachelor party isn't that important."

"I disagree." Aiden sagged against the pillows, and Midnight decided to climb onto him and begin kneading his chest. He chuckled. "I don't believe I ordered a massage this morning." One of Midnight's claws got caught in his tee, and Aiden freed it before lifting the cat and dropping him to the floor. "Massage over." He leaned back once more and regarded Will. "A bachelor party is a rite of passage kinda thing. Most people only get married once—unless you're my Uncle Tim, and we've all lost count of how many ex-wives he's accumulated. But what about my idea? A D & D game night instead? I could find us a place to hold it, no problem. And I could sweeten the deal." He grinned. "Craft beer?"

Will laughed. "I appreciate the thought, but I don't want you putting yourself out. You have enough on your plate with school."

It was a valid point. More than that, Aiden was touched to find Will so considerate.

Then he recalled the conversation during dinner.

"You know my mom won't be happy about this when she hears. And she's gonna blame me, seeing as I'm supposed to be putting this shindig together."

Will arched his eyebrows. "But it's not her party, is it?" Then he smiled, and the light returned to those dark brown eyes. "Wait a minute though. She doesn't have to know. We just *tell* her it's going ahead."

Aiden gave a gasp of mock horror. "We lie?"

To his surprise, Will grimaced. "I don't like the idea either. Lies are never a good thing. They just get you deeper into trouble. But in the circumstances…"

"I have another idea."

Will smiled, and it was a relief to see his usual cheerful expression. "Now what?"

Aiden grinned. "Let me arrange a bar crawl."

"Huh?" Will cocked his head to one side. "What's the difference between that and a party?"

He stroked his jaw. "Well, participation will be limited to a select few."

"How many is a few?"

He flashed another grin. "Two. You and me."

What the hell?

Will frowned. "A bar crawl with only two participants?" He liked a beer now and then, but a night of going from bar to bar, getting steadily more drunk, did not appeal.

But you like the part where it's only you two, don't you?

Yeah, he did, even if it was never going to happen in a million years.

"Think about it." Aiden laced his hands behind his head. "A hassle-free evening, enjoying a few beers. We can take selfies. That way, we'll have proof. Mom doesn't need to know we're sitting in a bar full of strangers." He smiled. "It'd be you and me, sharing a quiet night of—"

"Getting drunk," Will blurted.

"I won't let you drink too much," Aiden promised. "Remember, I've seen what you're like when you overindulge. Although, if you don't have a hangover the next day, Mom will be suspicious. Unless you can fake one?"

Will smiled as the idea settled in his mind. "I think I can manage that."

A night with Aiden ticked all his boxes.

Excuse me? A night with Aiden? There isn't going to be any bar crawl. By December 10, Becca would have gotten her act together, they would have broken up, and there would *be* no wedding.

The thought of messing Aiden around did *not* sit well with him.

"Great. Then that's what we'll do. Problem solved."

Except there was another event to endure, because unless Becca announced their break-up before the following Saturday, there was Deborah's cocktail party.

Cocktails….

"This party next week… are there likely to be a lot of people going?"

Aiden chuckled. "Knowing my Aunt Deborah? The house'll be packed to the rafters."

Great. Another night of Becca's relatives, of pretending to be in love, answering questions about the wedding, pasting on a smile until his face ached…

Aiden gave him a knowing glance. "You're not into cocktails, are you?"

Will chuckled. "What gave it away? No, not really."

"The same way you weren't into beer?" Aiden's eyes twinkled.

He laughed. "Okay, I *really* don't drink cocktails. They sound like something my parents would drink. I don't think I'm a martini kind of guy."

"Then I'll have to convert you. I'm not a martini kind of guy either. Way too tame for me."

Will gave him an inquiring glance. "'Tame'?"

Aiden reached for his phone on the nightstand. "I'll do a little mixology research before the party. I'll also find out what alcohol Aunt Deborah is planning to have there, and maybe make a few suggestions." Another grin. "I'll offer my services as bartender for the night."

Will returned his grin. "You could invent your own Pan Galactic Gargle Blaster."

"Now *there's* a thought." Aiden cocked his head as noise erupted from below. "Mom's up. You ready to go suit hunting after breakfast?"

Yet another thing Will had woken up thinking about.

"Look, I can understand Becca having a really special dress—she's the bride." Will's stomach clenched at the subterfuge. "But I *have* suits. In fact, I have the one I wore when Ethan got married last year. A new one seems like an unnecessary expense."

To his surprise, Aiden broke into a wide smile.

"You and I think alike. I don't really want a new suit either. So what do we do about it? Tell

Mom another lie?"

Will shook his head. "No, we tell her we looked into it and we'll get it sorted. Becca should be her priority."

"In that case, what do we do while they're at the bridal store?"

Will bit his lip. "Promise not to laugh."

Aiden stilled. "Now I'm intrigued."

"Are there any decent bookstores in Milwaukee?"

Aiden's grin sent a flood of warmth rushing through him.

"Plenty."

Lunch was over, and while Will yearned to head to his room to leaf through his new books, there was something else that required his attention.

Becca had been way too quiet throughout the meal, and she'd disappeared before the plates had been collected. Will had been the perfect guest and had offered to do the dishes, and had been duly thanked before Louise informed him they already had a dishwasher—he was called Carl.

He'd laughed at the joke, especially since he'd already spotted the dishwasher in the kitchen.

When half an hour passed and there was still

no sign of Becca, Will grew uneasy. He made his excuses and went upstairs to her room. He knocked, and when there was no answer, he peered into the room.

Becca lay on the bed, her gaze focused on her phone.

It didn't require a genius to know what—or rather, who—was on her mind.

Will closed the door behind him and went over to the bed. "Hey," he said softly.

"Hey." Becca didn't look at him, her voice flat.

He sat on the bed. "I know you didn't tell her. Didn't you get the chance?"

She shrugged. "The timing wasn't right."

Will let out a sigh of exasperation. "Becca, the timing will *never* be right, but you can't let this drag on any longer."

Time was not only not on their side, it was giving them hard stares and tapping its watch.

Becca sat up. "Would you come with me for a drive?"

He had a feeling she had a specific destination in mind. "Sure."

They went downstairs, and before Louise could open her mouth, Becca smiled and said, "Will and I are going out for a while. We won't be long." Then they were out of the house and heading for Becca's car.

"Want to tell me where we're going?" Will asked after a couple of minutes of silence.

"Something I want to show you."

Eight minutes after that, she parked on a side street, then led him to a store.

Will stared at the shop front with a frown. "Strike Bridal Bar? Isn't this where you—"

She grabbed his hand and tugged him toward the door, propelling him through it. A tall, slim woman was in the middle of hanging a dress in lilac satin on a rack of similar dresses. She frowned when she saw Becca.

"Miss Taylor? Did you forget something?"

"Could I try on my dress, please?"

The woman's gaze flickered to Will, and her eyes widened. "This isn't the groom, is it? Because it's bad lu—"

"Please, just bring out my dress," Becca pleaded.

Will didn't have a clue what was going on.

The woman shrugged. "Fine. The customer is always right." She went through a doorway.

Will took advantage of her absence. "Becca, why are we here?" he whispered.

"Because I want you to see the dress."

"I got that much, but why?"

"Because."

It was obvious he wasn't going to get any sense out of her.

The woman returned, carrying a dress made of ivory satin, the bodice covered in beautifully sculpted deep red lace, a matching lace around the hem. It was a very striking dress, perfect for a winter wedding.

Becca stared at it, her eyes shining.

"Why don't you try it on?" The woman glanced once more at Will. "It's your wedding, after all. If it doesn't bother you to let the groom see you in it, then it surely doesn't bother me."

Will got the feeling that was a lie, but he appreciated the effort.

"Thank you." Becca took the dress into one of the dressing rooms hidden behind red velvet curtains.

"Would you like some help?" the assistant offered.

Becca stuck her head through the gap. "Thank you. That would be great. I'd forgotten how many buttons this thing has."

Will was no closer to knowing what he was doing there but he figured Becca would clue him in eventually. He refrained from speaking to her through the curtain, preferring to wait until they were alone. While he waited, he gazed at the rows and rows of dresses: satin, silk, clouds of chiffon and organza… Another rack contained hangers for the veils, and in a glass display cabinet there were tiaras, combs festooned with silk flowers…

"Well? What do you think?"

Will turned, and the breath caught in his throat.

Becca was stunning. The dress was a snug fit around the waist, swelling into a layer of ivory satin that cascaded to the floor. She turned slowly, revealing a long line of red buttons from the bottom of the V-neck to a red velvet bow whose tails flowed down the skirt.

"Oh Becca."

She smiled. "It's beautiful, isn't it? This is what I'd wear for my wedding."

Will had to ask. "Has this been paid for?"

"The balance is due before the wedding." Becca stared at her reflection in the full-length mirror.

Will went over to her, careful not to stand on her dress. "This could be your wedding dress," he said in a low voice. "All you have to do is tell your parents the truth."

Becca swallowed, still staring at her reflection.

He put his arm around her waist and leaned in. "I think you have your mom and dad all wrong. From what you said, I expected them to be haters. But they're not. They're *not*, Becca. They're kind people. Good people."

Another hard swallow.

"Maybe they've changed," he continued in the same low, soothing tone. "Your mom works in the hotel. What if she's gotten to know someone there who's gay, and they've changed her opinion?"

Becca jerked her head toward him. "You think?"

"It's possible, isn't it?" Will kissed her cheek. "I've got an idea. It's your Aunt Deborah's cocktail party next weekend. Another couple of days in Milwaukee. Maybe the timing will be right then." He stared at her in the mirror. "You can't lose this dress, Becca. It's *totally* you. So what if you don't get to wear it in December? Keep it for when you and Kristen finally tie the knot."

Her eyes glistened.

"And if *I've* got this all wrong," he added, "then I'll help you pay for it yourself. And *I'll* give you away if your dad won't." Another kiss. "But it won't come to that, Becca. I truly believe that." He looked her in the eye. "Next weekend, okay?"

Becca nodded. "Next weekend."

"Now, let me take a picture of you in that amazing dress."

She chuckled. "I already have one. Mom took it." She turned and hugged him. "Thanks, Will."

He disengaged from her with great care. "Now, *please*, get out of that awesome dress before you damage it."

Becca gave another nod, then walked slowly toward the fitting room.

Will took a deep breath.

Finally.

Now all he had to do was hope Becca didn't lose her nerve.

CHAPTER SIXTEEN

Aiden Pops Will's Cocktail Cherry

Thursday December first.

The library had to be Will's favorite place on campus. The quiet, save for the sound of low chatter now and then, the smell of books, the sunlight falling in shafts through the long windows… Lately it had become his sanctuary, the one place where he could *think*.

Unfortunately, not all thoughts were of his studies. Aiden was there too. Not in the flesh, of course, but he might as well have been. Will had only to close his eyes to recall Aiden's strong jawline, those sparkling blue eyes, the red hair tumbling in soft waves…

Don't. Just quit, okay?

Easier said than done. Aiden was fast becoming a regular distraction. Will had tried to confine his recollections—and fantasies—to when he was alone in his bedroom, but memories of Aiden refused to be contained.

Will's dildo had never seen such frequent use, and he'd had to buy more lube.

He's an addiction.

And Will was about to go cold turkey, because this whole mess was nearly over. Hard to be addicted to someone he'd never see again, right?

Will had suggested Becca call her mom to announce they'd broken up—thus canceling the need for a cocktail party—but she'd refused.

'That just feels wrong. This has to be a face-to-face conversation.' Then she'd given a half smile. 'And Aunt Deborah would probably have the party anyway. She'd say it was to help drown our sorrows and cheer me up.'

That had brought on another discussion—where to lay the blame and exactly how much to reveal. Will had resigned himself to being the dumper rather than the dumpee, but he hoped Becca would use the conversation as a starting point to reveal the truth to her parents.

Except he knew *that* would be a discussion for another day.

He gazed at the open textbook, but the words danced on the page. All he could think about was the hug Aiden had given him when they'd said goodbye on Sunday. The smell of him. The feeling of those arms around him. The laughter they'd shared.

Those eyes that unraveled Will every fucking time.

And that one hug hadn't been *nearly* enough. Will wanted *more*. Hugs. Some kisses. Being in bed, touching each other, exploring, finding out what gave Aiden goose bumps or what made him moan. To discover things no other lover had found. To make him smile with breakfast in bed. To surprise him with impromptu trips to see the stars in some of the best stargazing places in the US. He wanted so much with Aiden, and it just wasn't going to be.

Damn it.

"Will?"

He jerked his head up. Kristen stood on the other side of the table, a pile of books under one arm.

"Hey."

She gestured to the empty chair next to him. "Is it okay if I join you?"

He had a feeling studying was not in the cards. "Sure." Will put his pen down, closed his copy of *Classical Electrodynamics*, and pushed his notes aside. He studied Kristen as she placed her books on the table and pulled her chair closer to his.

She looks pale. He couldn't swear to it, but he also thought she'd lost a little weight. Kristen removed her phone from her backpack and set it next to her books. He waited for her to speak, but after a minute passed with no sign of any communication, he reasoned he'd have to make the first move.

"How are you doing?"

She stared at her phone. "Okay."

Yeah right.

Will leaned in and lowered his voice. "Look, I know the rules say no food or drink in here, but…" He reached into his backpack and removed the opened bag of Hershey's. "Can I tempt you to a nugget?" He smiled. "I always find chocolate makes everything seem better."

Kristen chuckled. "Consider me tempted." She took a bronze-wrapped chocolate, disposed of the foil, and popped it into her mouth after darting a glance around the nearest tables to make sure she wasn't observed.

Will waited until she'd finished. "Okay, let's

start again."

Kristen gazed at him for a moment, her teeth worrying her lip. "Can I… can I show you something?"

"As long as it's not a dead mouse or something. Because if you do that, I'll end up standing on the table squealing."

She laughed, and Will suddenly realized it had been a while since he'd heard her do that.

This business is messing up lives.

Kristen smiled. "Believe it or not, I don't go around with my pockets full of dead rodents." Her eyes twinkled. "At least, not normally. That one time didn't count."

There was nothing quite so attractive as a good sense of humor.

"And while I hate to admit," Kristen continued, "One sight of a mouse and I'd be up on the table with you." She opened the purse strung across her chest, and took out—

Will caught his breath. "Is that what I think it is?" The box was small, covered in black velvet, and in the shape of a heart, and it could only contain one thing.

She opened it, and he gasped. "Oh wow." The ring was black, a dainty twisted vine with a costume diamond at its center. It had an art deco feel to it, and Will had never seen such a ring before.

Then he realized what he was looking at, and he froze.

"You're going to propose to Becca."

She sighed. "That was the plan."

"'Was'?"

Kristen nodded. "I *was* going to do it on her

birthday next week, but she'll probably be busy trying on wedding dresses." A bitter note crept into her voice.

She was hiding it well, but Will knew *pissed* when he heard it.

"It's okay to be honest about how you're feeling," he murmured. "This is *me*, remember? I'm the one who introduced you to her, after all." He sighed. "So I guess I'm to blame."

Kristen stared at the ring. "How I'm *feeling*? How about *mad as hell*? How about *frustrated*?" Her voice quavered, growing louder, and all around heads turned in their direction. "And I couldn't blame you. If it hadn't been for you…" She swallowed.

Will took the ring box from her and gazed at it. "You chose well. Becca will love this."

"I thought about buying something more traditional. You know, with a real diamond. But this… this is so her."

"I agree. And there are no rules that say it has to have a diamond." He smiled. "This is beautiful." He closed it and handed it back to her. "And so are you." With her long black hair and blue eyes, Kristen turned heads all over campus, and if Becca didn't know how freaking lucky she was to have such an awesome girl who loved her to distraction, she'd better learn it fast before some *other* girl stole Kristen away from her.

She flushed. "Thank you." Kristen put the box out of sight, then sagged into her chair, all her previous fire dwindled to ashes. "I didn't see this coming. The girl I love, about to marry our gay best friend."

Will rolled his eyes. "I know you study theater, but just for a minute, leave theatrics aside and think lucidly. Becca is *not* about to marry *me*. For one thing, I wouldn't have her."

Kristen gaped at him. "Why not? She's a catch."

"Yes, she is, but she also drives me crazy. We'd probably end up killing each other on the honeymoon."

She chuckled.

"And another thing. There isn't even going to *be* a wedding—at least, she won't be marrying *me*. Although it seems as if *you* have plans on that score." Will took Kristen's hand in his. "Now listen to me. I think the end is in sight."

She swallowed. "Really?"

He nodded. "There's something going on this weekend, and it's the perfect opportunity for Becca to come clean."

The light in Kristen's eyes…

"You're on my side?"

"Absolutely. Becca loves you. Trust me, I know. You haven't seen what I have to put up with when you go home for a weekend. In the dictionary under *pining*? It says *See Becca Taylor*."

That brought an even wider smile.

Then Kristen gave him a thoughtful glance. "Her parents… are they as bad as she says?"

"That's the weird part. No, they're not. And that's why I think the fallout won't be as bad as Becca anticipates."

She tilted her head to one side, her hair hanging straight in a glossy curtain. "They're nice people?"

"If that's you asking as their future daughter-in-law, then yes, they are." He smiled. "And they will *love* you." He inclined his head to where she'd placed the ring box. "It won't be long before that's on Becca's finger."

Kristen's fierce hug robbed him of breath, and he reasoned it had been worth missing out on some study time to bring her smile back.

You'd better not let me—or her—down, Becca.

Becca wasn't the only one who was a catch.

Saturday, December 3

"Where does your aunt live?" Will asked as the Uber sped along past single story houses set back from the road, the ground covered in snow.

"Cudahy," Becca told him. "We're almost there."

Carl twisted in the passenger seat to give them a wide smile. "Ready to be the center of attention? This party *is* for you, after all."

Will was about as ready as he'd be for a frontal lobotomy.

He'd worn his black suit again, which had earned him an eye-roll from Becca, not to mention the admonishment that all her family had already seen him in that suit and couldn't he have worn something different?

Will was past caring. He just wanted the evening to be over with and for him to be in an Uber speeding in the opposite direction, nursing a sore head because he'd drunk *way* too much in an effort to get through the torture—er, party—in as painless a manner as he could manage.

The one thing keeping him going at this point was the thought of Aiden mixing up an alcoholic storm in a metallic cocktail shaker, with more sexy moves than Tom Cruise. Not that he considered Tom Cruise to be sexy—Will wasn't into older guys—but he had to admit, he'd liked the clips of the movie he'd found on YouTube.

The car pulled up outside a house that could have been the twin of Becca's home, except the siding was all white, like a big-ass wedding cake.

I've got weddings on the brain.

Music could be heard from several feet away, and Will gave an internal groan.

This is going to be Hell, isn't it?

They got out of the car and as they climbed the steps to the front door, it opened and Louise stood there, glaring at them.

"Where have you all been?"

Will wasn't about to drop Becca in the shit: he and Carl had been twiddling their thumbs while she did her make-up. It wasn't until she was seated next to him in the back seat that Will realized why it had taken so long.

Becca was so nervous her hands were trembling.

"You don't expect them to be early, do you?" Carl quipped. "I got them here fashionably late." He winked at Will.

Yeah, Carl was a good guy.

They hurried inside out of the cold, and no sooner had Will and Becca crossed the threshold than music blared out. Will vaguely recognized the song as being from a show. A male voice was singing about getting married in the morning, and getting to the church on time.

Not if I have anything to do with it.

Deborah approached them with arms held wide. "Welcome! You must be getting so excited by now."

Becca chuckled. "Aunt Deborah. Nice outfit."

Will had never seen so many sequins. They seemed to catch every light in the room.

She preened. "I bought it especially for the occasion." She ushered them out of the hallway before they even had time to remove their coats, and Will was propelled into a living room bursting at the seams. An archway separated it from an equally full dining room, and everywhere there were familiar faces. People raised glasses to them as he and Becca wove their way through the crowd of relatives.

"Here, let me take your coats," Louise said.

"Mom, I need to talk to you," Becca began.

"Can it wait? You just got here and I'm in the middle of helping your aunt with the food." She kissed Becca on the cheek. "Later, okay? We've got all night."

Will caught Becca glancing at him, and he shrugged as if to say *Hey, you tried.* Louise headed out of the room, taking their coats with her, and paused to give Carl a peck on the cheek as she passed him.

"Be an angel and get me a drink?" She glanced in Deborah's direction and grinned. "A girl could die of thirst in this place. She's got me slaving away in the kitchen."

"I heard that!" Deborah hollered.

Louise pointed to the far end of the dining room. "The bar's thataway. Aiden's in charge. And while you're there, tell him I want whatever he made for Kelly. It tasted fabulous. Bring it to me in the kitchen."

Carl gave a tug on an imaginary forelock. "Right away, ma'am." He met Will's gaze, and his eyes sparkled. "I wonder what her last servant died of."

"Not following instructions fast enough!" Louise shouted from the hallway.

Will laughed. "Show me this bar. I'll get Louise a drink."

Becca tugged his hand. "This way. Prepare to be impressed."

Will followed, doing his best not to stand on people's toes or knock glasses flying. The crowd appeared at its most dense in the corner, and as he pushed through, he suddenly saw why.

Aiden was standing behind an actual bar. Shelves lined the wall, and all the bottles were illuminated. There was even a fridge filled with bottles of wine.

All it needed was a beer tap.

"You made it!" Aiden beamed.

Will leaned forward and raised his voice over the music to be heard. "I don't think the bar near my apartment building has this many bottles."

Aiden chuckled. "I think I doubled what

Aunt Deborah and Uncle Warren usually have here. I sent her a list of supplies a week ago."

"I'm going to find Mom," Becca told him.

"Good luck." Will returned his attention to Aiden, peering at the card on its little stand. "These are the cocktails?" It was pretty much what he'd expected: martini, Manhattan, cosmopolitan, old fashioned, sidecar, margarita…

Aiden coughed. "Well, those are *some* of the cocktails."

Will scanned the room, and it wasn't long before he noticed something. All the partygoers above the age of forty had what looked like your everyday, run-of-the-mill cocktails.

The younger generation had something completely different.

He pointed to a young man holding a tall glass filled with a bright green liquid and a whole lot of ice. "That doesn't look like anything on your list."

Aiden leaned over the bar. "That's because it's from the dirty list."

Will blinked. "There's a *dirty* list? And what *is* that he's drinking?"

Aiden's eyes sparkled. "Sex on the pool table. Peach schnapps, raspberry liqueur, Midori, grapefruit juice, triple sec."

Will had a feeling his evening had just taken a turn for the better.

"Your mom wants a cocktail, by the way. Whatever Kelly was drinking." Will froze. "Oh my God. What *was* she drinking?"

"A concoction of peach schnapps, cranberry juice, and Crown Royal. I'm not gonna tell Mom its real name for obvious reasons." Aiden turned the list around and pointed to the first drink.

Will almost choked. He cleared his throat. "You know what? I think that's a really good idea."

Louise would probably have apoplexy if she knew she was drinking a Royal Fuck.

Aiden got busy with the cocktail shaker. "So, would you like a blow job, or do you prefer a slow comfortable screw against the wall?"

Will grasped the bar, erupting into another choking fit.

A blow job would be awesome, just not the kind you're *talking about.*

Aiden gazed at him in concern. "Are you okay?"

He got himself under control, taking deep breaths. "I'm *so* sorry. I think I just swallowed my tongue. What were you asking?"

Aiden gestured to the bar. "To drink. What would you like to drink? A blow job or a slow comfortable screw?"

Will peered once more at the dirty list. The names were wicked: oral sex on the beach, Golden Showers. Juicy screw, Rugburn, Pop my cherry, Do me now, Tropical orgasm… Then he saw what had to be the best name over. "That one," he said, pointing.

Aiden wagged a finger. "Uh-uh. You have to say it out loud. Them's the rules."

Will pushed out a sigh of resignation. "If I must. Give me a Balls Deep, please."

Aiden grinned. "A good choice."

"And what's in it?"

"Coconut rum, Blue curacao, peach schnapps—"

"That's in every cocktail, isn't it?"

"Pretty much, but there's also sweet/sour mix, a splash of Sprite, some whipped cream…" Aiden's grin widened. "And of course, a cherry. Which you have to, you know, pop in your mouth. Or something."

Breathing had never been such a chore.

"But of course."

Becca joined him. "You look perfectly at home behind a bar, bro. Maybe you should consider a change in career?"

Aiden gave her a sweet smile. "And you, sister mine, will probably end up doing this job once you've graduated, so don't knock it."

Becca glanced at Will. "You look as though you're having way too much fun. What have you two been talking about?"

Will flashed Aiden a grin. "Cocktails." Then he turned back to Becca. "Well? Did you get to speak to her?"

"Are you kidding? It would be easier to see the President."

Aiden handed Will a tall slim glass filled with blue liquid, on top of which he'd squirted whipped cream, a cherry balanced on the summit.

"What the hell is that?" Becca demanded.

"Trust me, sis, you're safer not knowing." Aiden looked over her shoulder. "Uh-oh. Something's up."

Will and Becca turned around. Louise was heading for them, her expression grim.

"Mom? What's wrong?"

"Lou?" Carl appeared at her side. "What is it, honey?"

"The hotel just called."

Someone turned the music down low, and the guests shuffled closer.

"Well, if they want you to work the front desk tonight, they can whistle. It's your day off."

Louise rolled her eyes. "If *only* that were the reason. They were passing on a message from the caterers. There's a huge event booked in the same day as the wedding."

Carl frowned. "And? This is what happens on a daily basis, isn't it? They have three hundred seven rooms, sweetheart. I think they can cope."

"Apparently not. They're saying they've double-booked, and consequently, we have no food."

Will nudged Becca. "And *there's* your cue," he whispered.

Becca straightened. "Actually, Mom? There's something I need to—"

"I've got it!" Deborah shrieked. She beamed. "I have a solution to save the day!"

But we don't want *the day saving,* Will's mind screamed.

"What are you talking about?" Louise demanded.

"Kelly can do the catering," Deborah announced in a triumphant tone. "She can do it all at school, then we just car everything to the hotel. If we stick to a cold menu, that means we don't have to use the hotel ovens."

Louise blinked. "A cold menu… in December."

"Hey, at least I'm coming up with ideas," Deborah remonstrated.

This just gets better.

Louise turned to gaze at Becca. "What do *you* think?"

It seemed as if every pair of eyes in the room was focused on him and Becca, the room quiet enough to hear the proverbial pin drop.

Will nudged her. Nudged her again.

Finally, Becca took a breath, and Will heaved an internal sigh of relief.

"Sounds great," she croaked.

Deborah beamed. "Kelly? We need you." She hurried out of the room.

"And I need this." Will grabbed his glass and drank half its contents in a few gulps, spluttering as the cherry stalk went up his nostril.

Louise studied Becca in silence for what felt like several *long* seconds. "Then that's what we'll do." She smiled, then followed Deborah out of the dining room.

Will put his glass down on the bar, grasped Becca's upper arm, and steered her away from Aiden.

"She just handed you the perfect out," he whispered.

Becca's eyes were huge, "Sure—with everyone watching. If I'm gonna tell her, I'll do it when I'm alone with her."

And with that, she left him standing there.

Will stared after her, his gut in a twist. *I am* so *done with this.* He was seconds away from walking out of there and leaving her to deal with the whole sorry mess.

The voice at the back of his head chose that moment to pipe up.

You can't. She said she'd come clean. You have to give her more time. And her mom is pretty full-on. You've gotten this far.

The last thought to filter through his head was the clincher.

What would Aiden say?

The music resumed and voices rose as everyone started talking all at once. Will went back to the bar and leaned heavily on it.

Aiden cocked his head. "You look like you need another drink."

Will raised his glass and finished the cocktail. "That might just be the understatement of the decade, and it's only 2022."

"What'll you have?"

Will perused the list, then stabbed at it with his finger. "That one." The one that summed up how he was feeling in four little words.

Aiden glanced at the card. "One pain in the ass coming right up."

CHAPTER SEVENTEEN

Aiden Comes Out—Well, Sort Of

Something is going on.

Aiden didn't know what, exactly, but it was clear all was not well in Becca Land.

Actually, make that Will-and-Becca Land. Will had spent the whole evening at the bar, chatting with Aiden. He couldn't be positive, but it felt as if Will was avoiding Becca.

Or is she avoiding him?

When Aiden had ventured into the kitchen in search of more ice, Mom and Deborah were talking catering. Kelly was there too, coming up with suggestions as to what could be on the menu. Aiden only caught snatches of the conversation, but it was enough for him to make a mental note to visit Walgreens and buy up every packet of Pepto Bismol he could lay his hands on, to stockpile for the event.

When he returned to the bar, Will was still there, staring at the dirty list.

He's already had three. And if Aiden had his way, there wouldn't be a fourth. Aiden knew guys who could drink all night long and still walk a straight line.

When it came to drinking, Will was in the minor leagues.

He placed his hand on Will's back and leaned in to speak into his ear.

"I think you should stop. Quit while you can still walk."

Will jerked his head toward Aiden, his unfocused eyes blinking. "Stop? I haven't even got started." He held up his empty glass. "This was great. What was it called again? *Tonsil tickler*?" He grinned. "I love having my tonsils tickled, but the equipment has to be right."

It was official. Will was three sheets to the wind, and no longer in charge of what came out of his mouth. Because that sure sounded dirty—and gay—as fuck.

It's the booze talking. Yet another reason to get Will off cocktails and onto water—and probably a little food to soak up all that alcohol—before he said something far worse that his fiancée's family were gonna remember and whisper about while he was walking up the aisle.

Aiden walked behind the bar and dumped the contents of the bags of ice into the cooler. "I'm being serious."

Will's eyebrows shot up. "I'm serious too—about working my way through this list. So… what to have next." He leaned forward until his nose was almost touching the card. "How about…ooh, *that* one looks good. Malibu, Baileys, grenadine, 7-Up…" He straightened and gave Aiden a satisfied smile. "I'll have *Sex With The Bartender*."

That was too good an opening to ignore, especially since there was no way Will would remember it the next day.

Aiden shrugged. "Fine but I'd prefer to wait

until you're sober." Will squinted at him, and Aiden chuckled. "Sorry. I couldn't resist a joke."

"Aw." Will's lopsided grin was fucking adorable. "For a moment there I thought you were propositioning me."

Don't.

Don't do it.

You'll only regret it.

Aiden was tired of listening to the voice of reason.

He took advantage of the lull in the storm of partygoers clamoring for drinks to lean toward Will, elbows on the bar, their foreheads almost meeting. He was momentarily distracted by Will's scent, a warm, spicy smell that conjured images of bed, pillows under hips, open mouths, low moans of pleasure and kiss after kiss.

Fuck, you smell good.

Then he remembered he was this close for a purpose.

"I wouldn't do that, because A—you're marrying my sister, and B—I'm not out. At least, not to my family."

Will's breathing hitched.

"You… You're *gay*? Or are you bi?"

For the briefest of moments, Aiden had second thoughts. *You're about to share something important with a guy who's drunk. Is this wise? What if he can't keep his mouth shut? What if he says something very loud and very embarrassing that lets everyone in the house know what goes on in your bedroom?*

Bathroom.

Kitchen.

Truck, on occasion.

Wherever.

He'd gotten this far. There was no turning back. And besides, something deep inside told him he could trust Will.

"Gay. And that is *not* for sharing, okay?"

Will's mouth fell open, and he stared at Aiden in silence for so long that Aiden was starting to panic.

Oh shit. Maybe I should have kept my mouth shut.

Will shook his head. "First Becca, now you…"

Aiden didn't have a clue what that meant. "Excuse me?"

He waved his hand. "Doesn't matter. They're gonna have to know sooner or later. You can't spend your life in the closet. You can't keep hiding what you truly are."

Aiden bit his lip. "That's quite profound for someone contemplating his fourth cocktail." He sighed. "I *will* tell them eventually. Just… not tonight. Not with this big an audience." Then he saw Dad approaching, and clammed up.

Dad tapped Will on the shoulder. "I think I should take you home. You don't have to stay until the end. The party will carry on without you and Becca, trust me. Deb's parties are legendary."

Aiden jumped right in. "Dad's right. Go and get some sleep. And drink plenty of water."

Will pointed to the kitchen. "But…Louise is busy planning."

Dad chuckled. "And she'll keep right on planning without you. It's what she does. I just think you need to get out of here."

Aiden took hold of Will's hand. "Thanks for

listening."

Will looked him in the eye, locked into a brief moment of sobriety. "Thanks for sharing." He pulled free, wobbling a little.

Dad put his arm around Will's shoulders, and gave Aiden a proud smile. "In case Deborah forgets to tell you…. You've been an excellent bartender."

"Thanks, Dad." Aiden watched as his dad guided Will through the throng, only to have it swallow them up as people flowed into the gap they'd created, demanding cocktails. Aiden went back to work, pouring spirits into the cocktail shaker, his hands on autopilot.

His mind was on Will.

Why did I tell him? Why open up that particular can of worms? Instinct told him Will wouldn't betray a confidence, but the need to come clean about his sexuality had suddenly been of paramount importance.

Will's reaction told him one thing. His future brother-in-law was not a hater. Thank God.

But that still left the curious remark he'd made.

"First Becca, now you…"

What the hell?

Sunday, December 4

Will's tongue felt like a suede tie in his mouth. People in steel-toe-capped boots were dancing in his head, and a voice at the back of his mind wouldn't shut the fuck up, telling him he'd learned something vital at the party.

It took him several minutes for the recollection to become less fuzzy.

Aiden. Something about Aiden.

Then he had it, and he sat up in bed, his heart doing a happy dance.

He's gay. Aiden Taylor is gay.

Cold inched its way through him. *He thinks you're straight, remember?*

There had to be *something* positive on the horizon.

And when he learns the truth?

That relentlessly pessimistic inner voice rang out. *Your name is about to be mud, so what good will that do you? He won't be interested in you once Becca calls off the engagement.*

The quiet knock on the door took him by surprise. "Come in."

Carl came into the room, carrying a mug and a glass of water. He placed both on the nightstand, then gazed down at Will. "How do you feel?"

"Like someone smashed my brains out with a piece of lemon wrapped around a large gold brick?" He managed to smile. "Something I read once."

Carl's eyes lit up, and he sat on the edge of the bed. "My favorite character was always Zaphod Beeblebrox." He chuckled. "I memorized a few of his lines that I used to use on girls. 'I am so amazingly cool you could keep a side of meat in me for a month. I am so hip I have difficulty seeing over my pelvis.'"

"*The Restaurant at the End of the Universe*." Will smiled. "Another Douglas Adams fan. I have to ask… did the lines work?"

Carl coughed. "Most of them thought I was weird." His smile crinkled the skin around his eyes. "Then I met Louise, and the rest, as they say, is history." He shook his head. "I remember listening to episodes on the radio. The original production, mind you, not the movie they made years later. And Slartibartfast has to be the best name ever, although it's best not to attempt pronouncing it when inebriated."

Will sipped his coffee.

Carl wasn't done. "Will… If you ever need to talk… I'm here for you, okay?"

Which only went to prove to him once more that Becca must have her parents all wrong. He gave Carl a grateful smile. "Thank you." Will's heart gave a pang.

He'd be a wonderful father-in-law.

Another knock had both of them turning their heads.

"Will? You awake?"

Carl gave another chuckle. "Come on in, Becca. I'm just leaving."

She stuck her head around the door, and sniffed. "Ooh, coffee."

He grinned. "Sit here and I'll go get you some." He stood and walked around the bed to where she perched, bending to kiss the top of her head. Once the door closed behind him, Becca's shoulders sagged.

"How are you doing?" Will couldn't remember much about her state the previous evening.

"I felt as though I was locked in some awful nightmare. I kept remembering someone talking about plates of shredded lettuce with side cups of olive oil and balsamic vinegar as dressing, boiled spinach served in half a tomato, cold Chick-fil-A nuggets and veggie trays…" She shivered. "I mean, *Chick-fil-A*? Really? One of the most homophobic businesses around. And then I realized I'm still *in* the nightmare because that's what Kelly was proposing serving after the wedding."

Will had *had* it with the mythical wedding.

He put his mug aside and regarded her with a hard stare. "Let's be practical here. Are you going to marry me?"

She rolled her eyes. "Hell no."

"Okay then. And I'm not going to marry you either, so we both know it isn't going to happen. Now all we have to do is end this."

Becca narrowed her gaze. "You're looking at me again, are you? Because I have to be the one to end it."

He sighed. "No, I'm looking at you because I've come to a decision. You have one week, Becca."

She frowned. "One week to do what?"

"To call a halt. And if you *haven't* done it by this time next Sunday? *I'll* do it."

Becca brought her hand to her chest. "You're serious."

"Yup. I'll tell your parents the wedding's off,

and that there's no hope of us getting back together. I'll say whatever it takes to get the message across. And don't act so shocked. You knew we had to do this. I just didn't think it would take you this long."

"But what *exactly* are you going to tell them?" Becca's breathing quickened.

He gave her a kind smile. "I won't mention Kristen, and you don't have to tell them either. Lay it all at my door. I can take it."

Well, most of it. Shutting that door on Aiden was going to hurt.

Becca cocked her head. "Assuming I haven't told them… you're going to tell them *after* the bachelor party?"

"Sure."

Becca shivered. "Rather you than me."

"What does that mean?"

"It means Mom's going to be pissed, and she can hold onto a grudge until the end of time."

Will forced a smile. "Then isn't it a good thing I'll probably never see her again after this?"

She straightened the comforter. "By the way… You and Aiden were talking a lot last night. What did you talk about?" The forced casual tone let him know this wasn't mere idle curiosity.

"I don't remember."

A lie, but he'd promised not to share.

Becca's eyes flashed. "Well, try harder. Because I already have three messages from him this morning. Okay, one of them was a cute video of Midnight playing with a piece of string, but the other two were asking if I was okay, and offering to lend an ear if I needed one."

Will leaned back against the pillows. "I

didn't tell him, if that's what you're asking. I swear." He gave her a thoughtful glance. "It's your birthday this week, right?"

"Yeah. Friday. Not that I'm in a mood to celebrate it."

He smiled. "You know what you should do when we get back? Cook something nice for Kristen. Pull out all the stops, and then let her know it'll all be over in a week." He inclined his head toward the door where footsteps could be heard. "Unless you want to do it now?"

She glared. "It wouldn't be my first choice."

Carl came into the room and handed her a mug of coffee. "Your mom says breakfast will be in about fifteen minutes, so if you want to grab a shower, you'd better move."

"I don't take *that* long to shower," Becca protested. Both Carl and Will started coughing, and her eyes flashed again. "I do not."

Carl made his excuses and left the room.

Will drank some more coffee. "Of course, calling it off *still* leaves us with your cousin planning what sounds like the wedding menu from hell."

"*Planning* is fine. They won't be doing anything yet apart from trying out a few recipes." She shuddered. "Oh yeah. Mom says that's what we're doing next Saturday afternoon, by the way. Tasting sessions."

"Oh God." Never mind telling Carl and Louise—Will was hoping for the Apocalypse.

Becca snickered. "I wouldn't worry. Whatever you eat, you won't notice the aftereffects—the alcohol will destroy everything."

He snorted.

She patted his leg. "Thank you."

"For what? Taking the heat off you? Taking the deed out of your hands? Come on, I had to do *something*."

"I'll tell her," Becca promised. Her eyes twinkled. "Probably after I throw up whatever Kelly gave me to taste all over Mom's shoes."

"Ew."

She stood. "And now I'll go take my usual lightning-fast shower."

Will hurriedly put his mug down. "Will you not say stuff like that when my mouth is full of coffee?"

She flipped him the finger as she headed for the door. No sooner had it closed than his phone rang. Will's heart went into overdrive when he saw the caller.

"Hey."

"How's the head this morning?"

"Still on my shoulders." Will paused. "Thanks for trusting me last night."

"Well, if you remembered what I told you, you can't have been all *that* drunk." Aiden huffed. "Still can't believe I said that."

"Obviously I have one of those faces that inspire trust. I'll keep your secret, but I still think you should take my advice."

"I'll think about it." There was a pause. "Have a safe trip back to school and I'll see you next Saturday. I promise you a night to remember." He hung up.

Any night with you is a night to remember.

And once this was over, the hardest part would begin—trying to forget him.

CHAPTER EIGHTEEN

Aiden Smells A Rat

Saturday, December 10

Becca strode toward her mom's car, so fast that Will had to run to keep up with her.

"You don't think you were a little hard on Kelly?" he suggested as they came to a stop. He'd had the same reaction to Kelly's proposed dishes for the reception, but unlike Becca, he could be diplomatic and keep his mouth shut.

Becca whirled around to gape at him. She pointed to the house. "You were in there, right? That *was* you trying lavender asparagus risotto, right?"

"It wasn't *that* bad," he remonstrated, not entirely truthfully. Kelly had attempted to create something sophisticated.

It hadn't worked. Like, at all.

"Oh really? And what about the quiche?"

"Yeah, that was a little…underdone," he admitted.

Becca's eyes bulged. "Underdone? The bits of sausage were *swimming* in it. And they were still *oinking*! *And* while we're on the subject… sausage? In a quiche? At a *wedding*?"

"You've eaten Quiche Lorraine, haven't you?"

"Yeah. What's your point?"

"That has bits of ham in it, so I guess my *point* is, what's the difference between ham and sausage?"

"At least the quiche *I* ate was cooked. And what about the dessert?"

"What's wrong with ginger ice cream?"

"Oh, nothing at all," she said, her voice laced with sarcasm. "It just took the top of my head off and killed every last damn taste bud, there was so much ginger in it. And who has ice cream in December? Is she going to bring *that* over by car too? It'll melt by the time it reaches the tables."

Will snickered. "Not in December, it won't."

Behind them, the front door slammed.

Becca sighed. "Great. Mom's pissed."

"And you're surprised?"

"Rebecca Jane Taylor, you get right back inside that house this minute and apologize." Louise walked briskly toward them, her face like thunder.

"Louise, please, slow down," Will pleaded. "The path is really slippery." He had visions of her breaking a leg or something even worse.

She changed her pace, coming to a halt in front of Becca, who squared her shoulders and folded her arms.

Will knew the signs. It was Becca-speak for 'I'm not gonna budge so don't even waste your breath.'

"No, Mom." Thankfully Becca kept her voice at a reasonable volume. "It's *my* wedding, *my* day."

Will was going to strangle her.

You're supposed to be breaking up with me, not arguing about food for a wedding reception that isn't even going to happen.

That did it. Once he'd enjoyed a final pleasant evening with Aiden, he was ending this.

Can you hear yourself? You're as bad as she is. You *could say something right now. But you won't do that, will you? Because—*

Aiden. Because of Aiden.

"Fine." Louise spat out the word as though it had a sour taste. "But that doesn't give you the right to hurt Kelly's feelings the way you did."

"What did I say?" Becca demanded, eyes wide.

"Seriously?" Will chuckled. "I think saying that she should demand her money back from culinary school so she'll be able to afford the lawsuits from the guests was pretty cold. I'm surprised you didn't pull out the Peanut Corporation of America while you were at it."

"Huh?" Becca frowned.

"The what?" Louise seemed confused too.

He groaned. "One of the biggest outbreaks of salmonella in the US in 2009."

Becca narrowed her eyes, then turned back to her mom. "Ignore the nerd. I still have the right to choose what everyone eats, don't I? So if I want to order in subs from across the street, I'll do it." Becca snorted. "Come to think of it, subs would be a damn sight more edible than what Kelly is proposing."

Louise got behind the wheel, Becca beside

her. Will climbed in the back. Louise gripped the steering wheel. "It's not ideal, I know. It isn't an ideal situation. But unless you have another idea?"

Will was staring daggers at the back of Becca's head.

Yes, you do. Tell her. Now. Or at least tell her we all need to sit down and talk.

Judging by the way Becca squirmed in her seat, she could feel every inch of those daggers.

"Not right now, I don't," Becca murmured. She glanced toward the house. "But you're right. I should go back in there and apologize."

Louise patted her shoulder. "I'd wait a while. Let her calm down. Why not come over for a chat tomorrow morning before you leave? Just you and Kelly."

"Yeah, I can do that."

"At last. Sanity restored." Louise switched on the engine and pulled away from the curb.

It took Will a second or two to notice her shoulders were shaking.

"Louise? Are you okay?"

She made a choking sound as they stopped at the lights. "I shouldn't laugh. I really shouldn't." Then she bent over, the laughter bursting from her. "It *was* pretty awful, wasn't it?"

Will couldn't help but join in. "I agree, we shouldn't laugh." Except he couldn't hold it in a second longer. He guffawed. "Did you see Deborah's face when Kelly brought out the quiche? I thought she was gonna barf right there and then."

"Maybe Kelly needs to rethink her career choice," Becca said in a sweet voice.

Will wasn't fooled. "Do you have an

alternative?"

She shrugged. "I don't know… Bioweapons specialist?"

They were laughing so hard, the car rocked.

Louise glanced at Will in the rearview mirror. "What time does everything get going this evening?"

"Aiden says he'll pick me up at six-thirty." Will had thought of little else for the past few days. Not that he was all that keen to get drunk.

He just wanted to be with Aiden.

She narrowed her gaze. "Will there be food at this party?"

Becca chuckled. "Mom, it's a bachelor party. We're talking beer pong and strippers." She gave Will a mock glare. "I don't have to tell you to behave, do I?" Her eyes twinkled.

Will drew a cross over his heart with a finger. "I'm not about to be led astray by a stripper, I promise," he announced for Louise's benefit.

Unless Aiden is the stripper. Then all bets were off.

The Becca he knew was back. She'd been in a good mood all the way from Minnesota, and he was glad to see her smile again.

Will got his phone and sent her a message. *You had a good birthday, didn't you?*

Her phone buzzed. Becca glanced at him over her shoulder, grinning. She typed *The best. Thanks for not coming over last night.*

I didn't want to interrupt anything. He wanted to add an emoji to clue her in that he knew what had been going on, but then he figured an eggplant was so wrong in the circumstances.

Will grinned to himself and sent a scissors emoji instead. Then he reconsidered and sent a whole line of them.

He thought Becca was going to choke.

"Are you okay?" her mom asked.

"I'm fine," Becca spluttered. Her fingers danced over the screen.

You are so *dead.* Seconds later a link appeared.

What's this?

She typed again. *TikTok. Lesbian emoji combinations. If UR gonna do it, do it right.*

He chuckled. *Lesbian 101. I like it.*

"Are you two texting each other?" Louise demanded. "Stupid question, because you obviously are, which means it's something you can't share in front of me, so you know what? I'm going to change the subject. What are you going to do until Aiden arrives?"

"Carl said something about me helping him clear snow from the paths."

Becca snorted. "That'll keep you out of trouble."

Will didn't mind. He liked spending time with Carl, especially since he'd learned Carl was a fellow Douglas Adams fan. The time would fly by.

And then I get all night with Aiden.

For the last time.

Aiden got out of the car. The lights on the front of the house revealed his dad and Will standing at the edge of the lawn, chatting. It was obvious from their body language that they felt relaxed around each other, which boded well. Aiden had a couple of married friends who said conversing with their in-laws was like digging through a layer of ice.

"Nice work." Aiden gestured to the path scraped clean of snow. "I've got lots more at my place if you need something else to do."

Dad laughed. "I think you're old enough to clear your own path."

Aiden gestured to the lights. "Isn't it a little late to be clearing snow? Shouldn't this be a daylight activity?"

Dad coughed. "We were supposed to do it a couple of hours ago, but we got to talking about… something." Another cough.

Aiden had to laugh. "Dad, I've known for a long time that I come from a long line of nerds. And yes, I mean you. So are you really surprised Becca is marrying one?"

"I'm too old to be called a nerd." Dad grinned. "Now I'm just eccentric."

Aiden looked Will up and down. "You

going out like that?" Not that Will didn't do justice to jeans, boots, a thick coat, hat, and gloves, but it was hardly the attire for a night of bar crawling.

Will chuckled. "I'll grab a quick shower in a sec. We're almost done here."

"Clearing or chewing the fat?"

Dad waved his hand. "Go find your mom. Will can come out to play when he's finished."

Aiden climbed the steps to the front door, smiling to himself. From the kitchen came the sound of Mom singing. Then he recognized the lyrics to 'Dancing Queen'.

He leaned against the door frame, watching her bopping around the kitchen island, the music pouring from the Echo Dot. "Which one did you want to be—Agnetha or Anni-Frid?"

Mom froze. "Are you trying to give your poor mother a heart attack?" She grinned. "Maybe I always wanted to be Benny." She grimaced. "No, Bjorn would be better. I'm not into beards. Have you ever wondered why your dad has never had a beard?" She turned her head toward the countertop. "Alexa, stop."

"Don't let me interrupt you, not when you were having such a good time."

Mom went to the oven and peered through the glass. "I'm glad I've got you alone for a second. Don't do anything stupid, will you?"

"That depends what you classify as stupid."

Her eyes grew flinty. "You know what I'm talking about. Tying Will naked to a lamp post or something equally juvenile."

Aiden laughed. "In this weather? It would freeze his… toes off. Where's Becca?"

"In her room." Mom rolled her eyes. "It's incredible how she manages to disappear every time I want her to lend a hand."

He chuckled. "It's a gift." Mom opened her mouth, and he held his hand up. "Don't worry. I'll have Will back here in the morning, safe and sound, though not necessarily completely sober." He turned and headed for the stairs.

"Tell your sister to get her butt down here and set the table," Mom hollered after him.

Aiden paused at Becca's door when he heard her voice.

"Last night was amazing."

He smiled. He still thought her talking on the phone to Will was a weird habit, when they were literally feet away from each other. Then her words registered.

So they finally bumped uglies. I guess it had to happen sooner or later. He had to admit it was the perfect birthday present. Even better, it seemed as though they were a good match in the sack.

Sex wasn't everything, he knew, but for many it was a pretty vital component.

Who am I kidding? If the sex wasn't good, then it just wasn't going to work.

"I could have spent hours just kissing you."

Aiden's chest tightened. *I shouldn't be listening to this.*

His stomach clenched. *She was kissing Will.*

Something Aiden had thought a lot about since the night they'd met.

"I love you so much."

And that was Aiden's cue to creep away, his face hot.

At the top of the stairs, he caught the sound of laughter from outside, and he peered through the window. The lights picked out the sight of Will on his ass in a pile of snow, and both he and dad seemed to find it amusing. Dad was hauling Will to his feet.

From behind him came the soft murmur of Becca's voice, the words indistinct as she continued talking.

Then it hit him.

Wait a sec—talking to who?

Oh. My. God.

Aiden walked downstairs in a daze, his head reeling. *This doesn't make sense.*

The only problem was, it made *perfect* sense. It answered a lot of questions, for one thing. And what burned him most was the idea that Will was going to be the one who got hurt in all this.

He went outside to where Dad and Will were stomping the snow from their boots. "You done?" he asked Will.

"Sure, but I haven't had my shower yet."

"Just bring a change of clothes. You can shower at my place." Aiden wanted to get him away from Becca.

He wanted to discover just how much Will knew.

Dad laughed. "This brings back memories. I was Will's age when I had my bachelor party." He patted Will on the back. "Go have a great time. Don't get arrested."

Will blinked. "You think that's even a possibility?"

"Not really. Have fun." He aimed a hard

stare at Aiden. "And you? Keep him safe. It's Saturday night in Milwaukee, and we both know that means the assholes crawl out of the woodwork."

What Dad didn't know was that going on a bar crawl was the last thing on Aiden's mind.

A conversation loomed on the horizon, one that Aiden did not want to be having, but Becca had left him with little choice.

How do I tell my future brother-in-law that his fiancée is cheating on him?

Okay, maybe it wasn't *cheating*, but it was definitely confirmation that *something* wasn't right with their relationship.

What that something was, Aiden aimed to find out.

CHAPTER NINETEEN

Will Comes Clean—And Comes Out
Will And Aiden Play Hide The Polish Sausage

Will kicked off his boots and then dumped his overnight bag next to the couch. "So what's the plan? Which bar are we hitting first?"

"I hadn't given it much thought." Well, he *had*—right up to the moment he'd heard Becca telling some other guy she loved him.

Beer was pretty far down Aiden's list of priorities.

Will frowned. "I thought you had an itinerary all worked out." Midnight was winding himself in and out of Will's ankles, purring up a storm. He bent down to stroke him. "Your kitty likes me."

He's not the only one.

Except what he felt for Will went *way* beyond mere liking. And if Becca *was* doing the dirty on him, Aiden was going to be there for Will, one hundred percent.

Then Will straightened. "Can I be honest? I'm not really in the mood for a bar crawl." Before Aiden could say a word, he held his hands up. "I know, I know, you've gone to a lot of trouble to organize this, but… could we do something else instead? Like… grab a pizza again and watch a movie? No one has to know, right? We'll say we were having such a good time, we forgot to take pictures."

Aiden was done being reticent.

"Look, there's something I need to talk to you about."

Will gazed at him, his eyes warm. "I haven't told anyone in your family about…about you, if that's what this is about."

"It isn't, but thanks. I knew you'd keep my secret." He paused. "But someone else around here is keeping something secret—a pretty big something—and you need to know what's going on."

Will walked over to the couch and sat, his gaze fixed on Aiden. "You're starting to worry me." He didn't seem all *that* worried, but maybe he was one of those people who internalized everything, the human equivalent of a swan, serene on the outside, but churning like crazy beneath the surface.

Aiden sat beside him, leaning forward, elbows on his knees, fingers laced. He couldn't look at Will so he stared at the rug instead.

I really should clean it soon. He dreaded to think how much of Midnight's fur was on there.

That wasn't helping.

With an effort, he forced himself back into the moment.

"The last few times I saw you and Becca together, I had a feeling that all… Well, that all wasn't quite right between you. Something felt off."

Will didn't respond for a moment. Then he spoke in a low voice. "I have no idea what you're talking about."

"*You* might not have, but I think Becca does."

He wasn't sure if he'd imagined the hitch in Will's breathing. "What?"

Aiden sighed. "The night we met, when I came looking for you and found you in the lobby?"

"Yeah."

"Well, just before that, I found Becca sitting in a corner with her phone, talking to you. You know… mushy stuff."

"Where are you going with this? So we talk on the phone. So what?"

Will's voice had lost its serene quality, and an edge of irritation had crept in.

"This evening, when you and Dad were playing in the snow like a couple of school kids, I heard her having the same kind of conversation. The kind of conversation I shouldn't have been listening to, I know, because it was clearly intimate, but it shocked the hell out of me."

"You're losing me."

Aiden turned his head to meet Will's gaze. "You don't see where I'm going with this? I heard my sister say 'I love you'—but it wasn't to you. It *couldn't* have been, because you were with my dad. And that makes me think about the *first* phone call. What if that wasn't you either?"

Will was like a statue beside him, and the truth of the situation dawned on Aiden.

"Oh my God. I'm right, aren't I? There *is* someone else. *That's* why this feels wrong. And you didn't know, did you?"

Will's silence was beginning to unnerve him.

Aiden drew his legs onto the couch and held his knees against his chest. Will didn't look at him: his attention was focused on Midnight.

The dullness in Aiden's chest and the tight knot in his belly would not quit.

"I'm sorry, but I had to tell you." He stared at Will. "You do see that, don't you?"

Will nodded, moving his hand gently along Midnight's back.

He has to be feeling sick to his stomach right now.

The silence was killing Aiden.

"What are you going to do? Will you get her to give up whoever this guy is, to save your marriage that hasn't even happened yet, or will you just call it off? Because—"

Will let out a noise of pure exasperation.

"Will you *please* stop talking for a second?"

Fuck, where do I start?

There go my plans for a pleasant evening.

There was only one way out of this mess—tell the truth. Okay, it wasn't his place to share personal stuff about Becca, but considering everything that had gone on thus far?

Fuck it. She'd understand, given the circumstances. And he wouldn't be going through *any* of this if she hadn't dropped him in the shit and been too chicken to dig him out of it.

Will lowered Midnight to the floor, then sagged against the cushions.

"The most important thing you need to know is… Becca isn't cheating on me."

Aiden frowned. "Then who was—"

"No, you don't understand," Will interjected. "She isn't cheating on me because… because we're not engaged."

Aiden's eyebrows almost disappeared into his hairline. "But… but she told Mom…"

He nodded. "I know. I was sitting right there during that conversation." He chuckled. "So you can imagine what a shock it was, hearing my best friend tell her mom that I'd proposed." He grinned. "It was obviously *so* forgettable, I slept through it."

"Your best friend… So you're not in love with her?"

Will smiled. "I love your sister, okay? I'd *have* to love her, to put up with the mess she's created, but…" His heart raced. "She isn't my type."

"Then what *is* your type?"

He shrugged. "I like redheads."

Aiden blinked. "Not seeing a problem here."

Will raised his eyes toward the ceiling. "Fine. She's… missing something."

"Like what?"

Will locked gazes with him. "Something *you* have. Something I happen to like, a lot." He glanced at Aiden's crotch. Up to his eyes. Down to his crotch again.

Come on, Aiden. You're a smart guy. Work it out.

Aiden's gasp told him he'd struck oil.

"You're *gay*?"

"*There* ya go."

"Okay, we *are* gonna talk about this, but right now?" Aiden's brow furrowed. "I still don't understand. Why would she tell Mom she was engaged?"

"Because your mom kept trying to set her up with guys from the hotel. She'd grown tired of it, so she took the easy way out and told your mom we were engaged." He huffed. "Easy my ass. It was only supposed to be for the party, then we were going to 'break up'" he air-quoted. "Your mom changed everything."

Aiden crossed his legs. "I still don't get why she claimed to be engaged. Why not just say, 'Hey, Mom, stop setting me up with guys'?"

"Because *this* way was safer than telling her the truth."

"Which is?"

Here we go.

"You have more in common with your sister than you know. You see, I'm not Becca's type either." He smiled. "Get the picture?"

Aiden's jaw dropped.

Bingo.

"Becca's a lesbian?"

Will laughed. "You two really should talk more, you know?"

"Why didn't she tell me?"

Will stared at him. "Why didn't *you* tell *her*? All *she* says is she can't come out to your parents. And seeing as you're in the same boat, I guess that goes for you too. Because there has to be a reason why you haven't told them."

Aiden frowned. "It's not something we ever discuss. I mean, *ever*."

"Becca told me something like that too. But now I've gotten to know them? I have to admit, that theory doesn't hold water. Some of my D & D buddies are unfortunate enough to have homophobic bastards for their parents, and they talk about the shit that goes down." He looked at Aiden. "*Your* parents are in a different league."

Aiden's breathing quickened. "Can we get back to the *I'm gay* part?"

Will shook his head. "These last few weeks have been torture."

Aiden's gaze grew sympathetic. "Pretending to be straight?"

Will's heart hammered.

You've gotten this far. Don't stop now.

He took a deep breath. "No—pretending I'm not attracted to my straight soon-to-be brother-in-law. Who I then learn is about as straight as a corkscrew."

Aiden's breathing caught. "Oh my God."

"That's twice now you've said that. You need a wider vocabulary." The attempt at humor was nothing but obfuscation, and he knew it. Will sighed. "I'm sorry. I shouldn't have come out with it like that. It put you on the spot and I have no right to—"

Aiden darted forward, their mouths meeting in a fervent collision of lips, stealing Will's breath and sending his heartbeat into overdrive. Will reacted instantly, cupping Aiden's head as he held him there, unwilling to break the kiss.

You'll have to let him go some time.

It seemed Aiden had the same thought. He sat back, pulling free of Will's embrace, his eyes shining.

Will shivered. "Whoa. You have *no* idea how long I've wanted you to do that."

Aiden smiled. "Then tell me."

"I guess since you helped me to my feet in the hotel lobby." He returned Aiden's forthright gaze. "You knocked me flat twice. The first time was when you sent a luggage cart flying into me. The second was when you smiled."

Aiden leaned in and kissed him again, only this time it was sweeter, their lips brushing softly, Aiden's hand on his cheek, his fingers tracing the line of his jaw. Warm breath ghosted Will's ear.

"I can beat that. I wanted to kiss you the moment you walked into that hotel."

Will shivered as Aiden pressed warm lips to his neck. "So… Where do we go from here?"

"That depends." Aiden drew back and looked him in the eye. "Do you want to stop at kissing?"

Will grinned. "Didn't I say that for a smart man, you ask dumb questions?"

"Then how about a few intelligent ones?" Aiden picked up his phone, scrolled, then handed it to Will. "The results of my last test, two months ago. And by the way, I haven't been with anyone for the last six months."

"Ooh, a dry spell. I can beat that. It's been eight for me." Will grinned. "But seeing as you've shown me yours, I'll show you mine." He pulled up his results and showed the screen to Aiden.

"I'm on PrEP."

"I'm not." Will put his phone down. "Ask your question."

"Are you okay not using condoms?"

He smiled. "Perfectly—now. You've just scored an A+, Teach, for talking safety first. Some guys don't, and that's why they don't make it past my bedroom door."

Aiden blinked. "Are we moving this to the bed?"

Will grinned. "Did you have someplace else in mind?"

"I was all for fucking you right here on the couch."

Will chuckled. "Ohh, you sweet-talker, you." He stood. "Think you can keep a lid on it until I get back from your bathroom? I won't be long, I promise. I just didn't expect to be… active this evening." He cocked his head to one side. "Which leads us to your second question."

"I think you just answered it." Aiden's eyes gleamed. "But for my final question of the night—

"Thank God." Will narrowed his gaze. "I'm so hard right now, Midnight could use it for a scratching post." He winced. "Wait. That was a *really* bad example."

"By the time you're ready, Midnight will be safely stowed in the kitchen."

He laughed. "Thank you. I had visions of him holding up little kitty-sized score cards." Will peered at Aiden. "And the answer to the question you haven't asked yet, is yes, I am happy to both give and receive. So… is that it? Are we done talking?"

Aiden pointed to the door. "You know where the bathroom is."

Will was out of there before Aiden could finish his sentence.

Aiden stared at the door. *I do not fucking* believe *this.*

Talk about a night of bombshells.

Becca isn't engaged to Will.

Becca is into girls.

Will is into boys.

Two of those revelations were definitely a cause for celebration—okay, maybe all three—and when Will emerged from Aiden's bathroom, there were going to be fireworks. He wasn't going to think about his parents, or Becca, or the wedding—

Except there isn't going to be *a wedding, is there?*

The thought of kissing Will again consumed him. Undressing Will. Burying his shaft in—

The door opened. "I said I'd be fast, didn't—"

Aiden launched himself at Will, pinning him against the wall as they kissed, not gentle, not sweet, but white-hot with desire, brimming with need. Something fell to the floor with a *clatter*, and Aiden grinned when he saw the bottle of lube.

"Good thinking," he murmured.

Then it was back to the very real, very urgent business of getting them both where they wanted to be.

Aiden began to unbutton Will's shirt, and Will got busy with his, but that was taking too damn long, so they undressed themselves, Aiden still kissing him, pausing only long enough to remove his shirt, unbuckle his belt, unfasten his pants, and squirm out of all of his clothing except his underwear, while Will performed a similar ballet of tangled garments. The harsh sound of their breathing filled the air, and Aiden lifted Will into his arms, Will wrapping his legs around him as Aiden carried him to the armchair.

Aiden bent over to kiss him, because *fuck*, that mouth was addictive as sin, and Will didn't hesitate, reaching into Aiden's briefs to draw out his rigid dick. That first contact with Will's warm, wet mouth forced a moan from Aiden's lips, and he quickly removed his underwear, spreading his feet, his hands on Will's head as he thrust deep into Will's mouth.

At some point they flipped, and Aiden found himself in the chair, Will crouched over him, Will's feet on either side of him as he bounced on Aiden's cock, steadying himself with his hands on the arm rests. Aiden cupped Will's ass and helped him bounce a little faster, come down a little harder, until both of them were moaning constantly.

Then Will turned around and impaled himself once more on Aiden's shaft, only this time Aiden could see their reflections in the TV screen, could watch his dick sliding in and out of Will's ass, and that was hot as fuck. Aiden reached down to feel his slick cock driving into Will's hole, and Will groaned, working his own dick.

"Gotta slow this down, or I'm gonna have an honest-to-God heart attack," Aiden ground out.

Will was off him in a heartbeat, kneeling on the couch, offering his ass.

Aiden was not about to ignore that invitation.

He knelt behind Will, caressing his firm ass cheeks before pulling them apart to lick Will's pucker that contracted against his tongue. He played Will's hole with tongue and fingers, until Will seemed incapable of keeping still.

"Turn over," Aiden instructed, his voice a little hoarse.

Will flipped onto his back, drawing his knees up to his shoulders and rolling his ass up off the cushion. Aiden stroked the head of his cock over Will's hole, dribbling a little more lube onto his shaft. Then he pushed, slowly, so goddamn slowly, until at last he was all the way home.

"Fuck, that's deep."

Aiden pulled all the way out, then slid back in. Out. In. Out. In, until Will was moaning again, his hand a blur on his shaft. He raised Will's legs and hooked his knees over Aiden's shoulders, one hand on the arm rest, the other on Will's face as they kissed, deep, primal kisses, their tongues in synch with every stroke of Aiden's dick inside him. Aiden rested his elbows on either side of Will's head, their kisses connecting them as surely as Aiden's cock joined them. Aiden rocked, his hips pumping in a languid, fluid motion, Will's kisses growing more heated, his moans more frequent, his hand faster, and Aiden knew they were there.

His forehead met Will's. "You're close. Let go. I've got you." And then Aiden kissed him, groaning as Will's body tightened around him, loving that sensual arch of Will's back as he came, the way he pushed the back of his head into the arm of the couch, eyes wide open, a soft cry falling from his lips, his cum pooling on his stomach.

Will locked his arms around Aiden's neck, clinging to him, their bodies slick with perspiration and spunk. The smell of sweat and cum was a heady combination, and Aiden tried to hold back his orgasm, but he was fighting a losing battle, and at last he shot hard, his cock pulsing inside Will.

Will stared at him, his brow damp. "I can feel you."

Aiden nodded, then lowered his head to claim another kiss. He pinned Will to the couch, his energy spent.

Will lowered his legs to wrap them around Aiden's waist.

"And now I've got *you*," he said.

You can have me. Every little piece of me.

CHAPTER TWENTY

Will And Aiden Get A Shock

Sunday, December 11
Early

Will couldn't remember the last time he'd felt this relaxed. The past four weeks had been an endless round of trips between Minnesota and Milwaukee, of worrying when he simply didn't *do* worry. Studying had proved difficult, and that wasn't like him either.

Becca's momentary lapse of reason had had far-reaching consequences.

None of that mattered now, not when he was cuddling Aiden under a thick comforter, the scent of bed-warmed skin in his nostrils, the feel of Aiden's body against his… That ache in his ass was a welcome reminder of a night well spent.

It also held the promise of more to come.

Has it only been four weeks since we met?

Long enough to know this could be so much more than the joining of bodies and the pounding of hearts—oh yes, and asses too.

"What are you thinking?" Aiden stroked Will's arm, a leisurely up-and-down motion that served to reinforce their connection.

"That this feels good." He tilted his face

toward Aiden's. "It'll feel even better if you kiss me."

Aiden chuckled and their lips met in a lingering kiss that made Will's toes curl. On impulse, Will rolled on top of Aiden, hips rocking in a sensual grind. He took Aiden's wrists and held them above his head.

"Now I've got you," Will murmured before kissing Aiden's neck and collarbones, tracing a line down Aiden's sternum with his tongue. He loved the way Aiden arched his back, chasing the sensation. Will smiled against his chest.

"You taste as good as you look," he whispered between sucking Aiden's nipples, tugging gently on them, eliciting a low moan of pleasure from Aiden's lips.

Then Aiden chuckled, and the sound reverberated through him. "Ah, but do I taste better than lavender asparagus risotto?"

Will jerked his head up and relinquished his grip on Aiden's wrists. "Please, don't remind me." He gazed at Aiden, drinking in the sight: that handsome face framed by red hair spreading out over the pillow; his chest and neck flushed, his nipples taut; and the enticing quiver of his stomach that made Will want to lay a trail of kisses from his navel to the reddish cloud of hair at the base of Aiden's cock.

His stiffening cock.

"Get back here and kiss me. My lips are getting lonely."

Will pinned Aiden to the mattress and kissed him, feeding him a happy sigh when Aiden wrapped long legs around him, squeezing him a little.

"And now I've got *you*." He looped his arms around Will's neck.

Will chuckled. "So what are you going to do with me?"

Aiden slid his hand between their warm bodies until his fingers met Will's equally firm dick. He gave it a gentle tug.

"I was thinking of putting this where the sun doesn't shine."

Will grinned. "Sounds like the perfect way to start the day."

Lying in Aiden's arms was wonderful.

Burying his shaft in Aiden's body promised to be even better.

A Bit Later

"We should get up," Aiden murmured.

"You drained me. Not sure I can get up again. At least for another hour or so."

"I mean it."

"Mm."

"We both need a shower."

"Mm."

They lay facing each other, and he couldn't stop touching Will's face, his shoulder, his neck…

I'm just making sure he's really here, in my bed.

The previous night still felt like a dream. Every minute of it was crystal clear in his memory: the frantic coupling; the late-night search for pizza; sitting on the rug in front of the fire, feeding each other and laughing when Will got garlic cream on his nose; and Midnight going between them, mewling for rubbies and turning up his little nose at the pizza.

What stood out was Will lying face down on the rug, moaning while Aiden rocked in and out of him, his knees spreading Will's legs wide, a cushion beneath Will's hips to tilt that gorgeous ass and present Aiden with a deliciously tight hole.

Will chuckled. "What's the score so far?"

"Will's ass, two—Aiden's ass, one. And I wasn't kidding about that shower. I'm still wearing your cum."

Will stretched and let out a happy sigh. "That's sweet. I'm still wearing yours. Best aphrodisiac cologne ever."

Aiden cupped Will's nape and looked into his eyes. "You never intended going on a bar crawl last night, did you?"

Will shook his head. "This was going to be the last chance I had of spending time with you before everything went tits up. I wanted to enjoy your company, not yell over music to make myself heard, surrounded by people drinking their own body weight in beer and making way too much noise."

"And did you enjoy your non-bachelor party?"

He smiled and kissed the tip of Aiden's nose. "Well, it wasn't how I'd thought the evening would go, but I have no complaints." Then the light died in his eyes, and Aiden knew reality was kicking Will's ass.

Aiden could already feel the tip of its boot against his own.

"So what do we do now?"

Will rolled onto his back and stared at the ceiling. "Now? Becca and I are about to break up. Which is weird because I'd planned on doing exactly this today." He glanced at Aiden. "And your mom needs to know before she makes any more plans."

Aiden had been thinking about that. "Then the first item on the agenda is to go to the hotel and cancel the booking."

"But I didn't book it—your mom did."

Aiden shrugged. "It's still your wedding, dude. If they get snippy about it, we go to my mom, tell her everything, and then *she* cancels it."

Will rolled onto his side and stroked Aiden's chest, his touch light. "Do we have to go right this minute?"

Aiden chuckled. "I think putting on some clothes first might be a good idea—*after* the much needed shower."

"But I'm enjoying this." Will followed the trail of hair down Aiden's torso with his fingertip, pausing when he reached Aiden's cock.

"What—teasing me?"

Will grinned. "Of course."

Aiden grabbed him, pulling Will on top of him once more. He locked his arms around Will's neck. "There's something I need to tell you."

"Oh God." Will froze. "I thought we were done with all the revelations."

"Not quite." Aiden locked gazes with him. "The luggage cart that hit you in the back? It wasn't an accident."

Will's mouth fell open, his eyes wide. "You were *trying* to hit me?"

"No! I was trying to hit Becca. Well, Becca's luggage. I was jealous, you see."

Will frowned. "I don't understand."

Aiden sighed, stroking Will's back. "You walked in, and you were everything I've ever wanted. Good-looking, attentive, affectionate…"

Will raised his eyebrows. "You *know* the whole loved-up thing was all an act, right?"

"I do now, but since then you've proved that is how you really are. I watched you with Becca, with my parents, and I wanted to know you. Then you opened your mouth and it just got better."

Will kissed him, a gentle brushing of lips. "I wasn't kidding. These last few weeks have been torture. I wanted to tell you everything but I couldn't, and I knew once Becca came out with the whole Will-dumped-me scenario that I'd lose any chance of really getting to know you. Every time I saw you… I wanted you."

"But you didn't even know I was gay then."

Will smiled. "I know. I was convinced I was lusting after a straight guy."

"And is that all it was—lust?" Aiden had to know.

Will bit his lip. "I never believed in insta-lust until I met you. Then every minute we spent together, I learned there was so much more to you than looks. And even though I knew you'd never want me the way I wanted you, that didn't stop me liking you." He sighed. "Becca would end this mess and lose her fiancé—but *I'd* lose a friend."

The truth of his words was right there in his voice.

Reality nudged its boot into the crack of Aiden's ass.

He let go of Will. "We've got a packed morning ahead of us. We get to cancel the wedding, come out to my mom and dad… And then there's Becca."

"She's going to see Kelly this morning."

"So what's the plan?"

Will sat up. "When she gets back, we break up. Except she can't know that your parents already know… if that makes sense."

"Perfect sense."

"And before you ask, I'm okay with canceling the wedding, I'm even okay with telling your mom I'm gay, but I'm *not* going to out Becca."

Aiden smiled. "I guessed that would be the case. And then you'll be on your way." His heartbeat quickened. "So… Will you be continuing this recent trend of trips to Milwaukee?"

Will's grin was all the answer he required.

"Can I point out that the traffic flows both ways?"

Aiden laughed. "I'm going to be such a frequent visitor, you'll be begging me to stay in Milwaukee."

"Never gonna happen." Will's voice grew husky. "About that shower…"

"Let me do the talking," Aiden said as they entered the hotel lobby.

"Fine by me. I mean, how is it going to look? 'Excuse me, I'd like to cancel my wedding.'" Will appeared uncomfortable.

Aiden squeezed Will's arm. "We're in luck. Pete is working the front desk. I've known him for years. He used to give me lollipops when I came here with mom when I was little." He headed for the desk, dodging the bellhops who busied themselves carrying luggage to and fro.

Pete finished with the couple in front of them and smiled when he saw Aiden. "Hey. It's been a while. How's teaching? Your mom tells me some of the things your students get up to. Rather you than me." He leaned forward. "I think I'd be up on a murder charge before a week was out."

Aiden laughed. "It hasn't gotten that bad. Not yet, at least."

"If you're looking for your mom, she isn't working this weekend."

"I know." Aiden made sure none of the bellhops were in earshot. "Pete, can you do me a favor? Can you pull up the bookings for this month?"

Pete smirked. "Last time I looked, you

didn't work here."

Aiden gestured to Will. "This is Will Bryant."

Pete gave Will a nod. "I remember you. The anniversary party, right?"

Before Will could respond, Aiden got in first. "That's right. Long story short, he *was* going to marry Becca, but now he isn't."

Pete widened his eyes. "Little Becca is getting married?" Then he blinked. "Except she isn't."

Aiden stilled. "Mom didn't tell you about the wedding?" He'd have thought she'd have told everyone who had ears.

He shook his head. "I must've missed this. I'm getting old. Retirement can't come soon enough."

"Well, the wedding is now off. But the Imperial ballroom is booked in their names for December twenty-second. Can *we* cancel it or do you need Mom to okay it?"

Pete frowned. "Wait a minute." He peered at the monitor. "The Imperial ballroom is booked on that date."

"I know. The Taylor wedding, right?" It seemed Pete might be closer to retirement than he thought.

Another frown. "No—it's booked for a convention—Shrekfest."

Aiden gaped. "There's a con for *Shrek* fans? Who knew?" Maybe she changed the venue. "Can you check all the rooms, please?"

Pete tapped on the keyboard.

"This is weird," Will murmured behind him.

Aiden had the same thought.

At last Pete raised his chin. "Okay, I've checked twice. There is definitely no booking on the system for Taylor."

"Check Bryant," Will suggested.

Pete tapped again. "I'm sorry, but there are no weddings at this hotel during that week. I've checked current *and* canceled reservations."

Will stared at Aiden. "What the hell is going on?"

"There's only one way to find out."

Mom had some explaining to do.

CHAPTER TWENTY-ONE

Aiden's Mom Is In The Hot Seat

Aiden switched off the engine. All the way from the hotel, his mind had been in constant motion.

None of this makes sense.

"Generally when the truck stops, that means it's time to get out," Will remarked.

"I'm getting to it."

Will squeezed Aiden's knee. "I understand. I'm feeling a little apprehensive myself."

Aiden turned his head to stare at the house. "I thought we'd be doing all the talking. Now? I have no idea what's waiting for us."

"Then let's get in there and find out. We've got a deadline, remember? Becca will be back soon."

Aiden gazed at him. "Kiss me first?"

Will smiled. "I was going to do that anyway." He leaned in, the kiss sweet. "You smell good," he murmured.

"Down, boy. No time for any of that. You're going back to school in less than an hour." Aiden would be crossing the days off on his calendar until Christmas.

"Don't remind me."

They got out of the truck and Aiden walked

up the path to the front door. He used his key, and once inside, they removed their boots.

Aiden sniffed. "Mom's baking." He peered into the living room. Dad sat in his armchair, reading a newspaper. He glanced up as they entered the room.

"At last. I was starting to get worried. I've been expecting the phone call."

"What call?" Aiden asked with a frown.

Dad grinned. "The one where you ask me to come to the police precinct with bail money." His gaze went from Aiden to Will, then back to Aiden. He stilled. "Are you boys okay? You look so serious. The party went off without a hitch, didn't it?"

Will cleared his throat. "Actually, sir, there *was* no party. That's what I've come to talk to you about. To both of you."

Dad folded his paper and placed it on the side table. "Lou? Can you come here a sec?"

A moment later, Mom breezed through the door, bringing with her the aroma of chocolate and sugar. She blinked when she saw Aiden and Will.

"I didn't know you were here."

"Mom?" Aiden pointed to the couch. "Sit down, please."

"What's going on?" Mom perched on the edge of the seat cushion. She glanced at Dad. "Do *you* know what's going on?"

"No, but if you stop talking and let them speak, maybe we'll find out," Dad said dryly.

Aiden turned to Will. "You'd better go first."

"Are you sure?"

"Yeah. They need to—"

"Well, *one* of you go first, or *I'm* going back to my cookies." Mom's lips twitched.

Will squared his shoulders. "There's something I need to tell you. Becca and I won't be getting married. The engagement's off."

Dad gaped at him. "What happened? Did you have a fight? And when was this? Becca didn't say anything this morning. Did you break up over the phone or something? Because you were certainly still her fiancé when you left here last night."

"That's what I'm talking about. I'm not Becca's fiancé. I have *never* been Becca's fiancé." Will's voice quavered.

Mom's mouth fell open. "But… she told me…"

"I know, but it wasn't true. She… she was tired of you trying to set her up with guys."

"I never—"

Will held up his hand. "Please. I've known her for three years. I know what's been going on. So when you tried to fix her up with a date for your anniversary party, Becca was desperate to get you off her back." He shrugged. "She figured telling you she'd just gotten engaged would do the trick."

That was only half the truth, of course, but Aiden wasn't about to out his sister. "To be fair, she *was* going to break it off right after the party," he added.

"But then Hurricane Louise happened," Will concluded.

Dad sighed. "And suddenly there was a wedding on the horizon." He stood and went over to the mantelpiece, where he picked up a framed photo of Becca. He gazed at it fondly. "She could have said something then."

"Yes, she could," Will agreed, "but she didn't want to upset Louise. She was waiting for the right time."

"Which I'm guessing never came." Dad shook his head. "Oh well, at least we know now. Lou, you'd better call the hotel."

Mom said nothing, but plucked an invisible piece of lint from her skirt.

"Lou? You need to get on the phone to them and cancel the wedding."

Aiden stood in front of her. "That would be a little difficult—wouldn't it, Mom?"

She jerked her head up, blinking, her mouth open.

"But why?" Dad demanded. "They get cancellations all the time. Okay, so this one is a little too close to the wire, but—"

"It's hard to cancel something that never existed in the first place." Aiden speared her with a look. "Right, Mom?"

Dad's brow furrowed, his hand on his nape. "Something is going on here and I'm in the dark, so *one* of you had better start talking."

Aiden laid his hand on his mom's shoulder. "Will you tell him, or will I?"

She stared at him, paling. "I was doing it for her own good!"

"Wait—Aiden's right?" Dad stared at her, openmouthed. "There never was a wedding? Lou?"

Aiden arched his eyebrows. "I think you might need to explain that logic."

Mom sagged against the cushions. "I guess it all started with Yvonne."

Aiden frowned. "Yvonne, who lives down the street?"

She nodded. "Her daughter Trixie—you remember Trixie?"

"Wasn't she a goth? Yeah."

Will blinked. "A goth—called Trixie?"

"I think the whole goth business was her rebelling against her name."

"I think I'd have just changed my name," Will muttered.

"Except the last time I saw her, I don't think she was a goth, so maybe she's happy being Trixie too."

"Will *one* of you please get to the part where you tell me what the hell is going on?" Dad's voice rose.

Mom glanced at him. "Carl. Remember your blood pressure."

"Which is exactly why I take medication… dear."

Aiden *adored* his parents.

Mom returned her attention to Aiden. "Yvonne and I got chatting over coffee a while back. We were talking about our kids. Trixie goes to school in the Twin Cities too, did you know?"

Aiden squinted. "No I didn't. Becca has never mentioned it either." Then her words sank in. "Wait a minute…"

I think I know where this is going.

Will hadn't moved from beside him.

"Well, Yvonne asked me if I'd met Becca's girlfriend yet. I told her Becca must have lots of girlfriends at school, and Yvonne coughed and said, 'not that kinda girlfriend.' *Then* she told me Trixie had seen Becca with this same girl on numerous occasions. Her name's Kristen, apparently."

Will frowned. "When did this conversation take place?"

Mom coughed. "A while ago. I told Yvonne Trixie had gotten it wrong and that she must be confused. So… Yvonne messaged Trixie, who sent this." She picked up her phone from the table, scrolled, then handed it to Aiden.

He and Will peered at the screen. It showed Becca and another girl, kissing.

Aiden lowered the phone and replaced it on the table. "Why didn't you say something to her about this?"

Mom widened her eyes. "Because that would have been *wrong*. I figured Becca just wanted to tell us in her own time. But when I told Yvonne about Will and the engagement, she got all confused and surprised. So she talked to Trixie, who just confirmed what she'd been telling me for two years."

Will's breathing caught.

Aiden gaped. "You knew *two years ago* that Becca was a lesbian?"

Mom wrung her hands. "I wanted to let her come out on her own terms."

"So what was the idea behind telling her you'd booked a room for the wedding?" Dad demanded.

She sighed. "I thought once I told her what I'd done, she'd say 'Mom, you know what? I'm not really gonna marry Will. It was a joke, because I'm in love with Kristen.'"

"Except she never did." Aiden shook his

head. "And then you were locked into the lie."

Mom merely nodded, twisting her hands in her lap.

Dad was pacing. "But a *wedding*? You organized the flowers, the dress, the food—is that not taking things a bit too far?"

She gave him a defiant look. "Oh, this is all down to you."

Dad's shocked expression was almost comical. "Me? Where do *I* fit in all this?"

Mom put her hands on her hips. "You've been telling me for years that I needed to let loose once in a while, so I took a page from *your* book. I figured this would be the perfect prank, but also might be a way to get Becca to finally come out to us." She bit her lip. "Surprise?"

"You have *got* to be kidding." Dad's jaw was scraping the floor. "This is a bit more than chocolate poop and a meatloaf cake, don't you think?"

Mom managed a shrug. "I figured I had to go big. Isn't that what people say nowadays?"

Will stifled a chuckle, and for the first time during that whole surreal conversation, Aiden saw there might be a funny side to this. "Mom, you take 'go big or go home' to a whole new level."

Dad sat beside her on the couch. "You do realize Becca doesn't *have* to come out if she doesn't want to, don't you? You can't force her."

"If she's serious about this Kristen, then eventually we'll *have* to know. I just wanted to give her a helping hand. She shouldn't have to hide her love, especially from her family."

Dad chuckled. "I do understand, but your method of doing it was a little… extreme, don't you think?" He shook his head. "This whole thing is like one of those really bad comedies you see on TV. Right now the only thing that would make this whole situation even weirder is if you boys suddenly announced you were gay and into each other." He chuckled.

What the hell? Aiden snuck a glance at Will, who gazed back at him with wide eyes, his lips twitching.

It looks as if my parents are in for another shock.

Mom cleared her throat. "Funny you should say that."

Aiden's stomach tightened. *Or maybe not as big a shock as I thought.* Then he reconsidered. *She can't know anything.* Aiden had been *so* careful around his parents.

She addressed Will. "The night we met? I *knew* you and Becca didn't belong together. Oh, don't get me wrong. I really liked you, but two things stuck in my mind. One, of course, was knowing Becca had a girlfriend. And the second was something that became more obvious as the evening wore on."

"And what was that?" Will spoke in a low voice.

Another shrug. "I don't know. Maybe it was all the glances you kept sneaking at my son." Her eyes twinkled. "Then again, he was doing enough glancing of his own." She gazed at Aiden, chuckling. "You're not exactly subtle, you know. Neither of you."

What the—

Aiden hadn't been as careful as he'd imagined.

For the umpteenth time that weekend, he gaped. "You… You *know* I'm gay?"

Mom rolled her eyes. "Please. I'm your mom." Then she gave Will a knowing glance. "If you ever have kids, and you worry about the kind of magazines they're reading? Don't look beneath the mattress. They'll probably be there, right next to an oddly crunchy sock."

Holy shit. Mom really did *know something.*

Dad made a strangled noise. "Wait—Aiden's gay? He really *is* gay? … And Will too?"

Mom gave him an affectionate glance. "Aw. You are *so* sweet."

Aiden was still trying to get his head around this. "But you never said a word. Why would you keep—wait." He scraped his fingers through his hair. "It's that whole 'letting you come out on your own terms' business again, isn't it?"

Her smile faded. "I *was* a little upset you didn't feel able to tell me. I have to be honest here. That hurt."

Aiden knelt in front of her. "I didn't know how you'd react." He paused. "Except that's a lie. I knew *exactly* how you'd react. I've seen it every time you see something LGBTQ+ on TV, or hear it on the news. Becca has too."

Mom froze. "What?"

He took her hand in his. "Oh, come on. You've been doing it for as long as I can remember. So when I knew I was gay, you were the last people I was going to tell."

"You… you think I'm homophobic?" Mom swallowed. "Oh my God. I had no idea."

Dad put his arm around her shoulder, and

she leaned into him. "I know why she does it. I don't agree with it, but it's your mom's grudge, after all."

Aiden rose. "Grudge? What grudge?"

"I do *not* hold grudges," Mom retorted. "I just happen to have a very good memory, that's all."

"Seriously?" Dad stared at her. "I have never met *anyone* who can bear a grudge the way you can. You turn it into an Olympic event. What about that time your brother stabbed you with a pen? You *still* talk about that."

"Because it hurt!"

"But you were six!"

"For God's sake, will you two stop bickering and tell us what on earth you're talking about," Aiden yelled.

Mom blinked. "You're not too old to get a smack, you know."

"But in this case, he's right." Dad kissed Mom's cheek. "Over to you, honey. Tell your story."

Mom clasped her hands. "When I was seventeen—before I met your dad—I was dating this boy, Greg. He was… he was special, okay? So special, I was hearing wedding bells. And right before I was due to leave for college, I was waiting for him to tell me that the distance didn't matter, I was still his sweetheart, we'd visit each other, maybe even propose." Her face fell. "Only, he didn't." She narrowed her gaze. "What he *did* tell me was he was gay. That being with me had convinced him he wasn't into girls." Her eyes flashed. "What made it worse? Well, for me at least. I'd told all my friends how happy we were, how sweet and romantic he was, how he was too good to be true. And then I knew why. I mean, the nerve! I was so embarrassed and hurt."

"And ever since that day," Dad added, "whenever she sees anything remotely LGBTQ? It pisses her off."

Mom smacked him on the arm. "Hey, language."

"But it *does*," he insisted. "And when Becca gets back here, you're going to have to explain this all over again. You know that, right?"

She sighed. "If that's what she's been thinking all these years, then yes, I guess I have some explaining to do. But all either of them had to do was say something."

Dad chuckled. "Sure, but that would be the logical thing to do. Whoever said people were logical?"

Will's phone pinged, cutting off the conversation. He pulled it from his pocket and glanced at the screen. "Becca is on her way back."

"Does she know the wedding's off?" Mom asked.

"I gave her an ultimatum," Will said in a low voice. "If she wouldn't end it, I would. So it isn't exactly going to be a shock."

"Mom? Are you going to let her know that *you* know that…" Aiden waved a hand. "You get the picture."

Mom shook her head. "If she wants to tell me, that's her choice. I won't put her on the spot."

"Then it's decided. I'll do my the-wedding-is-off speech, you two act all surprised, and we take it from there."

Mom frowned. "But what reason are you

going to give for breaking off the engagement?"

Aiden smiled. "I can think of one big reason." He gazed at Will and held out a hand to him. Will took it and moved closer to him.

Mom gasped. "Oh. *Oh.* You and Will?? Oh my God! We could have a double wedding. I get to see both my kids happily married."

Will's gasp was the equal of hers.

Aiden laughed. "Whoa there, Mom. We only just met, remember?"

Dad joined in the laughter. "See what I've had to put up with for the last twenty-seven years? No wonder I'm losing my hair." Mom glared at him, and he kissed her. "And I wouldn't have you any other way. But don't be in such a rush to marry off our kids. Don't you remember all the stuff we got up to before *we* got married?"

Mom flushed. "Yes, I do, and you'd better stop right there."

Aiden's mind boggled.

Dad smiled. "That whole getting-to-know-you phase? I loved every minute of it."

Mom fixed him with a hard stare. "And *when* did you know you wanted to marry me?"

He gave her a sheepish glance. "Okay, you got me. About a month after we started dating. I knew I wasn't going to let you get away."

Mom's smile was positively smug.

"But what am I thinking?" Dad sprang to his feet and seized Will in a fierce hug. "I am *so* happy. In the space of less than half an hour, I've gone from heartache at the thought of not having you around, to utter confusion, then joy that you might be around a while yet." He released Will, and

Aiden was on the receiving end of a similar hug. "I'm so happy for you, son. By the way, I like Will."

Aiden grinned. "Yeah, I kinda picked up on that."

"Can we just stop for a minute and discuss what we're going to do about Becca? Because we're about to drop a bombshell."

Will smiled. "Let's see how she deals. She may surprise us all."

Aiden snorted. "Yes, she might—and we might also need something to revive her when she faints."

CHAPTER TWENTY-TWO

Aiden Gets A Shock

The front door opened, and Becca called out, "Will? You ready to go? Or do we need to raid CVS for Blowfish or OverEZ?"

"Will doesn't need hangover cures," Aiden hollered. He chuckled. "Any second now, Becca's gonna be the one with the headache."

Will was too busy rehearsing his lines in his head. Becca was only prepared for half of what was coming right at her.

"We're all in here," Louise said in a loud voice.

Becca walked into the room, and stopped dead. "Everyone looks so serious. Who died?" She gazed at Aiden with narrowed eyes. "You finally killed that cat, didn't you?"

He gasped in mock horror. "Midnight is just fine, thank you very much. We left him sitting in the window, chatting to himself. Probably because there was a bird outside that he couldn't get at."

"Give it time. He'll go the same way as Snuffles, you wait and see."

Will chuckled. "Snuffles?"

Aiden rolled his eyes. "Later, okay?"

"Well, if no one's dead, what's going on?"

Three pairs of eyes focused on Will, and he sighed. "Sit down, Becca. I need to tell you something."

Becca sat in the armchair. "Should I be worried here?" She glanced at her parents. "Do *you* know what's going on?"

Louise coughed, and Dad said quickly, "We're as much in the dark as you are."

Will cleared his throat. "I'm sorry, Becca, but I can't marry you. The wedding's off."

Give Becca her due, her feigned shock was pitch-perfect. She stared at him open-mouthed. "What?"

Louise gasped and clutched her chest, and Carl nudged her with his elbow.

Becca gazed at him with wide eyes. "But why don't you want to marry me anymore?"

Will took a deep breath. "Because… there's someone else."

Becca blinked. "There is?"

Yeah, that wasn't in the script, was it?

She frowned. "Who?"

Will turned toward Aiden, who laced his fingers through Will's. He gave Aiden a grateful glance before giving Becca his full attention. "Your brother."

Right on cue, Louise let out another dramatic gasp to rival any soap actress ever, and even Carl managed to appear surprised.

Becca stared at Will. At their joined hands. Back to Will's face. "This is a joke, right?" Except something in her voice told him that was exactly what she thought it was.

Will shook his head.

Aiden let go of Will's hand and put his arm around Will's waist. "This is for real, sis."

Becca's eyes were the size of saucers. "What the—" She lurched out of the armchair and crossed the floor to stand in front of him, glaring. "You're cheating on me with *Aiden*? I don't know which one of you I should hit first."

Will leaned forward and whispered, "Don't bury yourself in the part."

"Are you for real? I had no idea you were going to come up with *this* story."

Will coughed: "Actually?" He bit his lip. "It isn't a story."

Becca stared at him, doing a great impression of a goldfish. "You mean… You and Aiden…you're…." Then she raised her hand to smack his arm, but Aiden stopped her, his fingers around her wrist.

"Don't even think about it," he told her.

"Maybe I should knock *you* out instead. You stole my fiancé!" Becca tugged free of his grasp.

"Really? *That's* what you're going with?" Aiden arched his eyebrows. "We both know it isn't true."

Becca froze. "What?"

"Becca!" Louise called out. "Before you kill your brother and his boyfriend—"

It seemed as though that last word finally hit home. Becca looked Will in the eye. "Seriously? You're really dating Aiden?"

Will nodded.

"I know, it's crazy, isn't it?" Carl sounded gleeful. "This would make a great movie."

Aiden chuckled. "Yeah, a romcom."

"Can I finish, please?" Louise stood and walked over to Becca. "Sweetheart, I need to tell you something."

"If you tell me you're pregnant, I swear…"

Carl stood. "Both of you, sit down, please. Your mom is being serious."

Becca did as she was told. Will watched her face as Louise related the story of Greg.

"No. You're not telling me everything. There has to be more to it than that."

Will recognized that stubborn expression. Then Becca's eyes went wide.

"Mom? What's wrong?"

Louise's lip wobbled as she looked up, the shine in her eyes unmistakable as anything other than tears. "I failed you. Both of you."

"What are you talking about?"

Her shoulders slumped. "When we had you, I told your dad I wasn't going to be my parents. I was going to be open and honest with you. I would teach you how to love and be loved. I wouldn't hide things, like they did. And I turned around and that was exactly what I did. I am so sorry."

Will felt for her. "What I don't understand is why you would hold onto a grudge like this for so long." He bit back a smile. "Apart from wanting to enter the Olympics when they finally add Holding A Grudge as an event."

Her smile was tremulous. "It sounds even worse now than it did then. He invited me to go with him to Milwaukee Pride. I was excited to go, to meet his friends. I thought he was going to introduce me to them as his girlfriend."

Aiden let out a long breath. "But that wasn't

what happened."

She shook her head. "There was a group of us. Everyone was laughing and having a good time. But whenever we met people, he introduced me by my name. Not as his girlfriend, not as anything. I finally had to ask him why. He pulled me over into a corner and told me he had to say something." She bit her lip. "Before he could, another guy came over and put a hand on the back of his neck and pulled him in for a kiss. I told myself it was fine, he was just open with his friends. When they stopped kissing, he stared at me expectantly." Louise swallowed. "When I didn't say anything, he told me he was gay, and that this guy was his boyfriend." Her eyes flashed. "In my head, everyone in our group was in on it. They were all laughing at me. He'd been my first, he told me he loved me. I was actually picking out *china patterns*, for gosh sake. And now? I was being dumped because he was gay. And it wasn't even him being gay that stung. It was the humiliation I felt, the pain he'd caused, the hole he'd left in my heart. I ran and called home. My dad came and got me, but didn't ask why I was angry."

"Breathe, honey." Carl put his arm around her.

She gave him a grateful glance before addressing Becca and Aiden. "A few years later, I heard from a friend he was working on the PrideFest board and that he was still with that other guy—whose name I can't even remember—and every time something was said about Pride, that humiliation crept back in, and I was an eighteen-year-old girl again, being dumped and having to call home because I was humiliated."

Aiden shook his head. "So *that's* why you kept turning the TV off."

She nodded. "I don't begrudge him his happiness. Being with someone that long shows how in love you truly are, and I was happy for him, but still, my humiliation stayed with me for all this time. And now, because of it, I pushed my kids away, making them think it was the LGBTQ community I hated, when nothing was further from the truth." She snorted. "I wish I could explain how I felt every time I saw an ad for Pride. How my face burned, how my eyes watered. And it was all so *stupid.* I was with your father, we had two kids, but that stupid, insignificant thing from my childhood? It haunted me and I am so, *so* sorry."

Aiden knelt in front of her and took her hands in his. "We weren't innocent in this either. If we'd had the courage to talk to you, things would never have gotten this far."

Louise blinked. "Why would you talk to someone you thought would turn you away for being gay? I'm just grateful the two of you didn't cut ties with me."

Even Will knew Aiden would never do that.

Aiden squeezed her hands. "How about we promise no more secrets? You, me, and Becca."

"What about me?" Carl demanded. "I have secrets too, y'know."

Aiden grinned. "Yeah, but we don't wanna know where the key is to the beer cooler."

Louise gazed earnestly at Becca. "So yes, I carried a grudge for one person, but that was because I'd been in love, and what he did hurt me. Was it logical? God no, not even remotely. Was it healthy? Obviously not." She looked Becca in the eye. "I own that, and I apologize profusely if I ever, for one single second, made you think I wouldn't love you for being who you are. But I do. And your dad is right. I have to let go of this hurt and anger. I should have moved on a long time ago."

"Therapy," Carl coughed.

"Yeah, fine. Maybe you're right." He gave a smug smile, and she glared at him. "But being right once in all these years doesn't count as a winning streak. Remember that." She let out another sigh. "Honestly, I love my life. I love my family. And I will now and always love their partners. I can't let what he did weigh me down, because when you have kids, I don't want them thinking Grams doesn't love them with her whole heart."

Becca gasped. "Kids? Aren't you putting the cart before the horse here, Mom?" Then her shoulders sagged, her eyes glistening. She swiped at them with her fingers, then met Louise's earnest gaze. "Wait a sec. You said partners." She froze. "Why are you telling me this?"

Come on, Becca. Believe her. You know you want to.

"Isn't there something you wanna tell Mom?" Aiden gave her a loaded glance, and she blinked. He smiled and squeezed Will's hand. "Come on in, sis, the water's fine."

Will chuckled. "Shouldn't that be *come on out*?"

Becca stared at him. "You told them."

"No, he didn't," Louise got in quick. "Trixie Benton did, when she sent me a photo of you—and Kristen."

Aiden thought Becca's jaw was about to become unhinged. She gasped. "You *know* about Kristen?"

Louise gave a sympathetic nod. "I've known for a while."

"Just don't ask how long that is," Aiden added. "You wouldn't like the answer."

Becca jerked her head in his direction, then went back to staring at Louise. "Wait a sec. You *knew*—and yet you said nothing?"

Aiden laughed. "Oh sis, it gets *way* better than that. I'd say sit down, but you already are, so… This whole wedding Mom has been planning? It's a fake."

"What?" Becca's eyes bulged, her eyebrows disappearing into her hairline.

"She didn't book the ballroom. She was hoping that once she blindsided you, you'd tell her the truth."

"But… the flowers…" Becca's voice shook.

Louise smiled. "Elliott Pink is a friend. I use his services all the time at the hotel. He was in on it too."

"And the dress? That beautiful dress you had me try on *how* many times?"

"Ah, now *that* part was real. I figured you'd need a wedding dress—one day—and you obviously loved it, so…" She shrugged. "It's still hanging on a rack with your name on it."

Becca folded her arms. "What about the food? There *was* no double booking, was there? I mean, there couldn't be if there was never going to be a wedding. Then what was all that shi—stuff about Kelly taking over the catering?"

Louise chuckled. "That crappy food she served you at the tasting? That was all part of it. Kelly's actually an amazing chef."

Becca snorted. "I think we have different definitions of amazing, then."

Louise rolled her eyes. "Silly girl. I *asked* her to screw it up. She was offended, but when I explained why, she said fine." Louise's eyes twinkled. "She also said I was never to bring up the subject ever again."

"But… but…" Becca gestured toward the front door. "I just spent an *hour* with her, and she didn't let on once." She gave Louise another glare. "*You* told me to apologize to her. I spent fifteen minutes *groveling*." She shook her head. "I don't believe any of this." Becca pointed at her mom. "Mostly, I don't believe you let me go on lying to you."

Louise let out a heavy sigh. "I kept asking you if there was anything you wanted to tell me, remember? I gave you *so many* opportunities to tell me the truth." She tilted her head to one side. "You know what? This reminds me of that story about the man who is stranded on his roof when the floods come. He keeps telling everyone that God will save him. A guy in a rowboat comes along to take him to safety, but the man says 'It's okay. God will save me.' Then a helicopter arrives, and he says the same thing as they try to winch him into it. And finally, he dies and goes to heaven. He stands before God and says 'Why didn't you save me?' God says, 'I sent you a boat, a helicopter…. What more did you want?'" Louise gave Becca a forthright stare. "How many more openings could I have given you?" Before

Becca could respond, Louise softened her voice. "How do you think I felt when I saw that photo? And realized you couldn't come right out and tell me?"

Aiden chuckled. "I see what you did there."

Will nudged him. "Not the time," he whispered, and Aiden had the good grace to blush.

"Sweetheart, I'm sorry." Louise held Becca's hands. "I know this is on me, but really, you and Kristen seem to fit way better than you and Will ever did." Her gaze cut to Will. "No offense."

He chuckled. "None taken."

Louise gave Becca a beseeching glance. "Please tell me you'll bring her home for Christmas."

That flicker of hope was back, and Will rejoiced to see the light in Becca's face.

"Then you're really okay that I'm a lesbian?"

Louise enfolded Becca in her arms and held her tightly, and Will reasoned that was the best response ever. Then she drew back and wiped wet eyes. "Okay? Honey, I'm delighted. You've been with Kristen for so long. That's awesome. Now all I want is to meet her."

Becca swallowed again.

"Ball's in your court, sis," Aiden said in a low voice.

Becca smiled. "I'll ask her to come home with me for Christmas."

"Will? What about you?" Carl asked. "Will *you* be joining us for the holidays?"

Will beamed. "I might have to split my time between here and home, but yes, sir. I'd love to spend Christmas with you all." He gave Aiden a warm glance. "I want Aiden to meet my family too."

He had a feeling their reaction would be an anticlimax after all this.

Thank God. Will had had enough drama to last him a lifetime.

Will put his bag in the trunk and closed it. "I guess this is it, then."

He didn't want to leave.

Aiden took off his own scarf and looped it around Will's neck.

Will chuckled. "I do have one, you know."

"I know—but this one smells of me. I figured we'd swap."

He really liked that idea. Will reached into the back of the car and grabbed his scarf. "Look after it. And don't let Midnight sleep on it. Or stick his claws in it. Or—"

Aiden laughed. "Okay, okay, I'll treat it with the utmost care, all right?" He cupped Will's nape. "I'll miss you. Midnight will miss you too. He'll probably wander around the apartment, looking for you."

Will glanced toward the house. The curtains twitched, and he smiled. "I think we have an audience."

"Does that mean I don't get a kiss goodbye?"

"If you think I'm leaving here without one, I—"

Aiden stopped his words with a fierce kiss, and Will gave as good as he got. They parted, and he leaned, their foreheads meeting.

"You'll see me soon enough. It's only nine days before we're back here. And by then I can relax because the exams will be over. At least for a while."

"I won't call you then." Aiden didn't sound happy about the prospect.

Will grinned. "You'd better. I want to see your face on my phone every night."

Aiden snickered. "Just my face, huh?"

Will kissed him again. "Whatever you feel comfortable showing," he murmured against Aiden's lips.

Aiden gave a throaty chuckle. "Never had phone sex before. Not sure how much lube an iPhone would take anyway."

He laughed. "I guess there's a first time for everything." Another kiss, only this time Will poured his heart and soul into it.

This one will have to last me a while.

"Aiden, put him down. Maybe I want a hug too. The kisses, you can keep."

He laughed and hugged Becca. "Feeling better now?"

She snorted. "Now that I'm not marrying Will? You bet." She flashed Will a grin. "No offense."

"And again, none taken. I'm as relieved as you are."

Aiden took a step toward him, and Becca groaned. "For God's sake, you'll see him on the twenty-third. Now will you let us get on the road?" Her eyes sparkled. "There's a girl more than five hours from here that I'm dying to see."

Aiden gave a snort uncannily like Becca's. "See? I'm pretty sure you've got more planned for Kristen than just looking at her."

Becca glared at Will. "You. In the car. Now."

Will chuckled and climbed into the passenger seat. Becca got in and switched on the engine.

Aiden tapped on Becca's window and she lowered it. "Can you stop being my aggravating older brother long enough for us to be on our way?"

"I was just going to ask… Kristen's parents…Are they cool with her being into girls? Because if they're not, you *know* Mom's gonna love her to death."

Becca smiled. "They're cool. Thanks for asking." She wound up the window.

As they pulled away from the house, Will twisted to get one last glimpse of Aiden waving at him.

Then he was gone.

"Okay, now we can talk. You and my brother. Is it serious?"

Will gazed at the snow-covered road ahead. "I think so. I hope so. I've never felt like this before so…"

"How does he make you feel?"

Will thought about it for a moment, analyzing his emotions. "Like I'm walking on air when he's with me. I can't wait to hear his voice. Every time he's close to me all I want to do is touch him. I smile more when I'm with him." He was smiling just thinking about Aiden. "He's the sunshine in my day."

Becca was quiet for a minute.

"Have I said something wrong?"

She sighed. "Nope. You just summed up in a few seconds what it took me months to realize about Kristen." She chuckled. "That was fast."

Will smiled once more. "Not really *that* fast. After all, what started all of this was a luggage cart."

Four weeks ago.

And many more to come.

"Will… Now that it's just us…" Becca sighed. "I'm sorry, okay?"

"What are you apologizing for now?"

She rolled her eyes. "Where do I start? How about the way I let this business drag on? Not telling Mom when there were so many times I *could've* done it? Mainly I'm apologizing for being such an aggravating best friend. Let's face it, I've been an awful bestie. I was annoying, gutless…" She glanced at him. "Feel free to jump in at any time and disagree with me."

"I will—*if* I disagree with you," he teased. "And you left out selfish."

Her face tightened. "I guess I earned that. You'd have been right to walk away from this whole mess… but you didn't. I'll never understand that. I don't deserve you."

It was time for truth.

"Becca, I'm not going to lie. The only thing that kept me from walking away? Your brother.

Because right from the start, I wanted to keep him in my life. Which was a highly illogical reaction, seeing as once we 'broke up' I'd probably never see him again. But there was always this part of me that clung to the hope that somehow, if I rolled the dice right, I might get my heart's desire." He smiled. "And I did. So yeah, you're forgiven." Then he grinned. "But you've used up all your nine bestie lives where I'm concerned. So from here on in, there's going to be a whole new Becca."

She bit her lip. "Wow. Talk about a tall order."

"I have faith in you." He patted her shoulder. "Besides, we're going to be seeing even more of each other. We're going to be family."

Will couldn't wait.

CHAPTER TWENTY-THREE

Will Drops A Bombshell

Friday, December 23

"Will!"

He jumped. "There's no need to shout."

Becca glanced at him in the rearview mirror. "There is when I've said your name three times. Can you drag your mind away from your boyfriend for a second? We're stopping at the next rest area."

"Fine," he replied absently.

"Besides, it won't be long now until you see him in the flesh." She grinned. "Which has to be better than the *hours* of video calls I'm sure you two have shared."

Will had been strict during the last week while the exams took place. He'd limited himself to one call before he turned out the light.

Okay, so each call lasted at least an hour. Sleep was for the weak anyway.

"Will, are you okay?" Kristen asked from the passenger seat. "You've been so quiet."

"Just got a lot on my mind, that's all."

"Lighten up, why don't you? Exams are over—well, until May—and it's almost Christmas." Becca chuckled. "Plus, there's a certain nerd waiting for you in Milwaukee."

Aiden had been in Will's thoughts a lot during the past ten days, especially after Will's tutor had met with him to discuss Will's plans for after graduation.

The conversation had provided a cold dash of reality, and Will had been forced to consider the situation without the lens of his feelings for Aiden.

What do I do?

Will had known all his life what his future would look like—he hadn't counted on meeting someone who would turn those plans upside down.

I was happy with casual. I'd have stayed *happy with casual.*

Aiden wasn't casual. Aiden was permanent with a capital P. At least, Will had wanted him to be—until he put aside such selfish thoughts.

"Will, if you don't stop being such a grumpy bastard, I may have to kill you," Becca groused.

"I'm not grumpy," he retorted. "Just… thoughtful."

"Yeah, I can hear the cogs whirring from here. Okay then, *be* thoughtful—but by the time we reach Milwaukee, I wanna see you smiling. You got that?"

"I've got it."

The last thing Will wanted to do was spoil Christmas, so he figured he'd keep his thoughts to himself.

Aiden doesn't have to know.

The quiet voice in the back of his mind piped up.

But he'll have to, eventually.

Will would deal with that when it happened.

"For God's sake, Aiden, will you stop staring out the window?" Mom grumbled. "It won't make them get here any faster."

"I think it's sweet," Dad commented. "I remember when you used to wait at the window for me to get home. Then Becca came along, and I was replaced."

Aiden was about to retort that he hadn't been sweet since he was seven years old, when a car pulled into the curb.

"They're here!" He grabbed the coat he'd put over the back of the armchair, struggled into it, and made a beeline for the front door.

"Don't run!" Mom admonished. "You'll only slip and break something, and that'll be Christmas ruined."

She cares about me.

Then Dad yelled, "And she's talking about the display, in case you missed that part."

Well fuck. Feeling the love here.

Aiden hurried down the path to where Will, Kristen and Becca took bags from the trunk.

God, he looks good. He was also wearing Aiden's scarf.

"Hey," Becca said with a smile. "How—"

Aiden threw his arms around Will and

kissed him on the lips.

"Yeah, good to see you too, Aiden," Becca muttered. "Yes, this *is* Kristen. Nice of you to give her such a warm welcome."

Kristen chuckled. "You were just the same when you got back the last time. Leave them alone."

Aiden pressed his forehead to Will's. "I've missed you," he whispered.

"Missed you too."

Aiden straightened, grabbed Will's bag, and then held out his hand for Kristen's. "Hello." He gave her a smile. "Glad you could be here." He led the way to the house, the others trailing behind him.

"Sure, I'll carry my own bag," Becca murmured.

"And you called *Will* grumpy," Kristen said, chuckling.

They went inside, and Aiden ignored the introductions to take Will's hand in his. "Don't get comfortable. You won't be staying here. You're gonna sleep at my place."

Becca snorted. "Sleep. *Riiight.*"

Mom glared at her. "You can take Kristen's bag to the guest room."

She laughed. "I don't think so."

Mom put her hands on her hips, and Aiden had to smile. *She and Becca are so alike.*

"Young lady, if you think I'm going to let you—"

Dad laid a gentle hand on Mom's arm. "I know she's still your baby, but she's been living her own life for nearly three years now. Do you *really* want her miserable throughout the holidays?" His eyes twinkled. "Besides, what makes you think they'd stay in their own rooms? What are you going to do—set booby traps outside their doors?" He gave her a meaningful stare, then his eyes went wide. "Holy crap. You would! C'mon, do you *really* think Aiden is offering to put Will up to create more space here?"

Will's face flushed, and Mom blinked rapidly.

"Dinner will be in about an hour," she said, a little croak in her voice.

"Is there anything I can do to help?" Kristen offered.

Mom beamed. "I was just about to prepare the vegetables. Come into the kitchen."

Aiden snickered. "You wait. The kitchen door will close, and the dinner won't be the only thing getting grilled."

Becca gasped. "Wait for me," she called out. "I can help too."

From the kitchen, Aiden caught his mom's comment. "Well, *that* only took twenty-two years."

Dad had his back to Aiden and Will, but it was obvious he was laughing his ass off.

Will gazed at his surroundings, frowning. "I don't get it. We put up a ton of stuff outside, but there's still no tree in here." He glanced at Aiden. "You don't do Christmas trees?"

Aiden laughed. "Are you kidding? In *this* family? The reason there's no tree yet is because of tradition." There were colored and white lights dripping from any surface that would accommodate them: along the shelves of the bookcases, draped over picture frames, around door frames… Aiden pointed to the space in the corner next to the couch.

"It'll go there. It's still standing in the garage, trussed up like a turkey."

"Christmas Eve is when we trim the tree," Dad told him. "It's also tradition that it's the one night of the holidays when Lou doesn't do any cooking. We leave that to our kids."

Will's lips twitched. "Please, tell me it's going to be edible."

Dad chuckled. "You can let me know tomorrow night—*you'll* be helping prepare the meal."

Will regarded Aiden with arched eyebrows. "Thanks for the warning."

Aiden had had enough small talk.

He took Will by the hand and led him into the dining room, out of earshot.

"You don't know how happy I am to see you." He leaned in and whispered, "I'll show you *exactly* how happy tonight." Then it dawned on him that Will was way too quiet. "Those two wore you out on the drive here, I bet. You look tired."

"A little, yes."

Aiden slipped his arms around Will's waist. "I bet you're relieved the exams are over. You said they went well, though." He kissed him, a lingering press of lips, breathing him in. "Only five more months, and that's you done—for a while, at any rate."

"That's something we need to talk about."

"Can it wait? I mean, it isn't urgent, right?"

Will gave a tired smile. "I guess not."

"Then prepare yourself for the ordeal to come."

He gave Aiden a quizzical glance. "What

ordeal?"

Aiden grinned. "It even has a name. It's called 'Mom's eggnog.'"

"Where's Will?" Becca asked.

"Talking to his parents." Aiden glanced up at the ceiling. "I told him to use my old room. He said he wouldn't be long." He grinned, inclining his head toward the kitchen. "Sounds as if Kristen and Mom are hitting it off. I've never heard Mom laugh so much."

"I know, right?" Becca shook her head. "I went looking for them earlier and I found them in Mom's craft room. You will never believe what they were doing."

"Something crafty?" he suggested.

"She was showing Kristen her bags of yarn." Becca stared at him with wide eyes. "*Yarn*, for God's sake. And Kristen doesn't even knit."

Aiden smiled. "She doesn't *now*, you mean. She might be bitten by the bug by the time you all leave." He gave an evil grin. "Just think. It'll start as a bag of yarn, then it'll become a drawer. Then a chest. And finally a whole room, just for her craft supplies. Imported bamboo knitting needles, steel ones, laminated birch ones… The list is endless."

Becca eyed him. "You started knitting, didn't you?"

Aiden coughed. "Sorry, forget I said anything."

Becca's snort told him she wasn't about to forget that bit. *And she's got Mom's memory, dammit.*

He folded his hands behind his head. "I

didn't see this coming. You with a girlfriend, me with a boyfriend, Mom and Dad ecstatic about the situation…"

Becca's gaze took on this look he'd never seen before. It was…softer, a kind expression, her eyes filled with warmth.

So this is Becca in love.

He had to admit, it suited her.

The door opened, and Dad came in, carrying a tray laden with glasses.

"Get it while it's hot."

Aiden sniffed. "You made mulled wine." He beamed. "Perfect."

"Don't I make it every Christmas?" He raised his voice. "Will you two stop jawing and get in here? And Will? Where are you?"

There was the thud of feet on the stairs, and Will appeared in the doorway. He sniffed. "Oh wow. That smells good."

Dad waited until everyone was present before handing round the glasses. He raised his.

"A toast. To family."

"To family." The sound of clinking glasses filled the air. Aiden sipped the wine, loving the hint of cinnamon, cloves, and orange.

Becca returned to her sprawled position on the couch. "*Now* it feels like Christmas."

"What about my eggnog?" Mom demanded.

That triggered an eruption of coughing.

"Delicious, as always," Dad said quickly.

"*That* was the word I was looking for," Aiden added just as fast. "I knew it began with a D."

"My money was on deadly," Becca muttered.

Mom narrowed her gaze. “You know, if you *don’t* like it, you should really let me know. Because if you don’t, you’re going to be drinking it every Christmas until the Rapture.” She gave Dad a sweet smile.

“You know what?” He kissed her on the cheek. “It wouldn’t be Christmas without it.”

“I was going to wait until Christmas Day,” Kristen began. “But I *can’t* wait that long.” She put her glass down on the side table, then walked over to where Becca sat. Kristen removed a small heart-shaped box from her jeans pocket, and Becca bolted upright in a heartbeat.

“Oh my God.”

Kristen opened it and held it out to Becca. Inside was nestled a black ring that caught the light. “I was going to do this on your birthday, but you were already engaged at the time.” She chuckled. “But now you’re a single woman again…. Becca Taylor, will you marry me?”

Becca swallowed. “God, yes.”

Kristen took the ring from its box. “I know engagement rings are supposed to be diamonds, but—”

“Stop right there.” Becca held her breath as Kristen slid it onto her finger. “That is freaking *perfect.* If I was gonna choose a ring, this would be it.” She stood, flinging her arms around Kristen, and they kissed. Becca’s eyes glistened, and Aiden felt tears prick the corners of his eyes.

“Oh my God.” Mom was crying, and Dad already had his phone out, taking photos. Will was grinning like a loon. Then everything dissolved into one giant hug fest before Dad disappeared into the kitchen, with a shout of "This calls for champagne!"

"We don't have any," Mom hollered after him. "But there's a bottle of Prosecco in the fridge door."

"Good enough."

By the time everyone had a tall glass of bubbling wine, Becca and Mom had stopped crying, although Kristen hadn't stopped smiling, and Dad hadn't stopped taking pictures.

"So when are you thinking of getting married?" Mom asked.

Becca gaped at her. "Mom. She only proposed ten minutes ago."

Mom fixed her with a hard stare. "And as you now know, weddings take a lot of planning. So…?"

Kristen nudged Becca. "How about July? Of course, we'll have just graduated, we won't have anywhere to live, and as for jobs…" She laughed. "This is crazy. I can't believe we're even talking about this."

"I know," Becca said, her eyes shining. "Let's do it anyway. July is a long way off. Who knows what will happen by then?" She glanced at Mom, who'd grabbed her phone. "Mom? What are you doing?"

"Calling the hotel, of course. Keep your fingers crossed."

"We don't want a big room," Becca said quickly.

"Smart move, just rolling over and going with the flow," Dad murmured. "You're finally learning the number one Taylor rule when it comes to your mom."

"What's that?" Will asked.

Dad grinned. "To quote the Vogons, 'Resistance is useless.'"

"Like you said, July is a long way off. Who knows what will happen by then?" Mom's eyes sparkled, and she gave Aiden and Will an inquiring glance as she headed for the door.

It didn't take a genius to know what was on her mind. *She said as much, didn't she?*

Aiden speared her with a look. "Mom? Don't even think about it."

"Think about what?" she asked, pausing at the door, her eyes wide.

"Mom, you really can't do innocent." Before he could add anything, she'd left the room. Aiden shook his head. "You wait. The next thing she comes out with will be 'So Aiden, why don't you and Will make it a double wedding?'"

Becca burst out laughing. "Oh my God, you *nailed* her."

Even Dad was laughing. "That was really good, son."

Then Aiden caught sight of Will's face, and his stomach clenched.

Something was wrong.

"Hey, what's up? It was a joke."

Will grabbed his hand. "Can we go somewhere a bit quieter and talk?"

"Sure. Let's go to my old room." He led Will up the stairs, his heart racing. Once inside the room, he closed the door behind them. "Just so you know? I'm not about to propose, if that's what's panicking you. Mom's just being Mom, that's all."

Will sat on the bed. "Look, I've been

thinking a lot about this since I saw you last, and…"

Ice etched its way over Aiden's skin. "Thought a lot about what, exactly?" He joined Will on the bed.

Will studied the red rug. "When I was eight years old, I told my parents I wanted a job with NASA when I grew up."

"I know you said it was your dream."

He nodded. "And it still is. But that's what I need to talk to you about." He leaned forward, elbows planted on his knees, head bowed. "Once I finish my degree in May, the next thing will be a master's in Astrophysics. That will take two years. After that? A PhD, and that'll be another five years. Then we're talking at least three years as a post-doctoral researcher. So by the time I get my first paycheck, I'll be in my thirties. And that's assuming I ever make it into NASA in the first place."

Aiden frowned. "Is there a point to all this?"

Will jerked his head up. "You can't saddle yourself with someone who can't pay his own way. It isn't fair. I know how much a teacher earns. My mom is a teacher, remember? I wouldn't want you to bear all that financial burden."

There was a knot in Aiden's stomach, and a heaviness in his limbs.

"You know I'm right, don't you?" Will's voice quaked.

Aiden knelt in front of Will, sitting back on his haunches. "Are you done? Because it's *my* turn." He cupped Will's chin, tilting his head toward Aiden. "You know, for such a smart man, you can be incredibly stupid."

Will blinked.

"Listen to me. I might have only known you for…" Aiden did a quick calculation. "Forty-two days, eleven hours and about twenty-seven minutes—not that I'm counting—but that's long enough to realize I'm not about to let you go. When you know, you know, right?"

That stifled little gasp was enough to tell Aiden he wasn't the only one who knew, and a sense of calm flooded through him.

"Yes, it'll be tough going, but you know what?" He knelt up, looking Will in the eye. "We will figure it out." He smiled. "You can't control this narrative, Will Bryant, any more than Becca could, and you saw what a mess *she* made of it. So stop trying to make all the pieces fit, and take life as it comes. You have five months until you graduate. And yes, during that time you'll have to make some decisions, but I'm gonna be there to make them with you." He leaned in and kissed Will on the mouth, his hand curved around the back of Will's head. "Do you want to know *why* I'll be there?"

Will swallowed. "I'm sure you're about to tell me."

"Because I *love* you, my stargazing, Douglas Adams-quoting, D & D-playing wonder nerd of a man. And before you tell me it's too soon for me to know that, let me remind you that my dad—"

"Knew he wanted to marry your mom about a month after they started dating," Will finished for him, smiling.

"So there you have it. Knowing our own mind clearly runs in the family. It's in the genes."

Will's breathing hitched. "Apparently it runs in my family too." His face glowed. "I love you too.

I was yours the moment you came to help me up off the floor."

The door opened and Becca burst in. "Oh God."

Aiden lifted his eyebrows. "Come in, Becca. I'm only in the middle of something really important right now."

"Mom's done it again."

"Done what?"

"She's booked us a ballroom for the wedding. July twenty-second." Becca stared at him. "I'm getting married!"

"Make sure she's really booked it this time," Aiden said with a grin.

Becca looked from Aiden to Will. "Have I just interrupted something?"

Will started laughing, and Aiden had to join in. Will helped him to his feet.

"You're fine, Becca." Will gazed at him. "We'd said all the important stuff before you walked in on us."

"What are you all doing up there?" Mom hollered. "Becca, get down here. We've got a wedding to plan."

Becca rolled her eyes. "Coming, Mom."

Will grinned. "You know, I have the strangest feeling of déjà vu." He kissed Aiden on the cheek. "Thank you for listening to all that."

"Well, you've said it now, so you don't have to say it again." Aiden shook his head. "And there I was, looking forward to a relaxing Christmas."

Except he wouldn't change a thing.

CHAPTER TWENTY-FOUR

A Taylor Family Christmas Eve

Saturday, December 24

"Aiden!" Becca yelled. "Your cat is staring at me."

"Take it as a compliment," Will said with a grin. He picked up the catnip mouse Aiden had thrown into Midnight's pet carrier. "Here, kitty. Leave the human alone and come sit with me." Becca and Kristen sat on the rug in front of the fire, surrounded by rolls of wrapping paper, tape, bows, and labels. A Christmas movie was playing on TV, but no one was watching it. Louise and Carl were taking part in another holiday tradition—going from house to house along the short street, taking small gifts to their neighbors and sharing a glass or two of something.

Once they'd left, Aiden had snickered. "Now you know the *real* reason Mom doesn't cook on Christmas Eve."

Becca pointed at Midnight. "Why did you have to bring him anyway?"

"His usual cat sitter is away for the holidays, and seeing as I'm staying here for two nights, I wasn't about to leave him on his own." Aiden took the mouse from Will and dangled it by its tail. "Come on, Midnight."

"So you're telling me Milwaukee doesn't have pet boarding services or Kitty Day Care centers?"

Aiden leaned into Will. "You think if we bribe Midnight with enough kitty treats, he'll shit in her shoes?"

Will had to bite down hard on his laughter.

Midnight didn't budge, but sat at the foot of the beautifully decorated tree, gazing up at it.

Aiden snickered. "You just know he's busy working out the best route to climb to the top before he forces it into submission."

Will chuckled. "I think he's surveying all those presents and trying to work out which ones are his."

Becca froze. "Tell me you didn't buy presents for your cat."

Aiden glared at her, but Will got in first. "Hey. It's Christmas for kitties too, y'know. He's family."

Aiden took Will's hand and kissed his fingers. "And *that* is why I love you."

The sound from the TV died. Becca stared at them, the remote in her hand.

"The L-word? Already?"

Will gave Aiden's thigh a squeeze. "To quote your brother… 'When you know, you know.'"

"Aw, I think they're sweet. You're just jealous." Kristen kissed Becca's shoulder.

Becca widened her eyes. "Why would I be jealous?"

"Because it took you *how long* to get up enough nerve to tell me you loved me?"

She flushed. "Yeah, well—"

"But to be fair," Aiden interjected. "She *has* said it a lot since then." His eyes twinkled. "Mostly when she's on the phone."

"It doesn't matter how long it takes to bring you to the point where you can tell someone how you feel about them." Will's face grew warm, and it had nothing to do with the roaring fire. "What *matters* is that you get there."

Aiden said nothing but raised Will's hand to his lips once more.

"We'd better hurry up." Becca glanced at the clock on the wall. "They'll be back soon, and then we'll have to get going with dinner."

Will peered at the pile of gifts for Louise and Carl with a sigh. "I haven't got them anything."

"Oh, you have." Kristen smiled. "You love their son. That's gotta count for something."

"More than you think. He's *so* unlovable." Becca stuck her tongue out at her brother. Then she frowned. "I'm sorry, that was uncalled for."

Aiden blinked. "Okay, who are you, and what have you done with my sister?"

She rolled her eyes. "I can apologize, can't I? I can be mature."

Will stared at her, then laughed, clutching his stomach. "Please. There's only so much a guy can take."

"Seriously though? I'm really happy for the two of you. Especially my ex-fiancé." Becca smiled. "He's getting a good man."

Aiden tilted his head as he stared at Kristen.

Becca leaned toward her. "There are chips in the kitchen. Would you bring us some? I've got the munchies."

"Sure." Kristen stood and left the room.

Becca regarded Aiden with a forthright glance. "Okay—why are you staring at my fiancée?"

"I'm still getting to know her," Aiden remarked. Then he smiled. "But so far? I gotta say, sis… I really like her."

Becca's face lit up. "She's wonderful, isn't she?" Midnight sprang into her lap and butted her chin with his head. Becca shrieked, sending the cat flying across the room to cower under the side table.

Aiden got up and went to retrieve the kitty. "You really aren't a cat person, are you?" He rejoined Will on the couch, Midnight stepping over Aiden's thigh to climb Will's chest.

"Hey, dogs aren't much better, unless they're the big, wuffly variety and not one of those little yapping rats."

Will scritched behind Midnight's ears. "That was really good, kitty. Do it again. Can you make her jump higher next time, though?"

Becca glared at him.

Kristen walked back into the living room carrying two bags of chips.

"Hey, Kristen, you hadn't planned on having a pet or two when you and Becca get married, had you?" Aiden asked.

Kristen snorted. "Please. I've known her for how long? I know what she's like."

"Hey, if you wanted a pet, I would deal." Becca shrugged. "Who knows, maybe I'd even come to love them."

Aiden's eyes widened. "Holy crap, she really *is* in love."

The front door opened, and Becca made a mad scramble to stuff the unwrapped gifts back into their respective bags. "You're early!" she hollered.

"Want us to go back to Jen and Oliver's?" Carl called out. "I don't think your mom has finished telling them how she makes *her* eggnog and how it's better than anyone else's."

"I wasn't doing that at all," Louise retorted. "Even if it *is* true. I mean, *soy milk*? Really?"

Will chuckled. "I love your parents."

"Is it safe to stick my head around the door?" Carl demanded.

"Sure." Becca hid the bags behind her.

Carl gave Will a warm smile. "We have one more Christmas Eve tradition to come, but that'll be after dinner. Our highly anticipated, secret dinner." He withdrew.

Will turned to look at Aiden. "What *are* we having for dinner?" No one had said as yet.

Aiden grinned. "Pizza."

Will gaped. "You're kidding."

"Hey, we're not talking your everyday, store-bought pizza. This is homemade, with toppings you'll never find at Pizza Hut."

Will bit his lip. "You've brought figs, haven't you?"

Aiden waggled his eyebrows.

Carl's words had intrigued him. "So what's the tradition no one's mentioned yet?"

Becca groaned. "*Someone* not a million miles away took it upon themselves a few years ago to climb up into the attic and root out all Dad's old home movies—and digitize them." She glared at Aiden. "Didn't you, shithead?"

Aiden guffawed. "Yeah, that sounds *so* mature. Those are Mom and Dad's memories you're bitching about. Ours too. And if *I* can put up with your usual comments about the color of my bedroom walls, *you* can stomach Mom *aww*ing about you in your first tutu."

Will had a feeling it was going to be a fun evening.

Carl and Louise were in the armchairs, Becca and Kristen were on one couch, and Will was on the other, Aiden perched on its arm, his laptop on the side table beside him, the projector next to that.

"I love that we still look at these," Louise murmured. "Home movies are a dying art nowadays. Everything's done on phones."

"You can still save videos done on phone, you know," Becca informed her.

"Good. Because I want videos of my first grandchild taking their first step. You got that? I'm putting in my request now."

Carl chuckled. "How about we let the kids get married first?"

"Aw, look at that." Kristen smiled. "Aiden, what is that you were making?"

"A model of the solar system, out of papier mâché and coat hangers."

"How old were you?" Will asked. The little tousled-hair boy was adorable, carefully placing what had to be the sun onto its wire stand.

"Six," Louise told him before Aiden could respond.

Will glanced at Aiden. "You little genius."

Aiden laughed. Then he pointed at the screen Dad had erected. "Aww, look. Becca in her little pink tutu." A chorus of chuckles rippled around the room.

"Do you still wear a tutu?" Louise asked.

Becca rolled her eyes. "Yes, but not that one." She grinned. "Hey, Disneyland! Which means…. Drum roll, if you please…. Aiden getting a hug from Goofy."

"And that's where it all began," Carl observed. Everyone turned to stare at him, Aiden included. "What?" Carl asked with a frown. "Well, Goofy's a boy, right?"

Aiden shook his head.

"And that's Aiden aged fifteen," Louise told Will. "We were going to repaint his bedroom, but he insisted he wanted to do it, right down to choosing the paint."

"See? He was a nerd even then," Becca remonstrated. "Who paints their bedroom walls purple?"

"I was a trendsetter," Aiden retorted.

Will watched as Aiden rolled paint onto the wall before turning to glare at whoever was behind the camera, trying to shoo them from the room.

"And now for the finished article," Carl announced.

Posters covered every inch of wall space.

Will chuckled. "Why go to the bother of painting? You could just have used posters." He had to smile when he peered closer. Handsome faces stared back at him: Taylor Lautner, Zac Efron, Ryan Kwanten, Tyler Posey, Josh Duhamel…

He grinned. "There you go, Carl. I think *that's* when it all began." Then he laughed. "Aww, you had an *Aladdin* poster. How sweet."

Louise chuckled. "I remember that phase. You sure loved *Aladdin*. I bet you wanted to ride that magic carpet."

Becca made a choking sound. "Yeah, Aiden, it was the magic carpet you wanted to ride."

Aiden gave her a hard stare, but the remark seemed to have sailed over his parents' heads. The next section was Aiden's high school graduation. Aiden looked smart in his cap and gown, laughing with his friends.

One in particular caught Will's attention.

"Who's that?"

"His name was Steve Bennow," Aiden told him.

"He was such a good-looking boy," Louise commented. "I liked him."

Becca grinned. "So did Aiden, now I come to think about it." She leaned forward to catch Aiden's attention. "Was he your first crush?"

That earned her another fierce glare.

Will nudged him. "You've got good taste."

Aiden turned to gaze at him. "Yeah, I do,"

he said softly.

Louise sighed. "I wonder where all these young people are now, what they're doing… I lost track of all my high school friends, and yet when I was sixteen, I thought we'd be together for the rest of our lives." She got up from the couch. "More snacks, anyone?"

A chorus of requests followed her out of the room

Aiden paused the recording. "I don't have to wonder where Steve is concerned," he whispered.

"What?"

He removed his phone from his pocket and scrolled. Aiden laid a finger on his lips as he handed the phone to Will.

It took all Will's effort not to gasp. According to the OnlyFans tag at the bottom of the screen, Steve Bennow was now Tyler Raw, and judging by the moans pouring from the guy whose ass he was drilling with a *very* large dick, he was good at what he did.

"Oh my God. Did you know he was gay in high school?" Will kept his voice low.

Aiden gaped. "No! And if I'd known what he'd end up doing, I'd have gotten him to at least give me a blow job."

Will coughed. "I'm glad you waited until your mom had left the room before telling me that." He shifted on the seat cushion, resisting the urge to adjust his crotch.

Aiden grinned. "You got a problem?"

"Yes, I do, and tonight you can help me solve it—as long as you don't make as much noise as Tyler. Because if either of your parents decide to investigate, I'm packing my bag and going back to Minnesota."

Aiden moved in to whisper. "That's what pillows and ball gags are for. To muffle the sound."

Will froze. *Wait.*

"You don't actually *have* a ball gag, do you?"

He just smiled and stroked a finger under Will's chin. "We can talk about it later."

A whole lot later, Will hoped, when there was no chance of being interrupted.

It seemed Christmas had come early, whereas Will would be doing his best not to do so. Well, either that, or come as many times as was possible before Christmas finally arrived.

CHAPTER TWENTY-FIVE

Christmas Day

Aiden loved Christmas morning. The smell of hot chocolate and cinnamon rolls, the sound of wrapping paper tearing, Becca's squeals—they got louder as she got older—Christmas carols playing in the background… The day had always possessed a magic for him, and he'd assumed once he was an adult that the magic would fade away and die.

Will had brought it back, and then some.

Waking up in his old attic room, in the bed he'd known as a teenager, and finding his arms full of Will had been the best Christmas present ever. So what if it had been a bit of a squeeze? Will's bed was bigger, but it was also next door to his parents' room, so hell no to that.

A bit of a squeeze translated into a whole lot of cuddling, and that was just fine by Aiden.

"Morning." Will stretched.

Aiden chuckled. "Don't do that. One of us will fall out of bed, and that would attract way too much attention." He kissed Will's forehead. "Merry Christmas. You get a better kiss after I've brushed my teeth."

"Wow, feeling the romance."

He smiled. "You want romance? Okay, how

about this?" He cupped Will's chin, tilting his face toward Aiden's. "I love you."

The light in Will's eyes sent Aiden's heart soaring.

Will beamed. "I love you too." He burrowed deeper into Aiden's arms. "Can we just spend the day here?"

"That would be a little awkward, seeing as your present is under the tree."

His eyes widened. "You got me a present?"

"Well, that sure woke you up in a hurry." Aiden smiled. "Of course I did." He narrowed his gaze. "Do I have one waiting for me? Not that it matters if I don't, but seeing as you brought up the subject…"

Will said nothing, and that was just torture.

"You did get me something, didn't you?"

"You big kid." Will chuckled against Aiden's chest. "Yes, there's something under the tree for you too." He craned his neck to look Aiden in the eye. "And even if I hadn't *bought* you a present, I still have something for you. Only thing is, you have to find it first, and that might take some doing, because I've hidden it."

"Do I get a clue?"

Will grinned. "It's in my ass, and you'll need something long to reach it."

Aiden brought Will's hand to his morning wood. "Think this'll do the trick?"

Warm fingers curled around his shaft. "Why don't we find out?"

Carl and Louise had made French toast for breakfast, and as soon as everyone had finished, they got down to the all-important task of opening presents. It seemed another Taylor tradition was for Becca to dole out the presents, and it didn't take Will long to see a theme—Becca and Kristen had bought him D & D gifts: a bookmark, a thermos mug, and a portable rolling tray for dice. She'd even gotten something for Midnight—a cardboard box to play in.

With each gift, Will's excitement blossomed, until he couldn't keep still. He'd gotten the *perfect* present for Aiden.

"Where's mine?" Aiden demanded.

Will was off the couch in a heartbeat, making a beeline for the package he'd placed there the night before. He gave the flat rectangular gift to Aiden. "Merry Christmas."

To his surprise, Aiden didn't open it but stared at it.

"What's wrong?"

Aiden placed the gift on the coffee table. "Becca, can you hand me that present, please?" He pointed. "The one in the dark blue paper."

She gave it to him, and Aiden placed it in Will's hands.

He stilled. The two packages were an identical size and weight. "No," he whispered. "We couldn't have… It has to be a coincidence." His heart pounding, Will tore off the paper, and burst out laughing when he saw the framed certificate with its gold foil seal. "I don't believe this."

Aiden had named a star Will Bryant.

The certificate had the star's coordinates and the date it had been registered with the International Space Registry. Will gazed at it, unable to stop smiling.

"You like it?"

Will chuckled. "Like doesn't even come close." He inclined his head toward the table. "Open your present."

"I have a feeling I know what I'm going to find."

Will still couldn't believe they'd both had the same idea, but he loved the notion that two stars in the heavens bore their names.

Carl gaped at the two identical certificates. "Did you two—"

"Yes, they did." Becca snorted. "And if that doesn't tell you they were made for each other…."

Will gazed into Aiden's eyes. "Becca, it only confirms what I already knew."

"What's that?"

He smiled. "Your brother was Taylor-made for me."

Aiden beamed, leaning in as if to kiss him, while Carl applauded.

"Aiden? Your turn to set the table," Louise shouted.

He sighed. "Hold that thought." He got up

and walked into the dining room.

Will's phone buzzed on the table, shattering the moment. He glanced at the screen. "It's my dad." He clicked on Answer. "Merry Christmas."

"Merry Christmas, son. Is it a good one so far?"

Will smiled. "It might even qualify as the best yet."

"In that case I'm happy you're there, even if it *is* a little strange not having you here." Dad chuckled. "First Christmas *that's* happened."

"I'll be there for New Year's," Will promised. "With Aiden."

"Ah, that's what I wanted to talk to you about. Don't rush back here on our account. You've been working hard these last months. Once you're back at school, you're into the home stretch. Take some time to relax. And don't worry about introducing us to Aiden. We'll meet him some other time. I'm assuming he'll be here for Commencement?"

Will hadn't thought that far ahead. "I'll ask him. It's on a Saturday, so he won't need time off from his job."

"Then we'll get to meet him then." Dad chuckled. "You do know he and your mom are going to talk school?"

He laughed. "Yes, I figured."

"Merry Christmas, baby," his mom shouted in the background. "Sending you Christmas hugs."

"Sending some of my own your way, Mom."

"Hang on, your brother wants a word."

There was a pause, then Ethan almost deafened him with a yell of "Merry Christmas!"

"Try that again, but a little louder this time," Dad said. "That way, Will should be able to hear you all the way over there in Wisconsin."

Ethan ignored the comment. "This guy of yours—Aiden, is that his name?—is he the one we were talking about?"

"The same." Will watched Aiden as he laid the silverware on the table.

"So I take it he *is* into guys after all." Ethan snickered. "Lucky Will. Well, you certainly got what *you* wanted for Christmas." Another pause. "Is he how you imagined he'd be?"

Will smiled. "Better."

"Then I'm happy for you. So when do I get to grill—I mean, meet him?"

He snorted. "I'm suddenly rethinking the whole idea of introducing you to him."

"Joking aside, we *do* get to meet him, right?"

Will's heart pounded when Aiden turned to face him and mouthed *I love you.*

"Yeah, you'll meet him."

"I mean, we need to make sure he's not like that time when you had a 'boyfriend in Canada'.

"Oh, screw you. I was twelve. And I only did it because you were being a dick."

Ethan laughed. "Yeah, good times, good times. So you think this one is gonna stick around?"

"Hopefully for a long time to come." His heartbeat raced. What came to mind was a tattoo he'd seen once in a porn video.

Tomorrow is never promised.

Right then, Will would take whatever tomorrow would bring.

All was right with Aiden's world. It had been a day filled with gifts, good food, Christmas movies, and a lot of laughter. But sitting on the couch with Will, the fire still burning, the lights still twinkling, and everyone else upstairs in bed?

Talk about the perfect end to a perfect day.

Will got up and put another log on the fire, and Aiden chuckled. "We should be thinking about letting it die, not keeping it going."

Will grabbed the throw from the back of the couch. "Want to lie under this with me and stare at the pretty lights?"

Aiden made room for him, and they snuggled under the throw. He listened to the crackle of the logs and watched the flames dance behind the grate, his arm draped over Will's waist. "This was a good idea."

Will let out a happy sigh. "Do you think your parents would mind if I slept on the couch tonight? I want to enjoy this for as long as it lasts."

Aiden bent down to kiss him, slow and sweet. "And I want to enjoy this." He slid his hand down Will's torso, until he encountered firmness. Aiden's fingers fumbled as he tried to pop the button and lower the zipper on Will's jeans one-handed.

Will's low moan when Aiden reached into his briefs to curl his hand around Will's cock was the best accompaniment ever.

"You feel good," Aiden whispered.

"*That* feels good."

"It would feel even better if you took your clothes off."

Will froze, his eyes wide, the firelight catching in them. "Excuse me?" He pointed to the ceiling. "That's your parents' bedroom right there. And Becca is over there." He chuckled. "Kristen too. Although I don't know that for certain, I don't believe for a second that Becca would let them spend the night apart."

"I promise to be quiet." Aiden grinned. "And I'll also close the door."

Will snorted. "Uh, excuse me? I've been in bed with you. Unless we have that aforementioned ball gag, you can't *do* quiet."

Aiden grinned. "Okay, but if I have something in my mouth…."

Will stared at him. "You're incorrigible."

"Aha. I *thought* that last comment might do the trick." Aiden grinned. "And the definition of incorrigible is hiding a bottle of lube under the seat cushion for just such an opportunity."

Will shook his head. "The Vogons nailed it, didn't they? Resistance really *is* useless."

Christmas was always magical in Will's book, but that night brought a new kind of magic—a sexy, sensual kind involving firelight dancing over naked flesh, bodies entwined on a fireside rug, leisurely kisses that seemed to go on and on…The knowledge they could be discovered at any time added a frisson to their fuck.

Except this went *way* beyond a fuck.

Will strove to burn it all into his memory: Aiden on his back on the couch, his mouth around Will's dick while Will sucked him off; riding Aiden's cock, Aiden's hand covering Will's mouth; and Aiden kneeling on the couch, Will behind him, moving in and out of him, doing his best to slow things down because *dammit*, he wanted this to last.

It wasn't only a matter of keeping his climax at bay—it was more a case that he wanted to prolong the sensuous pleasure, the sheer *joy* accompanying every thrust, every look, every moan, every kiss… When they got too close, Will backed off and they stroked and kissed, until once more his need overtook his desire to make it last all night.

Will knew that wasn't about to happen, but that didn't stop him from doing his damnedest. The sound of footsteps on the floor above had them both freezing more than once, waiting until Will was certain Carl wasn't going to walk through the door.

Aiden touched his face. "Make me come?"

Will answered him with a kiss, and Aiden cradled him with his body as Will picked up the pace, sharing kisses as Will drove them to the point of no return. And when Aiden came, Will held him and kissed him, caressed him…

Told him Will loved him.

They lay under the throw, the fire finally dying, its embers glowing red. The only light in the room came from the Christmas tree, and Will would have been content to fall asleep staring at it, Aiden in his arms.

Except that couldn't happen. Fortunately, however, there was always the haven of Aiden's attic room, and once they'd tidied up and removed any sign of what they'd been doing, they crept upstairs, wincing when the narrow stairs creaked, betraying them.

Will loved it when Aiden curled around him, holding him close, but now he realized nights like this were coming to an end. Once New Year's had come and gone, it would be back to college, to phone calls, video calls, emails…

"Stop it," Aiden whispered.

Will turned his head. "Stop what?"

"You think you're the only one? I don't want this to end any more than you do. But there *are* trains between Milwaukee and Minnesota, you know. We'll see each other."

"You say that *now*."

Aiden cupped his chin. "Yes, I do. And I promise to try, but we both know what's in store for us. How much work we both have to do." Aiden kissed his forehead. "None of that is going to stop me loving you, okay?"

Will smiled. "Okay. Now kiss me again before I fall asleep."

So I can dream of you.

Of us.

CHAPTER TWENTY-SIX

Aiden and Will See In The New Year

Friday, December 30

Aiden switched off the engine and gazed at the three-story blue-and-white house. Two huge trees stood in front of it, and wooden steps led up to the front porch, on which sat a jolly, round Santa with a great smile. On the door was a wreath covered in blue lights, and a layer of snow lay on the veranda railing. Someone had cleared a path from the sidewalk to the house, and the driveway was filled with cars.

"When do your folks take the decorations down?"

Will chuckled. "When Mom says they've been up long enough, which is usually the day after New Year's." He pointed to the highest window set in the apex of the front gable. "That's my room."

"Did you grow up here?"

"We moved here when I was twelve," Will told him. He grinned. "I can't wait to see their faces. I love surprising them."

Aiden snorted. "Pull this kinda surprise on *my* mom, and she'd shit a brick." Although Will's dad had stressed there was no need for them to schedule a visit, Will had suggested spending New

Year's with his family.

Aiden liked the idea that Will wanted them to meet him. He was also curious to meet Will's parents.

Curious—and nervous as hell.

"Will there be room for us?" he asked. "Seeing as they don't know we're coming."

"Plenty—there are seven bedrooms. Mom and Dad each have a study, but there are sofa beds in both rooms. Ethan's room became Mom's craft room once he moved out. There's only Emma left now, since Dee got married last year."

Aiden shivered. "Why are we sitting out here in my truck when we could be inside, drinking hot chocolate?"

"Because I wanted to do this without an audience." Will twisted in his seat, cupped Aiden's cheek with a gloved hand, and leaned in to kiss him, a slow, sweet kiss that sent a rush of warmth flooding through him.

"Do I get to sleep with you?" he murmured against Will's lips.

Will smiled. "Sleep? Yes. My parents will be okay with that—at least, they'd better be, seeing as Ethan and Dee have already blazed that particular trail." His fingers were gentle on Aiden's face. "And in case I haven't told you yet, thank you for driving us here, especially because it means you'll be going back on your own."

Aiden huffed. "I'm gonna have music blasting out the speakers the whole time. And you *should* be thankful. I'm sparing you more than five hours in the company of the brides-to-be, because you *know*, all you'd hear is dress this, flowers that, music, bridesmaids…"

Will laughed. "Seems as if I got off lightly."

"Speaking of getting off… Are we *only* going to be sleeping under your parents' roof?"

Will stroked his chin. "Now, let me see. There'll be my parents, my grandmother, Ethan and his wife Marley, Dee and her husband Gavin, you, me, and Emma." He rolled his eyes. "What do *you* think?"

"So we don't get to let the New Year in with a bang?" Aiden quipped.

Will narrowed his gaze. "You packed that ball gag, didn't you?"

"Maybe?" Aiden chuckled. "Well, you did buy it for me for Christmas, didn't you?"

"Sure—as a joke gift." He chuckled. "Or should that be a *gag* gift?"

"You're hilarious." Aiden trailed a finger along Will's thigh, heading north. "And we did have fun with it, didn't we?"

Will let out a snort. "Yes, *you* did."

A squeal filled the air. "Will Bryant, you sneaky little—"

Aiden laughed. "That's gotta be your mom." He grabbed the box of cookies from the back seat. "Can't forget these." A present from his mom to Will's.

He'd never let Will see his nerves, not in a million years. Sure, it was daunting. A teacher for a mom, a professor for a dad…Aiden wanted to make a good impression, because *dammit*, this was important.

You're no slouch in the brains department, you just remember that. They don't give degrees in Physics to just anyone, right?

Will had said more than once that they would love him.

He should know, right?

And right then, Will's mom was walking over to the truck, bundled up in a thick coat, galoshes, and a knitted hat complete with ear flaps, beaming at them.

Yeah, it was going to be okay.

Dad handed Will a cup of hot chocolate. "You seem to have lost a boyfriend."

He chuckled. "He's in Mom's study. I guess they're talking teaching—again." From the dining room came laughter and raised voices. Will smiled. "Ethan's got everyone playing Clue again, doesn't he?" It was another family tradition.

"So why are you in here and not there?"

"I could ask you the same question, but I already know the answer." Will snorted. "Ethan is *way* too competitive. Every game becomes a battle to be won. And I was hoping for a little peace and quiet. I haven't stopped talking since we got here."

"Well, what did you expect when you bring home your first boyfriend?"

He blinked. "Who said he's my first?"

"He's the first who was important enough for you to let us meet him," Dad retorted. "So… are we going to have another teacher in the family?"

Will burst out laughing. "I swear… you and Louise are out of the same mold."

"That's Aiden's mom?"

"Yes." Will peered at his dad. "Did Ethan tell you what's been going on these last few weeks?"

Dad huffed. "Are you kidding? He's as secretive as you." He frowned. "So what *has* been happening?"

Will began with Becca's shock announcement, and told the story all the way through to Kristen's proposal. Dad listened, occasionally laughing and gasping. When Will was done, Dad shook his head.

"Wow. It's like something out of a movie." Then he narrowed his gaze. "Hey, wait a minute—what were you implying before? Same mold? Can you *really* see me or your mother suggesting you two get married? With everything *you've* got planned?"

"Maybe not, but—"

"But nothing. All I'm saying is that after watching the pair of you, I get the feeling Aiden is here to stay." He cocked his head. "I'm right, aren't I?"

Will smiled. "I hope so. It's early days."

"I'm glad. I like him. Your mom does too, and not just because he brought cookies. Those were delicious." Dad grinned. "They were also gone before I could blink." He paused. "Can I ask… with all these visits to Milwaukee, all these wedding preparations, when did you find time to study?"

He chuckled. "Don't worry, Dad. The

exams went just fine. And Aiden and me, we've discussed my plans for the future."

"So he knows what to expect?"

Will nodded. "He's behind me, one hundred percent." He glanced at Dad. "Just like Mom was for you, when you were at school. You both lived off her teaching salary, didn't you?"

Dad smiled. "She was my rock." His eyes gleamed. "Could Aiden be yours?"

Will grinned. "I can't hide anything from you, can I?" He sipped his hot chocolate.

"It's serious, isn't it?" Before Will could come up with a reply, Dad held up his hand. "I'm not going to tell you you're too young to fall in love. You're old enough to know your own mind, your own emotions. I also know that when you want something, you go for it. So what I'm saying is… if your mom and I can be of help—financially, at least—we're only too willing to support you and Aiden." He smiled. "We've been there, remember?"

"Don't you think you've done enough?" Will sighed. "You and Mom have been putting money aside for my studies ever since I told you I wanted to work for NASA."

"No one ever said getting a good education was cheap. And you have the potential to be a bright star in NASA's firmament, so whatever it takes to get you there?" He shrugged. "We'll do it, happily." He leaned back in his armchair. "How long do we have the pleasure of your company?"

"A few days, then I'll be back at school." He chuckled. "Aiden too."

He wasn't looking forward to being separated, now there were no excuses to make the trip to Milwaukee, and he wasn't sure how long he could go without Aiden's hugs and kisses.

And the rest.

Saturday, December 31
11:55p.m.

Aiden watched Will's mom—*Rachel, remember? She said to call her Rachel*—buzzing around the room, making sure everyone had a glass of whatever they were going to toast the New Year in with before the ball dropped.

"It's not exactly a tradition, more a superstition," Will whispered. "She thinks it's bad luck not to have a drink ready."

"Aw, Mom. Coke? Really?" Emma whined, as Rachel handed her a glass.

Aiden liked Will's little sister. She reminded him of Becca. Both of them were feisty, with a wicked tongue and an even more wicked sense of humor.

Rachel rolled her eyes. "Yes, really. You're seventeen."

"Aw, please? Can't I have something harder?"

"Sure you can—in four years' time."

Emma snorted. "You think I'm gonna wait

that long before I take a drink? Mom, what planet are you on?"

Rachel's lips twitched. "I don't think I'm being unrealistic or even overly idealistic in wanting you to refrain from alcohol until you're of legal age."

"Can I remind both of you that it's almost midnight?" Will's Dad—David—shook his head. "Can't you hug it out so we can go into 2023 on a good note?"

Emma grinned. "Sure, Dad. It'd be an even better start to the year if I had some of Ethan's hard cider."

"Dream on, kid." Ethan sat on one of the huge couches with his wife Marley, and next to them were Dee and her husband Gavin, all of them watching the TV where scenes from New York's Time Square were showing.

Aiden slipped his arm around Will's waist. "You were right. Your family is really cool."

Will turned to him, his eyes shining. "I know, right?"

"Well, if you want to get the New Year off to a fantastic start, I guess now is a good time to share our news." Ethan's face glowed. "Mom? Dad? How do you feel about becoming grandparents? We were thinking June might be nice for it."

New York was forgotten as the room erupted into an explosion of congratulations, and Aiden got caught up in the swell of emotion—until Will hollered.

"Hey, the countdown's started!"

Everyone joined in, getting louder the closer they got to midnight, and when 'Happy New Year!" burst from the speakers, Aiden clinked glasses with

Will.

"To 2023."

Will chuckled. "To a degree, with the promise of more to come."

Aiden couldn't resist the siren call of those lips. "To us."

Will took Aiden's glass, deposited it on the side table along with his own, then took Aiden in his arms.

When Will's mouth was inches from his, Aiden smiled. "I thought you didn't want an audience."

"I changed my mind." Will's lips met his, and Aiden met the kiss with equal enthusiasm.

Someone started the applause, but Aiden didn't see who it was—he was too busy kissing the man who had come to mean everything to him.

The man he would do anything to hold onto.

CHAPTER TWENTY-SEVEN

Will Contemplates His Future

Friday, February 10, 2023

Will ate his lunch, dividing his time between his sandwich and his book. He hadn't seen Becca for a few days, but he knew she was rehearsing for a performance the following week. Besides, when she wasn't dancing or studying, she was with Kristen.

Will was surprised by how much he missed having her around.

Get used to it. There's a wedding coming, remember? They've got a lot to do.

He knew it wasn't just Becca's absence fueling his present melancholy state.

He missed Aiden so much it hurt.

They'd promised to visit each other, but what with Aiden's job and his studies, those promises seemed to have been put on the back burner. Plus there was his application to do his master's.

That meant two more years in Minnesota.

Two more years away from Aiden.

Becca doesn't know how lucky she is, having Kristen so close by.

Yeah, Will was depressed as fuck.

His phone vibrated, and seeing Aiden's name lifted his spirits a little.

Can you talk?

He clicked Call. "You on your lunch break?"

"Yeah. Sorry to call during the day, but—"

"Don't you *ever* apologize for calling me," Will ground out. "You have no idea how happy you just made me. I mean it."

There was a pause. "I miss you too."

That sent warmth rushing through him. "It's Valentine's Day on Tuesday."

"I know. Our first Valentine's, and we're apart." Aiden sighed. "I know there'll be others, but still…"

Will knew that too. It didn't improve the situation, however.

"What are Becca and Kristen doing to celebrate?"

Will snorted. "How would I know? I don't see much of her these days. And if I did, I wouldn't ask."

"Why not?"

His sigh matched Aiden's. "I guess I'm too jealous."

"Poor baby."

Will chuckled. "I hope you're not in the teachers' lounge."

"God forbid. I'm in my classroom." There was a moment's hesitation before Aiden spoke. "Want me to make it better?"

"And how are you going to do that?"

"You leave that part to me. So, what excitement do you have planned for this evening?

What *is* there to do in Minnesota on a Friday night?"

Will laughed. "Grab a pizza, a couple of beers, and watch a movie. *If* I can tear myself away from my books." He glanced at the clock on the cafeteria wall. "Damn. I have to go. Got a class."

"Yeah, but one more class is one step closer to your degree, think of it that way."

Will smiled. "I prefer to think of it in terms of one step closer to spending time with you after May thirteenth."

"Is that when you graduate?"

"Yeah. Then I get a couple of months before I climb back on the carousel."

"Go to your class. I'll call you tonight, okay?"

"I look forward to that." Will lowered his voice. "Make it a late video call, and I'll look forward to it even more."

"Hey, Will?"

"Yes?"

Aiden's deep, resonant voice filled his ears. "Love you."

He let out a sigh. "That was the best thing you could have said right now. Love you too." He hung up, then deposited his debris in the trash.

Another class.

Another weekend looming without Aiden.

For the first time Will was getting tired of student life. He wanted what Becca and Kristen shared—the best of both worlds.

What wouldn't I give for that?

Will glanced at his phone. Nine forty-five, and still no call from Aiden.

Maybe I should call him. I did say two-way traffic, right?

He'd also told Aiden to make it a late call, and apparently Aiden was following his instructions to the letter.

Then his phone burst into life, and Will grabbed it. "I was beginning to think you'd forgotten me."

"Since we've known each other our entire lives, it's not likely I'd forget about you. Well, not really our entire lives—it just feels that way."

Will sighed. "Oh, Becca."

Her gasp filled his ears. "What do you mean, 'oh, Becca'?"

"Sorry. I thought it might be Aiden."

"Then *I'm* sorry to disappoint you. Listen—"

His phone buzzed and this time he checked the screen. "I have to go. It's him!" And without another word, he disconnected.

He'd make it up to her later.

"Hey."

"Hey yourself. How was the pizza?"

"It was good. I didn't finish it, though. But

wasn't it you who said leftover pizza was the breakfast of champions?"

Aiden laughed. "Yeah, I did. Which toppings did you go for?"

Will snorted. "You really want to waste a phone call on pizza toppings?"

"Hey, I'm an interested party. I want to know what I'm having for breakfast."

For…

Will froze. "Where are you?"

"Freezing my ass off, waiting by the main door for you to let me in."

Will's brain was on a go slow. "You… you're downstairs?"

"Didn't I just say that? I checked I'm at the right building. But if you leave me out here much longer, something vital is gonna get frostbite and drop off, so it's in your best interests to get down here and let me the fuck in."

"On my way." Will hung up. He didn't bother putting on shoes, but grabbed his keys and ran out of the apartment, almost flying down the stairs. When he reached the lobby, his heart skipped a beat to see Aiden standing on the other side of the glass, a bag slung over one shoulder.

Thank you, God.

Will opened the door and virtually dragged Aiden through it. Cold lips met his, and Will squealed when Aiden slid an icy hand under the waistband of his jeans.

"How long have you been outside?"

"Uber dropped me off about ten minutes ago. I've been walking around since, looking for the building. This place is huge."

Will flung his arms around Aiden and kissed him, not caring who saw them. A ripple of applause brought a chuckle from Aiden.

"Maybe we should sell tickets," he muttered.

Will took his hand and led him toward the stairs.

"What happened to the guided tour? Don't I get to see where you live?"

"Yes—in the morning."

Aiden laughed. "Eager much?"

Will didn't reply, but tugged him along the hallway. "This is mine." He opened the door and they went inside. Once he'd locked and bolted it, Will didn't hesitate. He pushed Aiden against the wall and kissed him hard on the mouth, pinning Aiden there. Aiden looped his arms around Will's neck, his tongue going deep, both of them feeding each other soft moans and grunts.

"I'm guessing you like my surprise," Aiden murmured, pausing to kiss Will's neck.

"How… how did you get here?"

"I was out of school two minutes after the bell," Aiden told him. "Made it to the airport in about fifteen minutes. I was booked on the five-twenty flight. Got in at nine." He gave a throaty chuckle. "And I'm all yours until about six-thirty on Sunday, which is when I fly home, so make the most of me."

Will grinned. "You didn't really want to see the sights tomorrow, did you?"

Aiden pulled him close. "The only thing I wanna see is the inside of these four walls." His breath tickled Will's neck. "Now, how about you show me which one of these doors leads to your bedroom?"

"Past the sink and turn right."

Aiden picked Will up in his arms. "Then what are we waiting for?"

"This looks like a good place to live," Aiden murmured into Will's hair. They lay beneath the comforter, Aiden curled around him, his hand over Will's heart, Will's hand covering his. Aiden had no idea of the time. He only knew they'd both seemed hellbent on making up for lost time—and lost opportunities.

Aiden doubted there was a drop of cum left in either of them.

"It is," Will said after a moment. "Which is just as well, because I'm going to be here for a while. Like, about seven years." Aiden reached over him to turn on the lamp, and Will blinked in the light that flooded the compact bedroom. "Something I said?"

"Yes. Well, something you wrote in a message last week, actually."

Will rolled to face him. "You'll have to remind me."

"You were talking about your master's. Have you sent in your application yet?"

"That's what my dad asked yesterday. It's on

my To Do list for the weekend," Will told him.

Aiden heaved a sigh of relief. "I hoped that was the case."

Will gave him a puzzled glance. "What do you mean?" He stilled. "You know I can't get where I want to be without more studying, right?"

Aiden smiled. "I know. And I'm not here to ask you *not* to apply." He stroked Will's bare shoulder. "I'm here to suggest an alternative."

Will blinked. "Consider me hooked. What alternative?"

Aiden sat up and leaned against the pillows. "I can see why you'd want to stay here. Your family is here, after all. *But*…there's also the University of Wisconsin-Madison."

Will opened his mouth, but Aiden held his hand up.

"Just hear me out, okay? I've done a lot of research into this. UW-Madison is the flagship institution of our state, with a large, well-established astrophysics department."

"And how do you know that?" Will teased.

Aiden rolled his eyes. "Duh, I don't know. Because I can *read*, maybe? It's also got a healthy number of faculty members, not to mention research opportunities, and resources dedicated to the field. Plus, their Space, Science, and Engineering Center and the Department of Astronomy have got a really good rep for their research in various areas of astrophysics." Aiden cocked his head to one side. "Did you know that out of 4,665 institutions in the US, only one hundred forty-six are rated R1 for their research activity? That's the highest rating from the Carnegie Foundation. And in Wisconsin, both Madison and Milwaukee have R1 status."

Will smiled. "You *have* done your homework, haven't you? I hate to break it to you, but the University of Minnesota *also* has an R1 rating. That's why I was planning on continuing my studies here."

"I know. But I have one more important detail that might sway you to apply to Madison."

"And what's that?"

Aiden looked him in the eye. "According to Google Maps, it's one hour and twenty-two minutes—fastest route, at any rate—from UW-Madison to my front door. And any way you look at it, that's a damn sight better than five hours plus."

Will's pulse quickened. *No kidding.*

Aiden took Will's hand in his. "I'm not asking you to consider studying for your master's and your PHD at an inferior institution—Madison is definitely up there with the best."

He was preaching to the choir. Will had done his own research. "Then why—"

"I'm asking you to consider moving for purely selfish reasons. I don't think I'm cut out for a long-distance relationship. And while a five-hour drive might not seem all *that* much, that's before you factor in your studies and my job." Aiden stared at him. "What about you? Are *you* cut out for long-distance relationships?"

Will didn't even have to think about it. "No. I don't think so."

Aiden squared his shoulders. "My final point? There are high schools everywhere, even in Madison, believe it or not. If a vacancy turns up that I can apply for, you'd better believe my application will be winging its way before you can say Jack Robinson." Aiden frowned. "And while we're on the subject, just who the fuck is Jack Robinson anyhow?"

Will stared at their joined hands.

He'd be less than ninety minutes away.

We could see each other every weekend. Hell, maybe on school nights too.

He'd even move schools to be closer to me.

It really was a no-brainer.

Then logic kicked in.

He cleared his throat. "This assumes I could get a place. It's really tough to get into Madison. The acceptance rate for a master's is just over twenty-five percent."

Aiden's eyes twinkled. "So you *have* considered this already."

"Maybe? Plus, we're talking scoring a 1500 GRE."

"And are you on course to achieve that?" Aiden didn't break eye contact.

"Yes, I think so. But I'm sure the deadline for applications has passed."

"Then you apply for fall 2024, and we find you a job in the meantime, preferably one related to your field. By the way, Madison likes the idea of attending different institutions. They see it as an important way of widening your intellectual breadth, helping you to grow as a scientist—and a human being." Aiden grinned. "I read that somewhere."

Will shook his head. "You have all the answers, don't you?"

Aiden arched his eyebrows. "Just look at my incentives." He crooked his finger. "Come here."

Will shifted in the bed to straddle Aiden's hips, and Aiden cupped Will's nape, drawing him in for a slow, tender kiss. Their foreheads met in the way Will loved.

"You can do this," Aiden said in a low voice. "And I'll be there for you every step of the way."

"Hell of a time to be having such a deep conversation," Will observed.

Aiden glanced toward the window. "It's still dark out. How about we get under the covers and sleep?"

Will was too excited to sleep.

"I have a better idea."

Sunday, February 12

Aiden checked his phone. "Uber will be here in three minutes." Not that he wanted to go.

Not having to share Will with anyone had been awesome.

If this is a taste of what life with him could be like? Bring it on.

"I'll see you at Easter," Will confirmed. "And after that…"

"I know. Full speed ahead to your finals."

"Will you come to my graduation? It'll be May thirteenth, at Huntington Bank Stadium."

Aiden's eyes shone. "I'll be here. I'll be the one with the huge sign."

Will stared at him in horror. "What sign?"

"I'm yanking your chain." He grinned. "Besides, they probably wouldn't let me into the stadium with a sign that says '*You did it! You graduated. Now you're like smart and stuff*.'"

Will narrowed his gaze. "I hope you're still yanking my chain."

"There's something else of yours I'd prefer to be yanking."

He rolled his eyes. "Seriously? After all the time we spent in bed this weekend?"

"Don't forget on the couch. In the shower. On the countertop."

Will snorted. "I won't forget that last one, that's for sure."

"Hey, who knew lube would make the surface slippery?"

Will gaped. "Er, hello? It's *lube*? That's what it does."

Aiden bit his lip. "How's the bruise?"

"Oh, trust me. If you didn't have to leave right now, you'd be kissing it until it was gone."

"And if you weren't so sleep-deprived

because we've spent every available minute fucking, you'd have realized you didn't have to ask me to your graduation. Because it's also Becca's graduation too, remember?"

Will chuckled. "I don't think either of us is her favorite person right now. First, I cut her off because you got here, and then you didn't even tell her you were here."

Aiden laughed. "Yeah, she was *so* pissed. She'll get over it. I'm guessing Kristen will help with that."

A car pulled up outside.

Damn it.

Aiden took Will in his arms for one last hug. "See you at Easter."

Will chuckled. "Shouldn't that be 'See you tonight'?"

Video calls would have to do until Aiden had the real thing.

Will kissed him, and Aiden poured all his love into the embrace. Then he walked through the door and over to the waiting car.

May couldn't come fast enough.

CHAPTER TWENTY-EIGHT

Aiden And Will Do It Again

Saturday, May 13

Will had to admit, Kristen had scored a hit. "This place is awesome." He'd read about Owamni by the Sioux Chef, but had never ventured through its doors. The Indigenous menu, with its elk tacos, braised duck, and bison and walnut soup, was unlike anything he'd eaten before, and he'd eagerly anticipated the meal.

He wasn't disappointed. The food was sublime.

The company was pretty good too, especially the good-looking guy seated next to him. Because Aiden in a suit?

Hot.

Kristen beamed. "I'm so glad I booked this months ago."

The place was packed with graduates and their families, but Will saw at a glance that theirs was the biggest gathering. The restaurant had put two tables together end-to-end to accommodate the eleven diners.

Three families gathered around one long table. Everyone was talking up a storm. Will's parents and

Aiden's had clicked almost instantaneously. Kristen's parents, Roger and Fliss, had hit it off with Carl and Louise, and from the scraps Will had overheard, the two moms were deep into wedding mode.

Carl caught him looking, and chuckled. "And that's the last we'll hear from Louise for a while."

"I heard that." Louise narrowed her gaze, then dove right back into her conversation.

Dad added his chuckle. "I went through this when our daughter Dee got married. You have my sympathies."

Carl blinked. "You mean it gets worse?"

Dad guffawed. "Oh, much, much worse. You've got weeks to go. But the relief when it's over?" He grinned. "You'll *love* that part."

"Oh, I like this." Mom read aloud from the menu card. "'We aim to serve food honoring the people whose land on which we are standing, land known as Mni Sota Makoce, Land Where the Waters Reflect the Clouds.'" She smiled. "That's beautiful."

Dad nodded.

"Well, this is my first time in a restaurant that didn't serve pork, or chicken, or beef, and you know what? I didn't miss any of them." Ethan grinned. "That bison taco was amaze-balls. All of it was, to be fair. I think this was our reward for sitting through that senator's speech."

Dad rolled his eyes. "It's Commencement. What did you expect—a movie?"

"No, but popcorn would have been a bonus." That raised a few chuckles.

"No one said you had to come, you know," Will commented.

Ethan's eyes sparkled. "What—and miss seeing my little brother dressed in his cap and gown?"

Will mouthed *Thank you.*

Aiden sat next to Will, their hands joined under the table every chance they got. Will leaned into him. "And thank you for *not* bringing a sign."

He chuckled. "You're welcome."

Will gazed at their families. "You'd think they'd known each other for years."

"And you'll get to see them all again in July." Aiden raised his voice. "Isn't that right, Becca?

She groaned. "Please, no more wedding talk, okay? I'm stressed enough as it is."

Louise gaped at her. "*You're* stressed? And what precisely has stressed you out? Are *you* the one organizing the flowers? The catering? The printing? The band? Oh, wait a minute—no, you're not, because that would be me."

"Don't let her fool you," Carl said with a smile. "She's loving every second of it."

Louise flushed, and Becca chuckled. "He got you there, Mom." She glanced at Aiden and Will, then back to Louise. "But seeing as you're doing all this organizing, we could always make it a double wedding." She grinned. "Why should I be the only one to suffer?"

Will shook his head. "Again with this? You're persistent, I'll give you that." Her words had been enough to set his heart racing. She'd come out with them right on cue.

"But it's such a *practical* idea," Louise

remonstrated. "Everything's booked. All you'd have to do would be invite your family, Will, and just show up. Easiest wedding ever."

Becca gave an evil grin. "Yeah, Aiden's already got his suit. I was hoping to make him one of my bridesmaids, but the dress wouldn't fit."

"It wasn't his color either," Kristen added.

Dad fired Will an amused glance, and Will rolled his eyes.

"Okay, you were right. You're not that bad."

Dad beamed. "Thank you." He paused, his eyes twinkling. "Although Louise *does* have a point."

Will gave him a mock glare, even though his heart was racing harder than before.

Aiden leaned in close and whispered, "Whatever I say next? Play along."

Will blinked. He had his own agenda, and he hoped Aiden wasn't about to ruin it.

Aiden cleared his throat. "Sorry, Mom, but there's no way Will and I can get married in July."

Everyone stopped talking, and all heads turned in their direction.

Not following suit was a huge effort.

What are you up to, Aiden?

Louise stared at him. "But why not?"

"Because we were married last month."

Will had to bite his tongue.

"Is this true?" Will hated his mom's dismayed expression.

"Where?" Louise demanded, before he could come up with an answer.

"The Minneapolis Courthouse."

"How could you do such a thing?" she shrieked.

Carl squeezed her arm. “Sweetheart? You’re scaring people. You might want to remember you’re in a public place.”

She blinked. “What? Oh. Right.” She leaned forward, her gaze locked on Aiden. “You got married—without inviting any of your family? Or even telling us?”

Aiden shrugged. “We took photos. You can see them, if you like.”

Will was starting to see the funny side.

“It was a lovely ceremony,” he said with a smile. “Midnight was the ring bearer.” Aiden’s hand tightened around his, and he coughed.

Louise’s jaw dropped. “What?”

“How did you get him to do that?” Becca asked.

Aiden grinned. “We laid a trail of kitty treats down the aisle.”

Carl burst out laughing. “You had me going for a minute, but that last part was a giveaway.” His eyes twinkled. “Nice prank, son. Seriously good effort—almost as good as mine.” Becca and Kristen applauded, and Aiden gave a half bow.

Louise sagged with obvious relief. “You just made that up, didn’t you?”

Aiden laughed. “Oh Mom, your face…”

Dad chuckled. “That was a good one.” He glanced at Carl. “Remind me to ask you later about some of these pranks you’ve pulled.”

Carl grinned. “Sure.”

Will glared at Aiden. “*Now* look what you’ve done.”

“I still don’t see why it’s such an out-there idea,” Louise protested.

Now.

"Of course, your mom is right, you know," Will announced, his heart hammering.

Aiden jerked his head to stare at him. "About what?"

Will managed a shrug. "It *is* practical. Like she said, the room is booked—"

"*Everything* is booked," Louise piped up.

"And I'd be there anyway, right, Becca?"

She nodded, smiling. "You've already got your suit too."

Good girl. Just like we planned.

Aiden had gone very quiet.

Moment of truth.

Will removed the ring box from his pocket, opened it, and got down on one knee, looking up at Aiden.

Louise screeched, and every single person in the restaurant was now staring in their direction.

Ignore them.

Will took a deep breath. "Would you—"

Aiden's breathing hitched. "I do *not* believe this."

Not exactly the words Will had wanted to hear, but—

He froze as Aiden brought out a very similar box.

Oh. My. God.

"You have *got* to be kidding me," Becca said with a gasp.

"Hey, that's *my* line," Will retorted.

She stood and walked around to where he knelt. "You two… You did it again?"

"If you can stop interrupting me, I can finish

this and get up off my knee," Will groused.

"Allow me." Aiden helped Will to his feet. He grinned. "I guess great minds really do think alike. So, which one of us gets to ask first?"

Will laughed. "You think we could do it simultaneously?" He glanced at the occupants of the now silent restaurant: all attention was focused on him and Aiden. "We need to do something. It's too damn quiet in here."

Aiden gazed at the gold band Will held out. "At least the rings are different."

Will chuckled. "You went with white gold, and I chose rose gold. Apparently it works well with redheads."

"Well, *one* of you ask the freaking question!" Ethan blurted. "Or we'll never get to the champagne part."

Will straightened. "I've applied to Madison. My interview is next week." He grinned. "I guess I'd better change my status on the application form."

Aiden's eyes widened. He put down the ring box, Will did the same, and a heartbeat later they were in each other's arms, kissing, amid rapturous applause that started with their families, and swelled to encompass all the diners and servers in the restaurant.

"Love you so much," Aiden murmured.

"Love you more," Will fired back. He grinned. "Can we get to the rings now?"

"Never mind the rings," Mom called out. "I want to hear you ask the question."

Will looked Aiden in the eye. "Marry me?"

Aiden smiled. "I thought you'd never ask." Then they kissed, and the applause started up again, rising in volume as they exchanged rings. Tears streaked Becca's cheeks, and she hugged Kristen who was similarly afflicted. Mom and Dad were crying too, and Ethan's grin would not quit. Kristen's parents clapped with everyone else, both beaming with delight.

"Didn't I say this was a great idea?" Louise wiped her eyes.

Will kissed Aiden once more before retaking his seat, giddy with joy. "You scared me to death just now. Becca knew I was going to propose. That's why she came out with that double wedding remark, to give me an opening. And then *you* decided to play a prank." He rolled his eyes. "Your timing sucks."

Aiden chuckled. "Sorry." Then he paused. "That's a lie. I'm not sorry at all. Because that was *my* opening to propose to *you*." He stared at their joined hands. "I'd better start looking for a job in Madison. It might be a while before one shows up, so we'll have to be patient."

"But you *will* find one," Will said with utter confidence. "Because it's like you said—you'll be there for me every step of the way. And I trust you to do just that."

"Hey, don't we get some of the credit?" Becca put her arm around Kristen. "After all, we're sharing our big day with you."

Will laughed. "Believe me, no one will be looking at us, not with you in that amazing dress."

"You need a To Do list," Mom remarked.

"And at the top is a marriage license," Dad added. "Don't forget the legalities."

Will smiled. "We have seventy days. There's plenty of time."

Louise chuckled. "Seventy days? That'll be here before you know it! Okay, what we need to do is…."

Her voice faded into the background as Will stared at the guy who was going to be his husband in a little more than two months.

I don't know how I should feel.

Excitement squirmed in his belly like… like… something squirmy. And as for his heart, it thumped madly, especially when he smiled or laughed.

And every time he gazed at Aiden.

Is it too soon to be thinking of marrying him?

Who could say? He'd read about people who were married a week after they met, and were still going strong decades later.

I want that. Today and every day.

Will wasn't naive to think there wouldn't be problems along the way. He could remember some of his parents' arguments, but each time they made up, their bond became stronger, deeper, more cohesive.

Seventy days? In the grand scheme, it was nothing, but each day would seem like an eternity, until he stood at Aiden's side and said those all-important words.

I do.

CHAPTER TWENTY-NINE

Will And Aiden Tie The Knot

Saturday, July 22

Will awoke to the aroma of freshly brewed coffee. Carl stood beside the bed, holding the mug.

He smiled as he placed it on the nightstand. "Wake up, sleepyhead. You're getting married today. And it's a beautiful morning."

"Is Becca awake yet?" Will asked as he hauled himself into an upright position.

Carl laughed. "Becca would already be in her wedding dress if Louise let her near it. She's gone to get her hair done. At least, that was the plan."

Will took a sip of coffee. "Dammit. I meant to get my nails done. I guess it's too late now." Carl blinked, and he chuckled. "Just kidding." His phone buzzed and he glanced at the screen.

Still wanna marry me?

He smiled. "It's Aiden."

"And that's my cue to leave. Tell him not to be late. By the way, breakfast shouldn't be long." Carl left the room.

Will snuggled under the comforter and clicked Call. "Hey."

"Hey you."

"What are you up to?"

"Trying to get a bow tie on Midnight but he isn't playing ball."

Will put one hand behind his head. "One, that's because he prefers playing with string, shoelaces, the cord for the blinds, you name it, and two—really?"

Aiden snickered. "Are you always going to be this gullible? Because it's freaking adorbs."

"Is Carol taking care of him?"

"Yeah. Why? You didn't think he was going to be at the wedding, did you?"

Will grinned. "I wouldn't put anything past you."

Silence.

"Aiden? Is everything okay?"

"Are you as nervous as I am?"

Will froze. "You're nervous?"

"You're not?"

He sat up and drank more of his coffee. "Why should I be? I'm just going to turn up and say *I do.*" He paused. "You're not getting cold feet, are you?"

"Fuck no. I'm just waiting to see what calamities the day brings."

"Like what?"

"Oh, I don't know. A sprinkler going off in the ballroom, and then we all get soaked in foul-smelling water that's been sitting around in pipes for years. Ethan forgets the rings. The wedding cake is a disaster. There's a fire drill in the middle of saying our vows. A bomb scare. Mom wears ridiculously high-heeled shoes and falls and breaks her ankle."

Will laughed. "Wow. You forgot to mention the arrival of the Four Horsemen of the

Apocalypse."

Aiden's sigh filled his ears. "I'm overthinking this, aren't I?"

"Er, yes?" Will relaxed. He could deal with overthinking. "Wait… Go back to the bit about our vows. You *have* made yours, right?"

Silence again.

"Aiden? I mentioned this two weeks ago."

"You've written yours, haven't you?"

"Duh."

Another sigh. "I need to hang up now. I have some homework to do."

"I'll see you there." Will smiled. "I'll be the one waiting for a kiss, on what's going to be the happiest day of my life."

"Mine too. Love you."

"Love you too. Now go write your vows—and make sure they're better than the sign you had planned for my graduation."

"That's right. Pile on the pressure." Aiden hung up.

It had been a messy couple of months. Most of Will's possessions were in boxes stored in Carl and Louise's garage. He'd been living at Aiden's apartment, until Louise insisted he spend the night before the wedding at their place. Kristen and her family were staying at the Pfister, courtesy of Louise who'd also arranged rooms for Mom and Dad, Ethan and Marley, Dee and Gavin, and Emma. Ethan was dividing his time between his best man duties and his role as a new dad. The wedding was Marley's first event since giving birth to Will's beautiful little niece, Jasmine, and she'd asked for a seat near the back, in case Jasmine woke up and decided to add to the proceedings.

And while life was a little messy? *Once we're married, it'll get messier.* At least until he moved to Madison in the fall. Aiden was already searching for another job, but there was always the possibility they'd be apart for a while.

Will could deal with that too. The separation wouldn't be forever.

A knock on the door made him jump. "You decent?"

"Why start now?" He smiled. "Come on in, Becca."

Becca looked cute in her red PJs covered in fluffy white sheep. "Morning."

"I thought you were going to get your hair done?"

She gave an eye roll. "Will? It's seven-thirty in the morning. The wedding isn't until two. I'm not getting it done too far ahead." She sat on his bed. "I don't know about you, but I'm buzzing."

"Me too." Will wrapped his hands around his mug. "It's weird how things turn out."

"What do you mean?"

"Well, this all started with me pretending to be your fiancé. I'm now going to be your brother-in-law."

She snickered. "I keep forgetting that part." He put his mug on the nightstand, and Becca grabbed his wrist. "Thanks, Will."

"For what?"

"Putting up with me? I made such a mess of this, and none of it would have happened if I'd found the nerve to tell Mom the truth."

"Now wait a minute. Yes, none of it would

have happened—but that also implies I might never have met Aiden."

She smiled. "I love that look you get when you talk about him. You know, the kinda smitten one."

"You don't have to describe it. I see that same look when you talk about Kristen."

Becca gazed at his suit, hanging from the closet door. "Aiden says you're organizing your honeymoon. Where are you going?"

He grinned. "Uh-uh. It's a secret—and it's going to stay that way."

Becca flopped onto her back, staring at the ceiling. "I can't believe Roger and Fliss arranged a week in Cancun for us. Sun, sea, sand and—"

"Yeah, I already know the last part," he said with a chuckle.

"Breakfast!" Louise hollered up the stairs.

Becca grimaced. "I'm too nervous to eat."

"But you're going to. We don't want you fainting in front of everyone."

She sat up, and to his surprise, she gave him a hug. "I love you, you know that, right?"

He kissed her cheek. "Of course I do. You almost married me."

Aiden took a last look in the mirror. Mom's comment about his hair came to mind, and he smiled.

As if I'd get it cut. Will loves my hair. Especially when he got to tug on it when he was balls deep in Aiden's ass.

The recollection was enough to cause a reaction. Aiden peered at his crotch.

"Oh no, you don't. I am *not* walking up the aisle with a boner."

Dad's cough sent heat rushing to Aiden's cheeks. "You know, talking to yourself is the first sign of madness," Dad observed, gazing at him in the mirror.

Aiden chuckled. "You're wrong. The first sign is when you hear a voice answer back."

Dad stood behind him, his hands on Aiden's shoulders. "Have I told you how honored I am that you asked me to be best man?"

He smirked. "Yeah, Dad. Only about a hundred times."

"I still think you should have let me organize a bachelor party."

Aiden arched his eyebrows. "I already had one, remember? Of course, Will was gonna marry my sister at the time, but it still counts, right?"

And while it had been the most boring bachelor party ever, it was still a night he'd never forget. Everything clicked, it had finally all made sense…

And they'd burned up the sheets all night long.

Dad shrugged. "I guess Will feels the same. He didn't have one either."

Aiden hoped his plans for a wedding night would make up for that. He'd gone all out for romance—a hot tub, rose petals on the bed, champagne in the ice bucket, chocolates on the pillow…

And plenty of lube on the nightstand.

Hey, lube is romantic, isn't it?

What he was dying to know was where they'd be the following evening. Will was being pretty tight-lipped about their honeymoon.

Be honest. Would you want him to be any different?

That was a no-brainer. Aiden wouldn't change a goddamn thing.

The door opened, and Becca came in. "You're ready. Thank God."

"And what does that mean?"

Her beautiful red lips twitched. "Why were we always late leaving the house every time we went on vacation? Hmm? Oh yeah. We were waiting for you."

Dad glared. "That does it. Today of all days, can you two *not* bicker, please?" He turned to gaze at her. "Let me look at you."

Becca did a twirl, the loop of her train caught around her finger. Aiden had to admit, the dress was stunning, showing off her slim figure. That deep red lace bodice was a show-stopper, and the velvet bow at the back was perfect. A gossamer veil hung from the back of her gorgeously coiffed hair, held in place by flowers.

Aiden had no idea what kept it all from falling apart. His money was on Krazy Glue.

Dad swallowed. "You look amazing."

Becca flushed. "If you look a little closer,

you'll find a few stains. Mom got her wedding-day tears started already." She raised her chin. "Think it'll knock Kristen's socks off?"

Dad snorted. "If she's wearing socks, I'm worried."

"She can wear boots under that dress if she likes. No one would ever know."

Dad held his arms wide. "I promise not to muss either of you, but right now your old dad needs a hug."

Aiden smiled. "This get-up doesn't muss. Just don't step on Becca's dress."

Dad hugged them, and when he stepped back, his eyes glistened. "Well I guess I'd better get you both down to the ballroom, seeing as I'm pulling double duty."

"Just make sure we're on the right sides when you walk us down the aisle," Becca said with a grin. "Otherwise I might end up marrying Will."

There was a knock at the door.

"It's open, Kelly. Come on in," Becca called out.

Kelly came into the room, looking radiant in a long dress in deep red satin. She carried two bouquets. Her breathing hitched when she saw Becca.

"Oh, you look awesome. I still can't believe you asked me to be bridesmaid."

Becca smiled. "It was the least I could do, after the horrible way I treated you. And it all worked out well. At least you're not doing the cooking for this shindig now." She widened her eyes. "Shit. That didn't come out the way I intended. I didn't mean—"

Kelly laughed. "Relax, Becca. I knew what you meant."

"Time to go," Dad told them.

"You'll need this." Kelly handed Becca her bouquet, a mass of red flowers, glossy green leaves, and white ribbons.

"Just be careful when you throw it at the end," Aiden admonished. "You could take someone's head off with that."

Becca opened her mouth, but Dad got in first.

"Anyone would think neither of you *wanted* to get married."

They left the room, heading for the elevator to the seventh floor. When they neared the ballroom, Aiden caught the strains of piano music coming from inside.

Ethan stood by the door. He smiled when they reached him.

"Great. I'll go tell Will you're here." He hurried away.

Dad pushed open the door, and Aiden saw a room full of white-covered chairs, every one of them occupied. At the end of each row was a tree-like decoration, a round arrangement of roses, trailing ivy, and ribbons. The front of the room was dominated by a covered dais where Lisa, the celebrant, waited under a wooden archway covered in roses and ivy. She smiled when she saw them and gave a nod over to the right.

The piano music died away, and Mendelssohn's 'Wedding March' took its place.

"I'm glad you both went with something traditional," Dad commented.

Aiden shrugged. "It's okay. Not what *I* would have chosen but—"

Becca snorted. "The less said about that the better."

"Why? What did he want?"

She raised her eyes to the ceiling. "Only 'The Imperial March' from *Star Wars*."

"Hey, it was the John Williams recording," Aiden protested.

"I hate to interrupt but…" Dad gave a mock glare. "Both of you. That way. Now."

They walked slowly toward the dais, all heads turning to watch them, Aiden on the left, Becca on the right. When they reached it, Becca kissed Dad on the cheek.

"Thanks for getting me here."

Dad kissed her forehead, then took his place at Aiden's side. Ethan joined them, giving Aiden a nod.

Then the music changed, and Aiden turned his head to watch Kristen walking toward them on her dad's arm, her dress like Glinda's from *The Wizard of Oz*.

That's a lot of satin. He smirked. *Yeah, she could be wearing anything under there.*

Then his heart skipped a beat when he caught sight of Will behind them, wearing a dark blue suit that showed off his lean frame to perfection.

Here we go.

Aiden wasn't nervous anymore.

Will gazed into Aiden's eyes, and grinned. "Babe? She asked you to recite your vows."

Aiden coughed, and laughter rippled through the assembled guests. He took Will's hands in his.

"You captured my heart the moment we met, just like you captured everyone's attention." His eyes twinkled. "Of course, you were on the floor at the time, having just performed the Pfister's first flight through the lobby." That got an eruption of laughter. "I didn't know then why I couldn't get you out of my mind, but now I do." He squeezed Will's hands. "You're my missing piece. I hope I'm yours. Because we fit. And I promise to do everything in my power to keep us that way." Aiden smiled. "You and me? We can accomplish anything when we work together. We can even reach the stars."

Will swallowed. He leaned forward, and their foreheads met. "You get an A for that, Teach," he whispered.

Aiden gave him a pained glance. "I was hoping for an A-plus."

Will coughed. "Later."

Lisa touched his arm. "When you're ready, Will."

He took a deep breath and surveyed the guests. "I read something recently that summed up exactly how I felt." He returned his attention to Aiden, focusing on his face. "And it went something like this." Another calming breath. "Someone once wrote that while love is madness, it's temporary. It rolls in with all the force of an earthquake or a tsunami, and then it gradually fades. And when that happens? We have a choice. We can either choose to call it a day—or we can stay together because two lives have become so entangled with each other that parting is an impossibility. And that's what love is. It isn't that hitch in your breath when you gaze at the person you love. It isn't the buzz you feel when you're with them. It isn't even the…" Will's cheeks burned. "The urge to spend your days and nights—"

"Yeah, I think we all get that bit," Aiden murmured, and a ripple of laughter followed.

Will cleared his throat. "All these things are part of being in love, and we've all been there—if we're lucky. But love? That's what's left when the feeling of *being* in love has long gone." He gazed into Aiden's eyes and smiled. "I look forward to what is left over when being in love has burned away."

"Just as long as it doesn't burn away *too* fast," Aiden added.

Will laughed, and the guests joined in.

"That was beautiful," Aiden whispered.

Will coughed. "Unfortunately it wasn't original. I 'borrowed' the sentiment from a book."

"Which book?"

He smiled. "*Captain Corelli's Mandolin* by Louis de Bernières. You should read it sometime."

Aiden sighed. "You had to be different, didn't you?"

Will blinked. "Of course. Would you have me any other way?"

"Hell no."

Lisa spoke quietly, and Will's heart soared when they exchanged rings. At last Lisa introduced them to the assembled crowd as Becca and Kristen Taylor-Braden and Aiden and Will Taylor-Bryant, to rapturous applause that turned to laughter when Kristen bent Becca over backward in their first married kiss.

Aiden took Will in his arms, and Will glared. "Don't even think about it." The only answer he got was the press of Aiden's lips to his, the feel of Aiden's hands cupping his face, and the sweetest kiss they'd ever shared.

He's mine. He's really mine.

Whatever life would throw at them, they'd face it together.

"Are you ready?"

Will blinked. "For what? It's all done bar the dancing until midnight, right?" The DJ was getting ready to set the ball rolling, and all around them was the noise of chatter and laughter.

"So, your first dance together. What are you all going to dance to?" Louise asked.

Aiden chuckled. "And *that's* what I was asking if you were ready for."

Becca grinned. "Kristen and I have a routine all worked out."

Carl smiled. "I'd expect nothing less from a dancer. How about you, Aiden? Will?"

Aiden gave that lazy smile that always turned Will's inside to mush.

"Nothing so elaborate. Just a slow number where I get to hold my husband close."

Will let out a happy sigh. "I am never going to get tired of hearing that word."

"I can think of a few other words I'd rather hear right now." Aiden locked gazes with him. "Such as, where you're taking us for our honeymoon?"

"Ah, yes. About that."

Aiden stilled. "We *are* going on honeymoon, aren't we?"

"Yes, but the first part will only last for a few days."

"First part? There's more than one?"

Will nodded. "Mom and Dad have booked us on a cruise round the med. Turkey, Egypt, and Greece." He grinned. "A gay cruise."

Aiden gaped. "Seriously? So what's part two? Because I don't think you can top that."

"That *is* part two. We leave next week. But tomorrow night? I've booked us into a little hotel for two nights. The Country House Resort in Door County."

Aiden frowned. "In Wisconsin?"

Will nodded. "It's great. Private water view balcony. Whirlpool bath."

"Sounds great, but I think your parents have got it beat with their contribution."

"Ah, but I haven't gotten to the best part yet. It's a twenty-minute drive from the hotel to Newport State Park—and the forecast for the next three nights is perfect."

He loved watching Aiden's face change, the light in his eyes.

"I guess we're taking the telescope with us." Aiden kissed him. "That's perfect."

Will gazed at the happy faces of their wedding guests, most of whom were a repeat of the anniversary party.

The day we met.

There were a few unfamiliar faces, including…

Will's breathing hitched. "Who is that?"

Aiden followed his glance to the tall, muscular man with the blue eyes. "I have no idea. He isn't from your side?"

"No. I'd remember that… face."

Aiden chuckled. "Sure, it's his face you're staring at."

"I wasn't staring!"

Aiden narrowed his gaze. "Not even married five minutes and I catch you making puppy dog eyes at a gorgeous guy. So, you've got a thing for muscles, huh? Do I need to bulk up? Join a gym? Get a personal trainer?"

Will smacked him lightly on the arm. "I am not making puppy dog eyes, okay? He just… caught my attention, that's all."

He chuckled. "I can see why. Even his muscles have muscles." Then he grinned. "And he's taken, by the look of things." Aiden pointed to the guy at his side, and it was then Will saw their joined hands.

"Well, crap. We're not the only gays at this shindig." They made a striking couple. He met Aiden's amused gaze. "And for the record, there's a song that pretty much nails how I feel right now. Something along the lines of me only having eyes for you."

Aiden's sweet kiss was tender, loving, and held the promise of more to come.

"You two. You have the rest of your lives to kiss. Right now it's time to dance."

Will laughed. "Yes, Louise." He tilted his head in the direction of the two men. "Do you know who they are?"

She peered into the crowd of guests, and then her face brightened. "Oh yes. That's Daniel and Charlie. They're staying with Luke and Gloria this weekend. When Luke realized he'd double-booked, he was going to decline the wedding invite. I told him to bring them along."

Aiden blinked. "Because they're gay?"

She scrunched up her face. "Of course not. Because they're hot." She rolled her eyes. "Your Aunt Deborah thought we'd hired strippers for the party and asked when the show began." She pointed to the muscular guy. "That cheeky bastard started unbuttoning his shirt until Charlie stopped him. Then he said they'd do it together later." She snickered. "I can't wait to see if they have the nerve." She gazed at the couple and beamed.

"Aren't they sweet? Daniel's a firefighter here in Milwaukee, and they have the cutest little boy. Charlie showed me pictures. And they have sugar gliders! Charlie had this photo of him with them on his shoulders." She gazed at the men. "Such a lovely couple."

"Wow, Mom." Aiden grinned. "You're a regular gay magnet. We'll have you waving a flag at PrideFest yet."

Her eyes widened. "I'm free in June!" Before Will could come up with a suitably witty response, she smiled at someone across the room, and a moment later, she'd disappeared.

"Who are Luke and Gloria?" Will asked.

Aiden chuckled. "I have no clue." He glanced at Will. "Do I need to find you a tissue?"

"For what?"

"Your drool. Am I going to find you've ordered a naked firefighter calendar next year?"

Will grinned. "Would you complain?"

Aiden's eyes twinkled. "Hell no."

Whatever else he'd been going to say was lost when the DJ announced that Becca and Kristen were about to dance. Beyonce's 'Single Ladies' burst from the speakers.

Becca and Kristen were phenomenal. Their moves were polished, and everyone stood around the dance floor, clapping and cheering. When they finished, they brought the house down.

Will chuckled. "Your sister is incredible."

"Her dancing? Or her attitude?"

Will smiled. "Both?"

The DJ spoke again. "And before you hit the dance floor I'd like to ask Aiden and Will to share their first dance with you all."

Aiden held out his hand, and Will took it. Aiden led him to the middle of the dance floor and put his hands on Will's waist. Will looped his arms around Aiden's neck.

"So… did you choose a song for us?" he asked.

Aiden merely grinned, and from the sound system poured—

'The Imperial March' from *Star Wars*.

Will laughed so hard, his sides ached. "To quote you, you had to be different, didn't you?"

Aiden gave a nod to the DJ, and Tyler Shaw's 'When You're Home' filled the air.

Ohhhh.

He lost himself in Aiden's arms. "Okay, you nailed it." They moved in a leisurely motion, their cheeks pressed together. "I could stay like this forever."

"And are you going to love me forever?" Aiden's breath tickled his ear.

Will pulled back to look him in the eye.

"I'm going to love you until the stars turn cold."

THE END

ALSO BY K.C. WELLS

Waiting for You
Step by Step
Bromantically Yours
BFF

Collars & Cuffs
An Unlocked Heart
Trusting Thomas
Someone to Keep Me (K.C. Wells & Parker Williams)
A Dance with Domination
Damian's Discipline (K.C. Wells & Parker Williams)
Make Me Soar
Dom of Ages (K.C. Wells & Parker Williams)
Endings and Beginnings (K.C. Wells & Parker Williams)

Secrets – with Parker Williams
Before You Break
An Unlocked Mind
Threepeat
On the Same Page

Personal
Making it Personal
Personal Changes
More than Personal
Personal Secrets
Strictly Personal
Personal Challenges
Personal – The complete series

Confetti, Cake & Confessions
(FREE)

Christmas
Connections
Saving Jason
A Christmas Promise
The Law of Miracles
My Christmas Spirit
A Guy for Christmas
Dear Santa
Santa's Secrets

Island Tales
Waiting for a Prince
September's Tide
Submitting to the Darkness
Island Tales Vol 1 (Books #1 & #2)

Lightning Tales
Teach Me
Trust Me
See Me
Love Me

A Material World
Lace
Satin
Silk
Denim

Southern Boys
Truth & Betrayal

Pride & Protection
Desire & Denial

Maine Men
Finn's Fantasy
Ben's Boss
Seb's Summer
Dylan's Dilemma
Shaun's Salvation
Aaron's Awakening
Levi's Love
Maine Men – Two Tales

Salvation
Wrangled
Haunted

CrossBow Protection (with Parker Williams)
Broken Warrior
Broken Wheels

Standalones
Kel's Keeper
Here For You
Sexting The Boss
Gay on a Train
Sunshine & Shadows
Double or Nothing
Back from the Edge
Switching it up
Out for You (FREE)
State of Mind (FREE)
No More Waiting (FREE)

Watch and Learn
My Best Friend's Brother
Princely Submission
Bears in the Woods
Holy Hell – with Parker Williams

Anthologies

Fifty Gays of Shade
Winning Will's Heart

Come, Play
Watch and Learn

Writing as Tantalus
Damon & Pete: Playing with Fire

ABOUT THE AUTHOR

K.C. Wells lives on an island off the south coast of the UK, surrounded by natural beauty. She writes about men who love men, and can't even contemplate a life that doesn't include writing.

The rainbow rose tattoo on her back with the words 'Love is Love' and 'Love Wins' is her way of hoisting a flag. She plans to be writing about men in love - be it sweet or slow, hot or kinky - for a long while to come.

Printed in Dunstable, United Kingdom

63506431R00211